I0775603

THE TWINS IN THE MOUNTAINS

K.C. NUZUM

A warning is included to allow those who do not wish to read a book with such subject matter the choice to go no further. This book contains dark elements not suitable for small children, including or by mention alone: child abuse, sexual assault, and murder.

TABLE OF CONTENTS

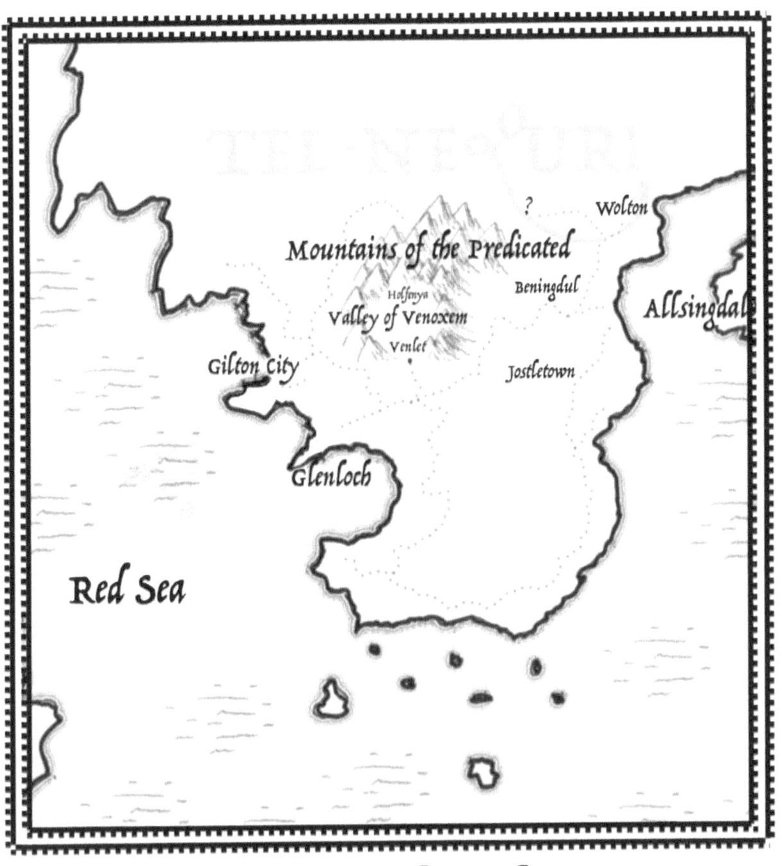

TEL-NFOUR
?
Wolton
Mountains of the Predicated
Beningdul
Allsingdale
Holfonya
Valley of Venoxem
Venlet
Jostletown
Gilton City
Glenloch
Red Sea

Central Zel

PROLOGUE

The murky tide of the ocean bubbled under the tortured docks, green and grey. Much like the sky. The groans of nearby sailors, wet and cold from years living on boats moved crabs feasting on smaller crabs into hiding.

A sailor boy, whose knees were wide and clothes were dry, ran from the boat, knocking his fellow seamen to the side.

"Watch it Sephen! Or, my gods' I'll—"

The voice of his father, harsh and scratchy lulled with the rowing boats, hitting rock wall and sea beds softer than usual.

To be back home, in Gilton City, made his body, stiff from the moon's long voyage out at sea come alive. He ran like a bloodhound to Tipa, the pretty woman who waved her ribbon from the dock at him before every journey; who, at her corner booth, rolled flour into dough she sold for just a dubel, as graceful as any angel would, or so he thought. But as he turned to meet her, where his face should have caught the sweet scents of her sugar and cinnamon pastries, he tripped, grabbing the sea-wrought, wooden booth she called hers no other merchant would claim.

As he stood, he straightened his shirt and removed his flimsy hat. He cooly ran his fingers through his black hair, expecting to see her smiling back, but as he turned to greet her, she was nowhere to be seen.

He swung around, suddenly immersed in a crowd moving him away as he peaked desperately above heads and around bodies, hoping to catch her on her way home at the very least.

It all happened so fast, he hardly had time to change direction. When the crowd came to a pause, he ran into a brick wall, breathing full air for the first time since. With his back against the wet wall, he watched as the taller adults moved to the back, allowing those shorter to stand and sit in the front.

He laughed at himself.

The puppeteer? What a bore.

He crossed his arms and looked up, the sooty clouds blocked his view of the sky. He turned away, towards the streets leading back to Tipa.

He was jolted back to watching the crowd as playful laughter and mothers whispering caught his attention.

It took him a moment, and was certain no one he knew was present, before he left the wall and joined the crowd, slithering past stench and ale—the true smell of the city. He kept his dubel purse close to him, having been robbed a time or two too many. When he reached his opening, where he could see the puppeteer and his box, he stopped. He smiled briefly before erasing it, crossing his arms as he watched the show unfold.

"You there? Are you ready?!" The puppeteer, a man dressed in burgundy robes and a coat with a crest resembling a lion, pointed into the crowd. His hair, curly and dark grey moved with him, his buoyant hat striped in blue and red.

Sephen stared back at the man and reluctantly looked away. He saw the eyes of those among him, expecting him to respond. His smug demeanor fell as he nodded at the odd man, whose smile crossed his whole face.

"Oh, sweet barnacles, am I relieved! The youth are so hard to talk to, especially those as wormy as thee!" The crowd laughed as Sephen's arms fell to his sides and all confidence he had left diminished. "Now, enough pleasantries, although I am pleased to be here—your teller of real stories. Truth only will leave my lips, or else I'll die at the hands of whips. Menfolk and womenfolk—children and their beasts, it is time for tell of demonfolk; a monster from the east. I'm glad to have your presence on these dark days of our, for today we tell of a major pestilence, one who has caused a stir in our Osir tower!"

He pointed his finger above him, and all eyes knew where to cast their gaze. Though giant buildings and the smoky sky covered it, every person in Gilton City knew where it was, and could find it with their eyes closed.

"This beast, this monster who claims the night, will not rest its chattery, rotten teeth until its consumed you and your children's life. It is not a trick of the mind. No, it is not. This foul creature, unkind, is as real as your unending gout. Terrible and cruel, festering and oozing, it does not stop for it is afraid of losing."

The crowd spoke amongst themselves, some elbowing Sephen who stood silent and defeated.

"Losing what, you may ask, although that shouldn't even be questioned," the puppeteer walked behind his box, his voice just as loud as before. "Well if not of your child, perhaps of your livestock or your life... whatever is it's dark intention..."

The small curtains opened and out came a puppet, its face full of sharp teeth with eyes red and ferocious.

"This foul creature does not sleep—it waits, it slithers, in those arcane mountains of old, where it feasts on soft bodies of children till dawn."

He moved the puppet across the small stage, revealing a black tail he whipped at the children leaning in, and they screamed both in fright and delight as wicked sounds came from the odd man.

"Whatever you've heard—of a small girl, cold and alone, scared and afraid—are all LIES!" He reached down into a box and flung a winged puppet across the stage, where it landed near Sephen who jumped as the puppeteer unleashed a guttural roar.

"It changes its form, you see, much like its kind—the half bred godkin of this very land. It can appear like the sweetest girl, so trust no one—you've been warned!" He said as he changed dolls again, this time a small girl, with rosy cheeks and black hair to the center, "for once it has you cornered, you will be no more!" He pulled a small chord on its back and it became drenched in red dye. Moans and prayers, abolishing this evil thing came from the crowd now upset and angry. The puppeteer, hidden where no one could see, smiled.

"Fear not my dear friends, for here, in this sacred city, we are safe—protected by our mother so pretty!"

"But what about Garaton?" came an angry voice from the crowd with many others in agreement.

What about him? Thought Sephen as he slithered out of the unruly crowd.

"Our lord, our true savior is always aware. He is here, he

is there—he is everywhere! Trust me when I say this—he sees all, so beware!"

Sephen didn't dare stay and see the rest of the show, but he surely heard the hollering of happy folks, knowing good and well someone must have destroyed one of the puppets they didn't like.

He shook his head at the thought and headed back towards Tipa's, yelling her name as he ran.

The crowd continued to linger as the story came near its end. As they mocked and spat at the silly puppets, a small boy stood afar, observing like no child would. His eyes, like lancers, cautious and swift, narrowed as the audience turned into a mob, ripping the puppet of the creature apart, taking the small box and throwing it to the ground into splinters. His eyes shimmered as he closed them, his body falling back into the shadows where he disappeared.

CHAPTER I

Mistacles sat pensive in his red oak chair, his thoughts countless and untethered. Another year had passed as fast as a jack rabbit, and in it a thousand more white hairs grew on his beard and head. Malkeevs, the hearth holiday of the year, where gifts were given and souls were forgiven was just around the corner. He could feel its approach without ever charting the stars for its harbinger was the already blistering cold of the summit becoming colder and more aggressive and the Moon growing ever distant.

Throughout Zel, snow had already fallen, more in some places than in others. In the Valley of Venoxem, in the bosom of the mountains, the weather did wondrous things. Holfenya was snowed in, and happy for it. Venlet's ground turned to ice at night but not a drop of snow touched it—not since that terrible Eleventh Day. Mistacles, perplexed couldn't find a reason why, although, the goddess Siracon was said to have left her hidden realm, where so few could find her, to spy on the Valley, where her light alone was too warm for anything but a storm to brew.

The fireplace before him was something strange for it was his masters, and his master before him, and none before him knew who, or what, carved it into the mountain. As a young man, studying with his master, Mistacles would climb atop the rock side of the house and wait near the chimney for smoke to escape. Not once, in all his years, had he seen it, except for the wafts of hickory chars that blew his way when an attendant, or two, or newer since, a child or two, rushed through his doorway.

He had watched the flames work hard on the logs as one of his sprightly wards rushed through the door and forced the fire's holy flames into embers.

He sighed.

So, the work begins again.

He rolled in his worn chair, reaching with his back any part of the cushion untouched. He settled where he felt most comfortable and gripped his quill tightly. The small, handmade book in his other hand was first a paper for the children but became a novel of its own, woven with a leather he could easily remove to add more pages.

As he looked at the little girl opposite him, his glasses fell to the tip of his nose. He squinted at her fidgeting.

"How are you doing today?" He spoke carefully and ended his words with thin lips.

She lowered in her chair, as comfy and intricate as his but not nearly as worn in, folding her arms in a most obstinate way.

"I see," he said as he scribbled some notes. "Not much better than yesterday."

"What are you writing?" she asked through lowered brows.

He smiled to himself.

He knew her too well; he could time her antics and

tantrums to the turning of the Sun. And not just hers but the other two as well. It could not be helped. They were there when he woke in the morning, and he was their bedtime storyteller late at night. Though the years had been long and difficult, full of terrible nights and unbelievable revelations, he couldn't see another without them.

"Can't tell ya," he said still smiling. "Besides—we have more important things to discuss."

She shifted in her chair. "Like, what happened before?"

She sighed loudly, kicking the wooden legs under her as hard as she could when she didn't get an answer. Mistacles gave her a reprimanding glare, like any guardian would, but softened when the girl turned away. He scribbled more notes and said nothing.

"What's she been saying?" she asked, scratching the worst of her tangled hair, cut short from years of neglect, sat warped and knotted above her shoulders.

"I can't tell you, it's private. We've discussed this before, sweetie—we must—"

"Must respect each other. Got it. It's not like she doesn't tell me anyways..."

She continued to swing her legs, hoping her strength could tear the wood in two. She got tired of kicking and allowed her eyes to lazily take in the familiar study. The lack of windows made the mahogany room feel ancient, like some terrible church and its terrible library she saw once in a dream. Bookshelves cracked and musty took up most of the space, twinned if not for the fireplace between them. And his globe, a giant, clear crystal behind his chair was covered by a sparkling blanket, sheer but dark.

The light from candles and magic trinkets, like stars in a bottle, made a strange orange cast across the walls, but she knew its real color and it was green. It was a warm springen day in their first year in the mountains when curiosity forced the three into a giant gamble—the proper guesser of the proper color of Mistacles painted walls would win their weight in Brandied Licorice. She guessed black.

She wrinkled her nose at the memory, still nauseated by the mention of that green shade, like wet river weeds mushed into frog's guts. And it smelled much the same.

"I got a letter today," he said as he watched her reach for the many rare and valuable trinkets besides her. "Did you hear me?"

She smiled sweetly in response before taking the magic lamp's chain in her hand.

"Are we done yet?" she asked.

"It was from the Army."

She fell back into her chair, sullen.

"I can read it to you if you'd like?" he asked as he reached into his pocket and pulled out an envelope.

"Why should I CARE?!" she screamed through gritted teeth with her arms once again folded.

"I am this close, little girl!" he said through pursed lips.

"Whatever! I'm done with this!"

She jumped to her feet and scrambled out the door like a hot tornado. He removed his glasses and wiped his eyes stained with anxious sweat, no longer amused by her outbursts.

On the door frame came a subtle knock and he knew instantly who it was.

"Come in, sweetie—it's okay."

He put on his glasses and watched as the meek girl walked cautiously to the warm seat. She looked to him and waited for his nod to jump up.

"You don't have to ask every time, you know."

"I-I...I know," she said behind her hair, long and velvety.

He cleared his throat before picking up his quill again. "Did you see her leave?"

She smiled slightly. "Yeah, she told me to keep my mouth shut."

He was quick to anger but hid it well. His temper cooled as the simple smile she wore washed away into her usual pout. He knew she wasn't a terrible little girl and would admonish her for even thinking it if it didn't make her feel worse.

He shook his head. She had changed so much since they first arrived.

"Do you want to talk about the night terrors?" he asked, choosing to stare at the ink bleeding into the parchment than see her miserable reaction.

"They keep my up all night," she said softly. Her tired body fell into the arm of the chair where she relaxed. She found the magic lamp chain and let it cascade through her fingers. "I think it's... getting closer to ending me each time it comes."

"Chil... I am so sorry you're going through this. I wish I could take your burden away—I really do!" With tears in his eyes, helpless and in despair, he got down on his knees and scuffled to the side of her chair where her head hung over. "You are an extraordinary little girl for what you've been through, and you should be proud of what you've accomplished. I... am so proud of you," he said with watery eyes. "I'm even proud of Tane!"

The Child looked up with her own teary eyes and smiled incredulously.

"Yeah right!" she laughed.

"It's true, I mean it. You, Tane, and Care... even Pul. You guys are extraordinary kids!"

Suddenly from the doorway came a rapid set of knocks.

There stood the golden fireball, Tane, poised like a bull ready to strike.

"Ah, did you forget something, sweetie?" he asked.

Tane rolled her eyes before waving at the Child.

"Chil, I'm hungry! Let's go!" she said as she stomped away.

As if on cue, the Child gently removed herself from the chair and moved to Mistacles, stupefied, and patted him on the head. They shared a moment of silence, and she giggled as he made silly faces in Tane's direction.

"Tomorrow, then?" he asked.

She smiled at the salt and pepper haired Imagi and ran to her friend who was screaming for her in the hallway.

He remained on the floor, totally spent. He glanced over his notes which resembled cloncluck scratches and groaned. He struggled back to his feet and made it to his chair before collapsing. After a few big breathes, he called for an attendant.

"Yes Master?"

"Would you be so kind as to fetch Care for me?"

"Oh, already on it, sir. We've been searching since breakfast. It seems he really got away this time."

Mistacles rolled his eyes. "You checked the foundry, the maiden's lavatory, the thermopolia, the gardens, and the northern grotto?!"

"Everywhere sir."

"Well, I had better take a look. Those damn children!"

He was slow to his feet and staggered to the door, hitting it as he left, looking left and right, expecting a child or two to run through his legs and possibly knock him down. Halfway down the hall he spun on his heels at the sound of shoes clicking. The small boy, as striking as always, was where he once stood, laughing at the poor Imagi nearly out of breath.

"Care, please—don't make Mr. Mistacles run again."

"Mr. Mistacles! Mr. Mistacles!" Voices sharp and irritating fell around him like whirlybirds in fallenden months.

"Knock it off, Tane! And you too, Chil. Care..." But as he turned to the boy, he was gone.

He sighed. "So, the search begins again!"

AFTER HOURS of searching and inevitable finding, Mistacles and his wards, tired and famished, traveled to the thermopolia where every cook from different zones of the mountains came to make delicious foods, exotic and hearty for just a few dubels a plate. The children had never had Balloceus' soup before their first trip to the market but were hooked once Mistacles gave them a sip—its southern peppers burned their tongue much to their amusement. And there they first tried Gozecha, the milk from nursing Tentactacon mare's which, oddly enough, tasted like honey and became a favorite of theirs whenever it was available.

The four sat around a large table outside of the busy market square in the company of many friends and neighbors, celebrating yet another year of seasons and those passed along the way, planning how they'll spend their Malkeevs soon arriving. But the Child was a frowny face among smiles as she flipped her empty tankard on its side.

"Can someone get this girl another ale?!" said Mistacles mockingly. She looked up at him and then back down again. "What is it now, sweetie?"

"I... I thought the Army were coming to celebrate with us," she answered.

"They're a little delayed but will be here soon enough. Now, how are your studies coming along?"

"Fine."

"Okay. Fine it is. Do you need help with anything?"

She peeled away her eyes to observe the distant rock walls, as lifeless, as colorless as the day before. She shook her head.

"Well, uh...It's nothing."

Excited, he moved his chair closer to hers. "Come on, you can tell me anything. You know that."

It took her a moment to speak, and she did so thoughtfully.

"I want to see outside."

At her words, she stared at the Imagi, the locked windows of her eyes opened briefly and, like the morning shone the Sun, shadowed but bright—ready for another chance at adventure, so were her eyes and they were marvelous.

He collapsed and sighed. "You know we can't, sweetie. Anything else and you got it!"

"I... I haven't seen the Sun or the Moon in a long while. I really miss them. And the great oaks in the valley. I can probably see them from Mother Summit." The rays in her eyes reached for him, and he couldn't escape them.

He examined her and considered it. "But if you go, the others will want too as well. And what makes you think Tane will come back once let out, hmm?"

"Well, just me then. Only for a few minutes. Please?!"

He smiled.

"I think we'll start with the Sun. Tomorrow before the others awaken. But you must stay by me. Promise?"

She nodded and the two shared a small embrace before

she ran off. He shook his head, damning himself for his own decision.

Care, who had been spying from across the room crept low under the table, careful to remain invisible as he reached for a pouch hanging from the Imagi's belt.

It all began an evening a fortnight before as the three were settling into their warm beds, anxiously fiddling their feet for the moment the story began. Mistacles, wrapped in blankets himself, sat by their bed and told them the tale of the man with the never-fading glue.

"There once lived a man on a farm, gods know where, in the time before the fall of Yexour, whose horse, divine, whom he cherished above all, whose magic made miracles and was the only of its kind, died in its sixteenth year. Desperate to keep its magic a little longer, the man turned its bones and hooves into glue, stronger than the horse alive; stronger than anything else in the known world, actually. He spent the rest of his days with the glue always by his side—uniting roofs to houses, limbs on people—continuing the work they did before. Eventually, the man became old and near death but didn't want to die. Wishing to live forever with his companion, he used the last of his glue and stuck himself to a moment in time, so death couldn't keep them apart."

"What?!" screamed Tane. "No one can do that!"

"Whoa!" said Care, amused with eyes wide open.

"I'm not done with the story. If nothing else, what is the one thing we've learned from these stories children?"

"Everything comes with a price!" said Tane picking her teeth. He went to remove her fingers from her mouth when he noticed the Child pensive and confused.

"If he stuck himself to a moment, wouldn't he be frozen in time?" she asked.

"Righto, Chil! So, because he used the glue, it trapped him in another plane where time has no power. A hollow place where he couldn't move or do anything besides...exist as the moment reset endlessly! Absolute torture if you ask me!

"He prayed tirelessly for the gods to help, and, of course, of all the Seven, who showed up to save the day?"

"Dreqtaton!" they answered.

Mistacles laughed.

"Why is he always in these stories?" asked Tane with a scrunched nose.

"Because he is devious and cunning and likes to interfere when it's none of his business. Well, except when it came to you guys. I'll give him a pass on that one."

"But didn't he introduce us... uh, humans to magic? That doesn't seem so bad" The Child turned away innocently and then over at Tane who rolled her eyes at her.

"Uh, yes and no. It's too complicated to explain in one sitting. We'll cover this later in your studies....Now, what was I saying before....Oh yes!—"

He shifted in his seat and moved the blankets as he recalled the rest of the tale. "The man makes a deal with Dreqtaton: if the god can release him from his glue, he can have whatever is left over. Of course, once the man is free, he and the glue turn into ash because that moment lasted for...eons!" The dramatic face he made caused the children to giggle. "Dreqtaton took the ash and turned it into a powder he gave to his followers until it was nearly gone. Anyone who yields it has the power to travel to any place in the cosmos, at any time, but...one must be careful not to run out or they could be stuck wherever they are...forever."

"Where is the powder now?" asked Care. Mistacles,

with a generous swing of his large arm patted himself on the side.

"Here, for now. We'll see what happens tomorrow."

Since that night, Care watched his protector like a hawk, expertly waiting for his time to strike.

Mistacles nonchalantly reached under the table as the boy's fingers ran across the pouch, pulling him up by the collar, kicking and screaming.

"What on Zel are you doing, my boy?"

"Ugh! I was this close!" he said as Mistacles set him down.

"You must be careful sneaking up on a Imagi like me, boy. You've got work to do if you want to make it an occupation someday, of course."

"This isn't funny, Mistacles. I really don't want to be here anymore. I don't know why you keep me here. I want to go home!"

Mistacles rubbed his head as the unruly Care said his peace. When Tane was off, the boy was surely on. How he loved running for any open door, or try to escape whenever he had the chance, or ask any magical person he came across if they would help him leave drove Mistacles mad. No amount of warning of treacherous people hiding in the mountains could stop the mad boy and went in one ear and out the other.

"Well, you can't leave until it's safe to do so. And I will not have you harassing our friends about portals and all sorts of nonsense! I wish I could send you home, but it isn't permissible right now. Please understand!"

Without a word, Care whipped out of his chair and ran into the shadows.

From a seat nearby, Mistacles heard a soft giggle and groaned.

"You know, sweetie, there are a gazillion other things you could be doing right now that doesn't involve eavesdropping in on my conversations?"

Tane laughed. "Oh, Mr. Mistacles, when will you ever learn?"

AFTER THE CHILDREN were tucked in bed and told another of Mistacles odd stories, the Imagi scurried back to the thermopolia where a small group of the Army of Miracon sat waiting for his return, still in their heavy armor and fur necessary to endure the harsh weather even in the secret passageways gifted to them by the Imagis. Their faces were red and full of stuble, and those once bald had hair too long to sheer easily.

Mistacles reached into his belt and revealed letters he passed to Hisousen, a man, still bald and war-wrought, who, after reading, passed it to the man next to him.

"What in Miracon's Dreams is this..." Hisousen held a letter from Daybar recently received within the day, "the Order of Garatos sent parades of soldiers through their pass? Do you think they have intentions of taking the mountain?" he asked, face stuck in shock.

"It would appear they have taken most of the roads already, the villages and their people hostage. They've got the way to Mother Summit completely covered, though it would be unwise of them to trespass further. Yexour would have warned me of this but...he is weak." Mistacles rubbed his beard as the letters went through gritty hands until reaching his again.

"Luckily, we're ahead of the rest of the army, one thousand strong, soon to arrive in the event war breaks out. This is the will of our goddess, though I wish it were more,"

Hisousen said tense in his seat, sharing a weary look with his team.

Mistacles nodded. "Okay, my friends—let's get right to it. I am tired of all this nonsense. People are dying; I've lost a generation of my Magi and many of your own stopping those disturbed twins in Gilton City from destroying our home and our golden egg—the godkin. If she were to fall into the wrong hands ever—all our hopes of a better future will be lost. With that being said, I need this place protected at all times. A small legion stationed here in the mountains sworn on the hand to Miracon with do. And my peers and I need more resources from the outside—our spells are losing their potency and ingredients most valuable will be required to keep the sleeping mountain happy."

Hisousen laughed and the table became quiet.

"Let me get this straight. You want us to sacrifice our own brothers and sons for some... ingredients?"

"Lieutenant Hisousen, do not mock me. Our spells will save this most sacred mountain so YOU and your men can stay here unmolested by the Order. Your men will not DIE on their way to our ingredients unless they are weak and inexperienced. You have my word!"

"Sorry, Mistacles," said another bald man, bigger and less torn up, "we're tired. We've been traveling all day and night. Even the safe path you laid for us was rocky and difficult to traverse. And Marcello has yet to send word of his position. We fear the worst."

"Oh, Reine—you worry too much! I do not feel he is in present danger. But, I will try communing with him tomorrow. For tonight, I would like to discuss matters with all of you further." The army men groaned. "Now, I received a letter from your party, that master Pul would be joining us. Where is he?"

"He...uh...didn't want to...participate," said Reine sadly. "He can't miss a single day of training, he says. It's been that way since Marcello left."

"And Munta?"

"He too left. Back to Venlet to check on things, or so we've been told. Him and the little guy haven't spoken in sometime. They needed the much-needed break, I guess." Hisousen watched Reine as his head fell at his words.

"Well, that's too bad. He's welcome here anytime. Now, back to business. I've received emergency correspondence from several villages and cities throughout the region, as you've read. They've all been disrupted by the Order—some worse than others. It seems they've been targeting those humans with a close relationship with us. Something needs to be done about it!"

Hisousen turned a fork in his hand. "We've sent posts to each establishment from here to Venlet, secretly, but none have been received." He stabbed it hard into the table. "It seems we have snakes in our grass. We've been scattered on this issue since Marcello..."

"Okay, okay. Things are worse than I thought. Gentlemen, drink up. We're in for a long night!"

CHAPTER 2

It was late and the Child stirred in bed, anxious for morning to arrive. She had tried to sleep but couldn't get it to come, and her thoughts got the better of her and she wished she were knocked out rather than hear them anymore. She moved her legs to ward off the tingles and stiffness from staying up all night. She had every intention to kick the air when an exhausted—*Ow!*—stopped her.

She sat up and patted her friend on the back.

"Sorry, Tane. My legs fell asleep."

"Well, tell 'em to wake up faster so I can get some rest!" Tane who had her head by the Child's feet moved to the headboard and rested on the Child's other pillow. "Why is your bed more comfortable than mine?"

The Child fell back heavily on hers and laughed.

"They're the same! You just don't like to sleep alone."

"That's not true. I sleep alone all the time and I can do it whenever I want!"

"I bet you can't do it tonight?"

Tane opened an emerald gem and gave a wicked grin.

"I bet you ten toadstool lolli's I can and be up before you!"

"I bet you my bed for yours you can't!"

"Oh, you are on Chil!"

"Could you guys PLEASE shut up!" A broken voice from across the room yelled to them.

Care, who had just fallen asleep, took his pillow and chucked it at Tane. Shocked, she took it and pelted the Child. Before anyone could breathe, they were all smacking each other with their pillows as fierce as men in battle. Within minutes, the bedroom door swung open and in came an exasperated Mistacles, looming over them with a candlestick in hand.

"You had better get back to your beds or SO HELP ME!"

Tane and Care scurried to theirs and tucked themselves in before he could wave his magic hand.

"Uh, Chil, can I have my pillow back please?" asked Care, and at his words the three fell into another fit of laughter.

Mistacles rolled his eyes and bellowed good night before shutting the door behind him. They laughed a little longer before saying their good nights to each other one last time.

"Good night Tane!"

"Good night Chil! Your bed is mine!"

"Ten toadstool lolli's all for me..." the Child said as she drifted off to sleep, finally.

And just as quickly as she fell, she awoke to a warm hand on her shoulder. She turned to face it, upset and disoriented.

"Aye, sweetie, it's me. Are you ready to see the Sun?" asked Mistacles.

"YEAH!" she almost screamed but hushed her enthusiasm as she crept out of bed and went to her wardrobe. She traded her night clothes for her warmest dress which was of cotton and hardly comfortable. She then grabbed a small, grey cloak made just for her and draped it overhead.

She closed the door behind her like the attendants when they were fast asleep but easy to wake, and met with Mistacles who waited patiently outside the door.

"Well, I can't imagine it's changed much since you last seen it!"

"Hmm... I'll be the judge of that!" she said, skipping down the empty hall. This was the first time she saw her world this early in the morning, vaguely remembering the times in Venlet when nighttime was her ally. She liked the quiet streets, where murky drops fell like horse hooves and lost, distant winds lingered.

They meandered behind the thermopolia and away from the stone homes and establishments she knew well and entered the dark, man-made alleyways that made the ones back home look like kingly-halls. Low hanging stalactites nearly impossible to see even when close looked down upon her as they walked along, aiming to stab her to death, or so she felt. The constant drip-droppings and skittering of varmints small and large concealed by the darkness didn't help her feelings in the slightest.

She clenched Mistacles hand as hard as she could without knowing and he quickly came to, lost in the hum of this decrepit place, and cast a spell of invisibility upon her, assuring her safety as long as she stayed by him.

After the fifth alleyway came a small plaza, also like the one back home, and from above were more giant stalactites, like mammoth blades hovering just shy of the roofs on the warped buildings nearest her. Not one had a front door but a strong, orange glow emanated from every window where figures danced and fought with no end in sight. Men with tall hats and dirtied faces approached those hunched over, begging for dubels and ale, reaching into pockets when no answer was given. Women screamed as they lifted their dresses and kicked to stale music and their audiences' clapping. As the Child got closer, they smiled, exposing their black and yellow teeth, caved in and full of abysmal holes, like hers not long ago. She shuttered at the thought and squeezed her guardian's hand to keep them moving.

Caught in the crowd growing more visceral and foul, her hand loosened in his and she found herself astray, stopping by a home closest to where they entered to wait for Mistacles to find her. And as she waited, she felt something move behind her.

She quickly turned and stared into darkness illuminated only by fog. She peered into it where little could be discerned but a man—or what resembled one—embracing another.

She squinted her tired eyes, burning, and saw threw the sheer façade. A man as pale as the fog's tendrils was ripping skin from the other's neck, whose limp arms moved little. Blood as bright as embers trickled down from the gaping wound and on to the ground where another figure, as pale as the attacker crawled low and licked the dark puddle like a dog.

She shook her head in disbelief. She left the wall to get closer for some morbid reason she couldn't control, but as she reached for the fog her arm was pulled—it was Mistacles, bringing her back on the path to the Sun.

"Don't look sweetie."

"I think that man's hurt. We should..."

"It's being taken care of as we speak. Don't worry, Chil —trust me on this."

"Okay," she said, looking back at the fog one more time. "Can I ask you something. Why am I invisible but you can walk, like you, like that?"

"Well, sweetie, I look like me to you but to everyone else, I'm an odd fellow—talking to himself!"

They laughed but silently as they slithered through human hordes and left the decrepit alleyways, heading for the rough climbs of the twilight zone closest to their location. But upon arrival, they stood before an impasse of massive rock and stalactite spears with no way through. The Child was without words.

"This would take us years to travel, if…" Mistacles waved a hand in the air, "we didn't have magic to help us!"

Suddenly, the Child was jerked off the ground, but not before her guardian grabbed hold of her hands. With an intensity of a giant's throwing arm, they were catapulted into the air where they remained, suspended, until a force unknown to the Child twirled them in a circle so fast, everything became a blur. Fear overtook her once she felt her face move and morph in a way that couldn't be human, and her body, which was supposed to be solid, turned into water the higher they ascended. After a few moments passed, the spinning stopped, and they were standing atop a cliff's edge at the height of the cave.

Mistacles gave the small child time to catch her breath and when they were ready, the two stood near a giant boulder, much like when she first arrived.

"Why on Zel did you do that?!" she asked, touching her face and hair to be sure they were where they were supposed to be.

"It was the only way. Now, precious child, are you ready to see the Sun?"

"Isn't it too early?"

"It'll be rising soon. Ready or not?"

She turned to face the boulder as it moved effortlessly, and with its leave a crescent of sun-kissed light filled in the emptiness of the darkened ledge no longer.

MEN CLUTTERED the entranceway into the outside garden, pushing their way through the many onlookers to get to Mistacles. He had sent a signal for all who were able to meet him on the greenery outside Mother Summit and to do so immediately. The Army of Miracon's men were the first to arrive. They barreled in and rushed to meet him, expecting some audacious foe but instead found him alone and in a terrible state, with his hands raised to the sky and his eyes filled with tears.

"Mistacles, what is wrong?" asked Hisousen who knew him well.

"She's gone."

His cryptic words caused all to gasp.

"What do you mean she's gone?" said a bystander. "Who? It can't be!" said another.

"YES!" he screamed, slamming his hands to his sides. "She was taken. We must do everything we can to get her back!"

"Who took her?.."

As a thousand or so questions came flying at the sobered man. Tane and Care watched helplessly on tiptoes. They had found their way to the greenery through their loyal attendants and could hear his words, much to their dismay.

"It can't be..." said Tane. Her sadness, like an endless well, had turned to anger, and with her change of heart, she ran on her heels to return to her room.

"Wait! Where're you goin'?" asked Care quickly from behind.

"She's left us. She said she'd never leave us again and she LIED!" Tane's words were venom.

"No, no—she was taken! She didn't want to leave!"

"How do you know?!" Tane whipped around and grabbed his collar, forcing her forehead on his. "How do you know she didn't leave to go be with her kind?"

"Wh—what are you saying?" Care pushed her away, confused by her words. They both stood in the hall on the verge of staying or leaving when a horrid scream came from the garden.

"A what?! NO!"

Many yelled after. Their confusion and shock causing all around them to join. Always curious, the pair crept back to the commotion and stood on tiptoes again where faintly they could see their guardian. And he was a broken man.

"Yes. I said correctly." Mistacles wiped his drenched eyes before settling lifelessly on a big rock. "It was a dragon."

He sobbed as the crowd argued then calmed, and stopped when all eyes fell on him again.

"She asked to see the Sun and I allowed it." He continued. "We watched it grow in the sky together—it was so beautiful!.. She asked to play in the flower patch over there and I allowed that too. My back was turned for less than a moment." He squirmed at the memory. "She screamed and reached for me, but I was powerless to stop it! My poor child!"

"Why couldn't you stop it?!" The crowd turned on him.

"I used all the power within me to bring it back, but it did nothing but deplete me. The great Imagi Mistacles couldn't stop a flying lizard—what good am I if I can't do that?!"

He fell further on the rock and repeated—*she's gone*—as his friends and fellow Imagi came to his side.

Care searched Tane's face and her eyes went blank, like the night sky without its Moon and stars. He saw nothing left of the emotion she showed expertly moments before. He felt cold in her presence and wanted nothing more than to go to his room and hide under his blankets. But he still worried for her.

"You okay, Taney?" he asked as she walked the way they came with an attendant running to take them back. He followed close but not before turning once more to glance at the clouds, just in case.

THE SKY WAS nothing like she imagined, and she thought on it often. She would dream of clouds longer and fluffier than these, like many feather pillows sewn together made to be jumped upon. She imagined how flying through them would be like swimming in a lake made of the sweetest of milk she could float upon to speak to the Sun and the Moon. But her imagination deceived her for the sky had no feather pillows, nor lakes of milk. Rather, it was like a waterless sea—endless, dry and cold. And barren.

And she thought the wind was her friend. How it would cool her back during the warmer months, and keep her chill during those long, lonely nights sleeping in the barn. But she was quick to realize it was her enemy. Up there, in its castle of nothingness, all intruders were knocked down with no mercy, forced to plummet to earth if it so pleased. And the Sun was its cruel alley and burned her like a slow-moving flame.

She was told to hang on to the harsh scales of the dragon and to keep as low as possible without a please or a thank you. In defiance, she stood and fell off its massive side. With little effort, it caught her in its gilded claws and put her back where she stayed for the remainder of the ride. When she could no longer see the mountains, she hit the dragon on the back of its head as hard as she could, hurting her frail hands in the process.

While the Sun was still high in the sky, the dragon dove without warning and she held on to blistering scales for dear life. The clouds felt like razors and the wind was in a terrible mood. When they finally broke free of them, the dragon opened its wings and floated above a hidden cascade, landing softly in a small pool where rushing water came to settle, choosing to float like a duck among wet rocks eroded through time.

It growled pleasantly as the bubbling water massaged its seared scales and belly.

"That wind was a tyrant today!" said the dragon. His voice, deep and strange, startled the girl who never heard a creature speak. "Are you okay, little one?"

She shook her head.

"Are you hurt?"

She shook her head again.

"Can you speak?"

She shook her head again.

"Now, that can't be true. I heard you speak up there in the stars moments ago. You cried for many people then."

She didn't respond and held tighter to his scales still warm.

He groaned before speaking again. "Can I help you down?"

"Please don't eat me!" she said as she shook in fear.

The dragon laughed and the pool rippled at the noise. "I don't eat children, little one! I have no plans to harm you."

"Then why did you bring me here?!" she screamed like Tane when she didn't get her way.

"I see you have a temper—I would change that if I were you. All business, good or bad, must be handled calmly. Keep your composure and your dignity at all costs. No matter what is happening. Do you understand, little one?"

"I didn't know dragons could talk."

"Not all do, but when we do, it's probably worth listening to."

She lessened her grip and examined a way down.

"Just jump in, little one. You'll be alright."

She fell into the water and allowed herself to sink deep enough to see the creature from underneath. It's two haunches and arms, like shimmering chainmail, were as big as tree trunks, folded in like any waterfowl lazily coasting the surface.

She pushed off the pool bottom and broke water, gasping for air.

"Don't swim much? Well, there's not much use in it unless you're a fish or a boatsman!" He laughed, shaking the water once more, and this time the Child smiled.

She left the pool and held her ground just shy of his reach. She expected a chase, but the dragon remained in the water, regal and indifferent as it watched her every move.

"Where do you think you're going?" he asked.

"Home. In the mountains. I like it there."

"But you're not from there, are you?"

"No. Mistacles says I shouldn't tell anyone—err—anything where I'm from."

It frowned. "I understand. It's a hard world out there.

You can't trust everyone you meet and those you do can turn on you in a dubel."

"Where are you from?" she asked, pacing through muddy pebbles. "I thought dragons weren't a part of this world.

"Well, I shouldn't tell you. You're a stranger to me too, after all. Fair is fair."

She kicked dirt and got closer to the wading beast. "Is there anything you can tell me?"

"Well, why don't we play a game. Winner gets to keep where they're from, the loser tells."

A small strip of the Sun's gracious light came through the clouds, landing on its scales, showing a gold brighter than the newest dubel and as wondrous and white as the road in Glenloch. It fluttered its wings, shooting water before her feet, and they were immense—like giant, black sails on a colossal ship. Down its spine sat an array of spikes, like daggers wedged in stone, leading from its grand tail to its crown where, sat like honored guests, two slender horns called home.

It stared at her, and she stared back, both exposing their otherworldly gaze. Circles of black and red spiraled its magnificent eyes—a light color she couldn't discern.

Blue, perhaps? she thought.

She walked closer to the glistening beast. "Is your skin made of..."

"Wait, little one. Let's go over the game. I ask you a question or you do something I say, and if you answer it honestly or do the thing, you win a point. But, since our prize is a particular answer to a question, neither of us can ask it. Any questions?"

"Nope. So, I guess it's my turn!"

The dragon smiled wickedly. "You are a remarkable child, aren't you?"

"No, the rules are the rules—it's my turn. Okay, first question: What are your scales made of?"

"Hmm..." It took a drenched and mighty claw to its snout and scratched. "if I can remember correctly, it is made of what humans call gold and...diamond?"

"Diamond?!"

"No, no! It's my turn!" it said mocking her and she giggled. "Now, how long have you lived in the Mountains of the Predicated?"

She answered carefully. "I thought I could choose between a question or a thing to do."

The dragon rolled his eyes before pointing at the waterfall behind him. "There. Jump off!"

She ran full speed up the rocks, nicking toes and crushing rock under foot-palms, and threw herself over its ledge without hesitation. As she fell, the world held its breath. She embraced the water though it caught her roughly. She tumbled until she hit the bottom as gently as one could hope for.

While sitting again on the sandy floor, she watched as the anxious dragon reached for her, pulling up weeds and earth as he struggled to find her. She could have stayed a little longer, but the dragon's rough movements caused the sand to lift and muddy the water. She pushed off her seat and entered air once more.

"Are you okay?" she asked as she found her way to land.

He sighed and returned to wading on water as if nothing happened. "Human children are simply the worst."

"Alright, now it's my turn!"

"Wait a minute, you didn't give me the option before. I want a recount!"

She laughed. "But we just started! And you didn't say anything, so you lost it. New rule!"

"You can't add new rules! It's forbidden!"

They both laughed then, and their game of turns went on until it was nighttime and neither won.

CHAPTER 3

Tane fumbled her fingers over her book's rough edges, tired of lying around but too bored to do anything else. It had been this way for days since her closest friend went missing. Hours they all spent looking for her, losing their minds in the process. Even she and Care searched where they had always been scared to—under their bed, in the scary terrain past the thermopolia, in the deepest parts of the cave—just to find their dear friend. But, when all crevices had been searched and there was nowhere else to go, they were left to themselves to do whatever they felt like. Their studies were put on hold. And their guardian, their protector had vanished as well, or so it seemed, for his time was spent with the army men and his magic subjects, devising any way to find his missing child. Streets were full of panicking parents imagining the Child as their very own, who prayed to their favorite god for her safe return.

It was beginning to look as though everyone had forgotten about Tane, more so than they already had. They treated her like she was just some other child, pushing her to the side like she never had parents of her own or a home of her own once. So, she left the streets and went to her room where she could be away from the madness at least.

"Tane, you in there?"

She looked up as an attendant she called Maggie walked through the door with a tray full of delicious-looking food.

"No," she answered as she continued to feel the book.

"You missed dinner again, dear. Come, we're still at the dining hall if you want to join us."

"What for? No one cares."

"That's not true, Tanesy-lion." The attendant, ancient and kind reached for her hand and held it close. "We care deeply for you. You are just as important to us as the air we breathe. We worry about you. We want what's best for you and we think that is a cold dinner we can warm up, if you like."

Tane smiled, sighing at her defeat as she got out of bed. She removed her hand from Maggies who smiled smugly as they left their home together.

As Tane expected, the streets were as full and chaotic as they were earlier and never ceased. Miracon's armymen ran amuck with weapons drawn, running in formations only they understood. Wise people stepped out of their way. Imagi and Magi held up large maps and unfolded endless scrolls, surveying them for clues. They were defenseless to the quick hands of pickpockets ever so happy with the change of pace, as those who were usually vigilant and suspicious were otherwise preoccupied. This was a time unheard of in the mountains. And word had spread, that terrible thieves and smugglers had heard of the Child being missing and were on their way to find her first and collect a reward from the highest bidder. Houses without locks were quickly fashioned with them and not a child was outside past nighttime.

"Did they catch the guy who snuck in?" asked Tane who stared off, lost in the energy zipping around her.

"Yes, Sir Hisousen himself is questioning him. For the first time in a long time, someone successfully found a way in. Very concerning."

"What about the armymen? They come here all the time?"

"That's because Mistacles helps them in. The mountain works with us and will not permit those it doesn't want in. It's an ancient magic that can never be broken."

"Unless you're the guy who broke it, right?"

He laughed. "And many others."

They entered the dining hall where seats were hard to find and where some resorted to sitting on one another. The smell of ale was like a haze in the air and made Tane feel nauseous. Maggie quickly led them to a far-off table where other attendants and Care sat with empty plates and a card game afoot.

"Where's Mistacles?" she asked as she took a seat next to Care. Maggie gave her a tray full of food and flicked his fingers expertly, heating it up to a sizzle.

"With Sir Hisousen. But don't think about that now, dear. Eat up and join us in a bit of card play!"

She ate her food in despair as the ever cheerful attendants came up with endless card games she didn't like. Not one. Bored again for the umpteenth time, she watched the busy dining hall and caught sight of a solemn armyman staring longingly at a piece of parchment in his hands. Curious, she snuck to his table to see it firsthand—a painting of a pretty girl with brown hair and pink lips, who wore a white and blue blouse. Her beautiful smile shined up at them.

Tane smiled.

"Is she your lady?" she asked.

He jumped in his seat and laughed at himself.

"Yeah. She's waiting for me in Salmer's Thame. If I ever make it back in one piece..."

He slid it into his front pocket and smiled unconvincingly.

"Where's Salmer's Thame?"

"East. It's far from here and it's absolutely perfect! The days are long, and the ocean loves us! We spend our nights dancing and being merry under the cool moonlight. No one works very hard there—it's nice!"

His eyes wrinkled at the memory and the twinkle in them made Tane's heart skip a beat.

"Maybe I can go there someday."

"Maybe, but for now it's safer for you to be here with us. This part of Zel is—"

He stood up just as a fight a few tables away broke out. He pushed Tane to the side gently before jogging over to help calm the storm.

Maggie was by her side within moments.

"Are you okay?!"

He looked over her arms and face which made her laugh.

"Why are so crazy, Maggie?"

He scoffed before leading her back to their table. Care had already gotten atop it even after the other attendants begged him to get down. The last time he did that, he pulled down his trousers and mooned them.

"Did you see the fight? Are they duking it out still?"

Distracted, Care bobbed and weaved on tiptoes, trying

to see over the many heads covering the show. Eventually, an attendant took him down and made him sit down.

"I think it's about time you two got to bed."

"We can't—" said Tane, "not until Mistacles tells us goodnight. It's our rule!"

The attendants were showing their anguish in the sad and depressing looks they gave the children knowing good and well they must do what they say. And with Mistacles gone most of the time, they were constantly on edge, praying the children have mercy on them for which they seldom did. Especially the spitfire Tane. They nodded at the children's truth and led them back home to wait for Mistacles in his office. Unattended.

"Care, we're going to Salmer's Thame."

"What? Why? I don't even know where it is."

"Doesn't matter. We're gonna get that glue and get the hell out of here."

THE PRISONER, tired and bloodied from his grievous wounds wriggled in his chair. He tried to scream but the stale cloth in his mouth prevented it. Chains to his ankles and wrists were tightly secured, and he could hardly move. His captors took their time turning a flaming, red metal rod he never saw between the chains, twisting them against his exposed bones until he felt it sear his tender skin. He screamed for mercy before anything broke.

"What was that? You wanna' speak up now?"

From the dark came a dark presence—Lieutenant Hisousen, and in his hands he held the torch that could burn flesh and ignite pain. Beside him stood Mistacles, pale and remorseful as the prisoner pulled muscles to escape the torture.

"Please, for the love of the gods, speak up!" Mistacles said, pleading with his eyes.

Undeterred, the lieutenant walked to the back of the prisoner's chair and slowly put the torch to its metal bars closest to his skin. The smell of burning skin suffocated the air and the prisoner's beaming eyes gave away what was happening.

"Are you ready to speak?!" Mistacles asked, begging for the torture to end.

Tears running down his eyes, the prisoner nodded and Hisousen took away the flame.

An Imagi scurried from a dark corner and took the cloth forced deep into the prisoner's mouth. He gagged and, breathing furiously when he could, coughed up red phlegm that scattered the floor beneath him.

"Okay. What do you want to know?"

"For starters—tell us where the girl is!" Hisousen shouted and the prisoner winced at his voice now synonymous with pain.

"We don't have her... We wished we knew where but that's it."

"Why don't I believe you?"

Hisousen brought the torch close to the prisoner's face who let out a throaty sob.

"That's enough, Hisousen!" Mistacles screamed, turning his ire to the prisoner. "Tell us everything you know. NOW!"

He glared deep into the man's eyes, stirring his heart to beat faster.

"A-alright! My close friends and I were taken in by the Order of Garatos six pale moons ago. They killed most of our guild because they didn't want to join. The rest of us have been rummaging through homes, emptying town and village reserves, and collecting information for our officials in exchange for our lives."

"Why here?" Hisousen asked.

"Why not? I had been near the mountains since last moon when I got word of the missing girl. They told me to enter when no one was looking, and I found my way in. No problem at all."

"You could have entered the whole time?!" Mistacles said in disbelief, his voice turning into a whisper. "We need those supplies more than ever now."

"Maybe I can help? You know, a favor for a favor?" said the prisoner before spitting more phlegm at Hisousen's feet.

"What information did you gather?" Mistacles sat close to him, and he eased up a little.

"Well, your fortress is easier to enter than was recently thought. And, there are less solid parts of the mountain the Order can drill into."

"Drill into? HOW DARE YOU!" An enraged Imagi got up to hit the prisoner but was carried off, screaming curses as he left.

"Now, the fun part." Hisousen said grimly. "Tell us everything you know about your officials and their operations, and maybe you'll leave here alive."

MISTACLES WAS brisk as he left Hisousen's tent. His heart was heavy, and he needed to be alone.

"Wait up! Are you okay?" Hisousen asked as Mistacles came to a stop and leaned forward.

"Are you kidding me? How can I be? Our fortress is days from upheaval, one of my children is missing, and—damn it Hisousen, I hate seeing people in pain!" he said, gagging.

"What had to be done was done. We got all we needed."

"Did we?" Mistacles stood upright. "Don't you think if we eased up on the guy, maybe we could have gotten more? Maybe, slight chance, he could have lived?"

"A traitor to his nation and to his people doesn't deserve to live!"

Mistacles shook his head. "I'm leaving before I say something I regret. You do the same!"

As he walked away, Hisousen shouted back. "I'll inform the guards down wind of the situation and send for Mal Three to come and get the new directive. Have a good night!"

Mistacles shuffled down the street near home, unaware of the two tiny prowlers following close behind, confused and upset by the conversation they overheard.

As he got closer to home, he turned sharply, bumping into them.

"Tane, Care—you better have a good explanation for this!!"

He carried the two in by the clothes on their backs and led them to the couch in his office. "Well?"

Care was the first to cave. "We just wanted to see you and find you and—"

Tane hit him hard in the arm.

"Hey, Tanesy, you had better say you're sorry."

"Why?!"

"Because it's not nice to hurt others."

"Oh, so you can but I can't. At least I didn't torture him to death!"

Mistacles stared at her in horror. "You heard all that?"

"Not all but enough to know. We waited up for hours

for you to come home and tell us goodnight. How fair is that to us, huh? We didn't ask to be here, you know. If you don't want us anymore, we can go somewhere else. You know, like Salmer's Thame!"

He didn't say anything at first. But then, like a fissure, he burst into laughter and it broke her confidence in half.

"Salmer's Thame?!" He laughed again. "Have you ever been to Salmer's Thame?"

"No, but it's perfect and sunny and oceany and..."

"It's a desert, sweetie," he said, laughing again. "You guys know just how to cheer me up! Sorry for yelling, by the way. I'm just... really worried about Chil, and I'm sad I haven't seen either of you enough since, really. Do you forgive me?"

The two kids looked at each other and Care jumped to hug the robust Imagi. Tane meandered to his side, and he picked her up and gave her a big bear hug. She laughed—really laughed—as her back made creaky sounds at his squeezes.

He carried them to bed as their attendants tidied up their space and set their waters on their bedside tables. He said goodnight to Care and tickled him until he screamed *emor*—an Imagi word for enough. As he put Tane to rest, he sang her a sweet song with his deep voice which put her to sleep when nothing else would. He lovingly touched her forehead and willed for all her dreams be merry ones, especially for that night.

He dimmed the candle-lights and left the room as the soft cooing of children filled the dark space. He dragged his heavy feet to his office and sat in his chair, loose in the legs and near its end. When all his work was finished, he held his head in his hands and cried for his missing girl.

CHAPTER 4

The night sky was like the ocean, filled with innumerable specks of glittering stars, stuck in some forlorn gaze. The Child smiled knowingly, as if she and these vibrant stars held a secret so few knew.

She had been in the company of a dragon, and not a moment did she feel despair, though the memories of her friends and family were never far from her mind.

Earlier in the day they flew through lands forested and deserted as they embarked on another of their spontaneous adventures. Buildings stood barely, destroyed and hollow, and small wars went underway as they glided above unnoticed.

When they found the ocean, the dragon took to soar, allowing the strong breeze to keep them afloat. She closed her eyes briefly, hypnotized by the fluid motions of the waves. She awoke once a tempest came, and lightning and thunder forced her head low, even before her dragon friend asked her too.

They eventually landed on a floating patch of burnt earth too warm for comfort, where black puddles full of red magma flowed ever south until inevitably entering the ocean where the water steamed at its touch.

"What's this?" she asked as she went to shimmy down the dragons' back.

"Ah, ah! You stay right where you are. Look, but don't touch."

"But it's so pretty! Why is it so hot?"

The dragon jumped between drifting rocks on the flame river like a cat avoiding water. Its gold scales ricocheted rainbow beams as the Sun came close to them, refusing to let them out of his sight.

"Because it comes from a volcano at the end of the world_named Zavai. One drop of this stuff will burn right through you."

"How come you can touch it?" she asked as he put a clawed hand into the lava.

He scoffed as he held like a goblet the liquid rock in his clutches, his scales and claws turned hot white, glowing as the lava continuously became hotter. And he felt nothing as he swished it, wishing for any semblance of pain to numb that which cannot be destroyed.

"Why'd you take me here?"

She wiggled as the heat rose and permeated her throat, sore and near closing.

"You remember the game we played called 'hot lava'?" he asked turning his great head to face her.

His neck, a sequence of armored scales hiding a black snack skin unbecoming of him bent and metal clamored at the motion. He smiled and so did she, thinking nothing of this.

He breathed softly onto her, and it was a cool relief. The heat no longer hurt her. He turned back and dropped his metal liquid, digging his claws into hard rock.

With the grace of a jaguar, he jumped high in the air and hung in free-fall for what seemed like forever.

The Child screamed with excitement as the world around her— though hazy—became clear. Oceans to the left and right, and land to the horizon dazzled through melted air.

At long last, they landed on a large patch of black earth that tilted at the weight of the great dragon. Before it could capsize, they were off again, leap frogging until they ran out of rough rocks and flew to miss the ocean; a sinister, dark blue, churning in anticipation and crashing like violent warlongs against warlongs as it missed an opportunity to swallow such a formidable foe.

She crossed her arms behind her head as the memory faded and the present sky above became cloudy—a grey brew. She folded leg over leg and gave in to sleep as the low humming of the dragon breathing lulled her into a restful state.

"Want some largaz'ret?"

His booming voice awakened her soul, and she sat up with her hand on her chest. She twisted to see and was face to face with a crispy lump, once an animal, at the end of a small stick, smelling of blood and foul waste. She followed the stick upwards and found the toothy dragon, smiling, holding the twig between two of its smallest claws.

She rolled her eyes and fell back on the grass.

"Okay then. All for me! Is something the matter?"

"Well..." she paused, "I'm a little confused is all."

"Confused? What for?"

She felt it walk to her and lay its long, gilded tail around her.

"Do you know who I am?" she asked for the first time since they met.

The dragon sighed. "I would be lying if I said I didn't. There's not a being in Zel who hasn't heard of you, little one."

"So, you know who my dad is?" She hesitantly looked at the dragon and it stared back sincerely, its deep blue eyes glowing above the fire's reaching arms. "I've never met him, so I don't know if I should call him that or... father? Garaton? I don't know..."

"I think you are thinking too hard on this, little one," the dragon said softly as it brushed her arm with the back of its claws.

"Do you have a dad?" she asked.

The dragon sighed again. "Yes and no. It isn't the same thing as it is for humans."

"Is there a difference between a dad and a father?"

"I believe so, but I am no expert by any means. It would seem a dad is a parent who is fun and caring—who is a part of their child's everyday life, no matter the circumstance. They don't seem to be as strict as fathers, and the children don't seem to mind. But fathers need to be strict, it seems, though they can do too much and cause more harm than good. They are your blood, but some choose to be little more than that. Some are there when you need them, and sacrifice so much, whether the child sees it or not. A man can be both, but some are neither."

"Mine chose to be neither. What does that make him?"

"A fool!" said the dragon as it lifted its tail in the air, taking the Child up with it.

"Put me down!"

"Not unless you say the magic word!"

"What?! I don't know it!"

"Well then—guess!"

"Uh... Pickles!" she screamed, even while her head

hung, and it echoed through their little camp, muffled under the distant waterfall softy churning.

They laughed like silly children, forever young as he dropped her softly on the ground and held his grand belly in a fit. They fell, heads resting on grass, still giggling and sides hurting, when the Child spoke again.

"Do you have any kids?"

He lifted his neck, and his warm, vibrant, armored scales turned cold. He cleared his throat and answered carefully.

"Yes, and I could have done a better job. I could have been there more. I hope one day they'll forgive me!"

"Of course they will!" she said as she climbed his horny crown and laid in the middle, a soft and smooth patch of skin. "You're the best..."

She pushed off its head and nearly cried at the realization. "Oh my—I don't know your name! I'm sorry!"

He chortled and moved them closer to the cave he claimed as theirs, blowing fire on dried twigs they gathered earlier. "It's okay," he chuckled, "I don't really have one—like you. But, you can call me whatever you want."

"Can I call you dad?"

Silence filled the world as she waited for a response.

"If that's what you want, little one."

At his answer, the girl sighed, relieved she hadn't been rejected. She climbed from his crown, and they returned to lying under the stars, watching them fade in and out of smoky clouds as time passed. And they discussed whatever came to the girls' mind, her thoughts like arrows shot without aim. Eventually she yawned and he told her to go to bed for which she refused and yawned again.

"Dad... can you tell me about Garaton? Have you ever met him?"

"There's nothing I can tell you you don't already know. He's the strongest of the Seven Golden Gods. Father of the great Gilton. Defender of Zel. He's bright and always ablaze, like the stars above. He was one once—a star, you know—back before Man was created. But that was a long time ago. You must know this. Everyone knows this."

"Defender? Against what? Most of the problems I've seen is caused by him, in one way or another, anyways."

"Well, he and his son stopped the Darkness in Gilton City several years ago, and they stopped the heathen, earthly spirits of this realm from enslaving men. And so much more, little one."

"Ugh," she rolled her eyes, "and he enslaved people too. Not convinced."

"And his Order of Garatos brings peace to the land."

She scoffed and the dragon watched puzzled.

"What's so funny?" he asked.

"I thought you knew about me... The Order of Garatos came to my land and destroyed my village. They killed almost everyone and took the children, including myself, to Glenloch to be slaves."

The great dragon shuffled its shoulders which disturbed her slightly.

She continued. "You make him sound not-so-bad, but I don't know... His followers like to hurt kids and they make their people work until they drop. I've seen it with my own eyes... You okay?"

The dragon snorted and spat a small flame before clearing its throat.

"Oh yes, I'm fine. I had no idea the magnitude of the depravity this world endured. I don't come here often, but when I do it's always a surprise as to what I find."

"Can I ask you one more thing before bed?"

"Of course. Ask away and I will answer honestly."

"Why did you take me from the mountains?"

And so came the longest pause of the evening.

"I saw you running freely on top of the mountains and wasn't sure what to do. I was under the impression you were under duress and needed to be rescued. But you seemed so happy with that big man—what was his name again?"

"Mistacles."

"Ah yes, Mistaples, the Magician!"

"No," she laughed, "it's Mistacles, the Imagi!"

"Okay fine. I picked you up not sure if I should take you to Gilton City or keep you where you already were. Do you like it there in the mountains?"

"Yeah... I get bored sometimes because we can't go outside but otherwise I like it a lot. I would much rather stay here with you, though."

He laughed. "A little girl cannot stay with a monster. Otherwise, we would be together forever, little one."

She started to fall asleep as the gentle humming of some ancient song rang through its head like a singing bowl and into hers.

"I'm curious, little one." He asked and she jolted awake. "Why did he take you outside?"

"Well..."

She stopped as the memory of that morning came to her. How kind and understanding Mistacles was for letting her outside when he knew the possible danger broke her heart. She could only imagine the sadness he felt not knowing if she would ever come back.

The dragon sensing this and intervened.

"I'm sure he's not mad at you. He probably misses you and wants to see you again."

She shook off tears and spoke again. "I asked to see the Sun and Moon because I hadn't seen them since we got there, so he snuck me to the gardens to see the Sun. We didn't make it to the Moon."

She looked to the sky and didn't see the giant ball. Every night she had been away, it was far from her.

She sighed.

"You know, I happen to know the Moon pretty well. Do you want to see her?"

The Child kicked the side of the dragon's neck and laughed at its gaging.

"No you can't!"

"First of all, please don't kick me in the neck. Second..."

From somewhere in the deep beyond, in the high, blackened sky came a circle, transparent at first but filled with a blinding opal as the moments passed. The world became illuminated in pale serenity.

The Child stared with eyes full of tears as her sweet face felt its cool light.

"You!... I... I can't believe!"

She jumped off its head and ran to the edge of a cliff to see it closely. The dragon stood back as she tried to reach for the Moon whose radiant glow lit up the entire valley for the first time in an age.

She reached for her until sleep overcame her and she fell back into the dragon, lying in his embrace as she closed her eyes, cooing like a baby in slumber. He watched her sleep soundly, her body rising and falling with her shallow breathing. He wished that moment would last forever.

He glared into the brightened vale and watched ever cautious, searching for any movements of the Order of Garatos whose presence now left a stain on their own god's name. And he was not happy.

CHAPTER 5

It was cold where he rested, somewhere in the northern plains where its people spoke a language he had not heard before, with customs so different from his own. He was on an important mission with his companions no one else his age could have been trusted with, or so he had been told. He would have been scared had he not been so enveloped by adventure—a young man, in the harsh wilds, surviving against all odds—like a real man.

His journey started to the east in Allsingdale, the heart of the goddess Miracon's people, where her army trained and waited for her call to action. He, with his companion by his side, traveled the long way from the Mountains of the Predicated to the city's high, sea-blue gates, having been told by Marcello Apontaceus their presence was wanted there. But by some terrible chance, not long after their arrival, the capital city's Lord of the Land was assassinated and a sacred statue of Miracon's favorite creature, the tenactacon, was burned to the ground.

The two mysterious fellows who left the mountains as pilgrims and entered the lush and vibrant ocean city as simple as anyone else were called soon after by the seer of the goddess herself to carry out the deed—to bring the traitor, the murderer home. And they had no other choice but to answer and agree for there was nowhere else in the world that could ever feel like the home taken from them.

Pul sat legs close to his chest in his ice box, shivering as he carefully carved a wood block down into an odd-shaped man. There was little else to do. His waiting was indefinite, and he learned after the first months of this tiring mission to never get his hopes up. He often looked around the strict, cold tent just to be certain his comrades were there, and he was thankful they hadn't left. A few were killed in the beginning and a few others hid and ran away, not cut out for the job. But one was missing now who he needed most.

And in he came like some giant bear, big and hungry before winter's nap. His beard hadn't grown in the years they spent together but had taken to trapping twigs and leaves and the occasional flying squirrel. He dressed lighter than the others for his skin could not stand the extra layers. And he loved the tundra air.

The many men inside booed at him as he quickly closed the tent flap behind him. He waddled to Pul and sat close by him, putting his large arm over his shoulders.

"Stop!" screamed Pul, trying to wiggle him off.

"You'll freeze boy! Nothing wrong with brothers helping one another!"

Munta smiled down at him, and he rolled his eyes at the gesture. He got up and threw the wood block on the ground.

"How much longer?" he asked a man lying still in a corner of the tent.

"Kid—it's gonna be awhile," answered the man,

laughing at Pul. "Why don't you go outside and play in the snow?"

The other men, haggard and bone-thin, laughed as well, their breath filling the tent like warm rain on a cool spring day. Munta, upon seeing the boy form a fist, whose anger he knew better than anyone else, was swift to pull him out of the hot room and into the tundra wild where the warm, wet air followed them before disappearing into a plume of powdery ice above them.

"I'm getting real sick of those pricks!"

"Hey! Where'd you learn to talk like that?" Munta said first serious then with a smirk.

He waited for a reaction but was left where he stood. He galloped to meet the boy's stride, easily done much to the boy's irritation. And he led the way, stubbornly, even marching against a blizzard but slower than either would have liked.

After a few steps, unknowing and unseen through the blinding blizzard were taken, the pair veered off the path, scuffling through black snow and banks until they reached the outskirts of the storm and its ire. Weary but relieved, they dragged their heavy feet to a nearby grove of evergreens and hid where they could speak freely.

"How much longer?" Pul asked again, but this time to the right person.

"Impossible to say. The longer we take, the better. If he catches on to us closing in, he'll run and hide and that'll be the end of it. Allsingdale will lose their chance for justice, and we'll be left to hang our heads all the way back."

"We can't give up that easily!"

Pul hit Munta who held his arm in jest, as if it could hurt the giant man.

"He knows these woods better than any outsider alive

and he has eyes on us already. One day, maybe two, if all goes well, and we'll have our guy. Now, would you like to take a walk to the market with me, and get some warm soup or stay here and mope like a little babyman?"

Pul pounced and was up and away, five gallops ahead of Munta before the brute could react. The snow drifts had passed and only flakes of its wrath, reaping nearby could be felt which, with the Sun well above felt refreshing. The rest of the walk through the crispy terrain of the Tel-nequri was peaceful and inspiring. Ice birds were a marvel under the Sun's spell, their bodice hollow and bright. Their wings left rainbow storms on the blank snowy land below until the clouds came to pass, and they were invisible in the all-white scenery once more. So little color could be witnessed except for traces of black beneath the ice for which nothing could live.

They conquered several mounds of man-high snow until they reached the market, alone among odd homes shaped like turtle backs, strong and closely connected. Seldom did a soul leave unless it was to run to the small market, a building where good, reliable merchants sold their wares.

Pul gritted his teeth as the lingering, snowy air hid his view. He was at his wits end. Along with Munta constantly teasing him, ice foxes who liked to jump onto the hilly exposure around them, kicking up dusty snow like salmon tossed water in the rivers close to home had found him and were nipping at his ankles and wrist—too fast for him to grab. And how they could tunnel so quietly and emerge like a boat crashing through a barrage made his heart nearly stop every time they attacked. And his partner stood besides, laughing.

Pul hit Munta in the arm, the full weight of this

enduring walk in his swing, and the man fell into a snowy mound, squealing like a helpless damsel in distress.

"*Stop*—next blow and I might die!"

Munta giggled quietly to himself as Pul angrily walk ahead, half amused by the big foot prints he left but otherwise amazed by how well he healed since the Eleventh Day —a miracle to all those who knew him before. He had his cane for so little time when he threw it aside Munta hardly noticed.

It happened while they were on their way to the others, the little ones Venlet was desperate to get back. An elderly woman had a small shack in the middle of nowhere where, if not, most of the troops would have perished if she hadn't intervened. She gave the boy something and whispered and prayed as he slept. Munta could still hear her other worldly chants but hadn't the strength to stop her. And for that, he is thankful for upon waking his little buddy was relieved of most of his burns. The cane was left on the mountain side and the boy was soon reunited with his friends, his family. But though he planned for them to stay for a while, Pul insisted to leave with the armymen, Marcello specifically, and they left right away. A scratch he could never reach, Munta always wondered—*why did we have to leave so soon?*

He shook his head and got to his feet to keep up with the determined lad.

"So, you were just gonna leave me there hanging, hmm?"

"No, I was gonna come back after I had my 'joe and soup. To collect the money for it, of course."

"Of course. My, my—in all my days I thought I'd never see this land. It was only a fable when I was young. But to be here..."

Munta threw back his head to catch the thousand, spiky snowflakes swarming above his tongue.

"Can you stop diddle daddling?! I'm hungry! You were the one who wanted to go!"

Munta turned to Pul serious and pale. He crouched low like a beast and roared. Pul rolled his eyes. He didn't think to act until he saw the big man take off one glove and knew.

"Stay away!" he said walking backwards, watching the bearded fellow wiggle his giant hand at him.

"No way! Pul, my hand is cold! Can I warm it on your face?!"

And then he ran after the boy who screamed and leapt towards the market, barely making it inside before giving him the coldest hand in history on his slightly scarred cheek.

"You're evil!" said Pul as he hit the big man again and again.

It was warmer in the market than outside though no door kept the shrilling cold winds from Arka at bay. Locals still wore their long, fur jackets and thick leather boots as they casually perused one shop after another in this massive place.

Pul caught a soft light from above and looked up. A dome of ice, thinning and wet, covered the market, shielding it from the lashings of the ancient, northern winds. It's indomitable skin so clear, the clouds could be seen, passing by, though blurry, as if they were swimming on some silky lake.

He gasped as the Sun's rays collided with the ice ceiling and hit wall after wall at an angle, random but purposeful it seemed. In his moment of weakness, Pul felt another wet and cold hand on his other cheek and reacted violently. All bystanders whose fur and boots changed little if not by a sliver more tan or brown-black or dark brown noticed the two tussle in the foyer and whispered among themselves. Munta, noticing this, waved his free hand at them to signal they were okay—a regular occurrence for the pair but maybe not for everyone else.

"Excuse me," from behind them came a soft voice, "you guys seem hungry. Would you like to try some of our food?"

A pretty woman with frizzy orange hair and an apron hugged tight around her puffy fur jacket had silently approached, bent slightly forward as if she were speaking to children. Both Munta and Pul froze but were quick to gather themselves as her eyes caught their every move.

"Yes please." They answered in unison, and as she walked them to her tavern, as rich with the smell of food and ale as any other tavern south of the tundra with not nearly as many stuffy noses, they heckled each other silently only to stop whenever she looked back.

"Where are you two from?" she asked.

"Uh…" Pul looked at Munta who blinked his left eye twice, "we're from Gilton City."

"Oh my!" She beamed as she sat them at a booth near a hardy fire. "I've never been there but I've heard it's incredible!" She stood there a moment as they stared back at her.

"So, uh, what ya' serving?" Munta asked in a most obnoxious way. Pul kicked him and got a nasty glare in return.

"Well, we've got seal, venison, pork, warlong, salmon—all the best animal bits in soup or on a platter. I would recommend the seal today, freshly caught!"

"Meh, we've had seal every day since we got here!" said Munta turning away from the girl. He winked at Pul and the boy knew what to do.

"Dad, I'm hungry for something else!" he said pounding his fists on the table.

The girl, first confused changed to excitement when she thought of something.

"We might have some duck, but it could take me awhile to find out. What did you guys say your names were?"

They shared a long look and came to an understanding inherent only in those who have lived on the run. Game was afoot.

"Oh! I don't remember ever saying, bless your sweetness! I am Earl and this is me boy, Junior. And what is yours?"

Her eyes flashed with fear, but she smiled regardless.

"Angelica. My father owns the place. If you guys need anything..." She moved to leave but stopped. "Shoot. Sorry. Do you guys still want the duck?"

Munta, seeing Pul grin like a fool, nodded.

"Absolutely."

THE TWO WALKED with a bucket full of soup carefully as they went over their plan.

"So, where'd you tell her to send the rest?" asked Pul as he tried to hold onto his smaller bucket.

"To the shed opposite our post. That's why we're going the long way. Luckily, we ran into Jusaenous before we diverted."

Munta proudly walked forward and Pul relented.

"I can't wait until this is all over."

"You and me both boy!"

· · ·

The men from Allsingale waited, bellies full in a ditch an eyes distance from the abandoned hut they sent their order from the tavern. Two pig sacks full of duck soup, carried on a cracked sled pulled by two dogs, ears flopping as they ran like wolves. And a party of men with jackets as fluffy as the dog's fur kept pace, somehow traveling through snow and trees, hiding in the dark where the Sun couldn't reach.

The freezing troop used a well-crafted glass to see farther up close and shared it amongst each other, leaving Pul his hand out as he expected a turn.

"Why can't I see?" he asked Munta who sat back, relaxing for the first time all day.

"Because you don't need to. What'll you do if you see something? Charge 'em?"

Pul raised a hand and Munta mockingly flinched before giving the boy a tickle.

"Will you guys be quiet!"

One of the companions glared daggers at Pul as he spoke. His dark eyes and scowl followed the boy everywhere, as cold and distant as he was to him, who wanted nothing more than to get along. Their interactions quickly became the worst part of this mission, beating the harsh weather bar none.

Pul took off his gloves, cold and bored, to check his scarred hands—they hadn't changed since he last looked. It was a marvel how most of the burns healed overnight, a truth he could hardly believe if it weren't for the seer's mirror. He hadn't looked into one since. The once bald man who screamed through his mind had been subdued. Nowadays, he only whispers.

He smiled to himself. He loved his burns and wore them like a badge of honor—they made him feel like a real man, like one who had gone to war and survived; like one who could never be beaten, not even by nature. But he outgrew these feeling, or so Munta said, though, as he waved his fingers, flicking them through the cold air like soldiers changing formation, he could hardly bare to part with them for some reason he couldn't explain.

"Hey," Munta whispered, and his words were almost lost as the man in Pul's mind spoke a little louder, "that guy's lost in the head, okay. Don't listen to him. We can do whatever we want." He waited for a response but continued without one. "Don't you want to see what happens next?"

Pul didn't move.

"Okay then, suit yourself. Wait, hey, hey, look—it's her!"

Pul looked up then as the sled came closer to the hut and he could finally see. It was the pretty woman from the tavern, and she sat nestled on top of the sled, holding the pig skin bags by rope like some northern Lady of the Land. The men, five in total and big, who ran as fast as shadows, stopped shy of the hut with their small blades and odd-shaped clubs within reach.

Munta shook his head.

"I hate when I'm right."

"Mr. Munta, you have a keen sense for danger," said Jusceanous, a man of slender build and sour-green eyes before gathering the party's attention as quietly as one can. "Alright, on the count of three, we'll approach the enemy from the rear as they enter the house. Keep low and stay away from their line of vision. If they turn to face us, dive until invisible. Okay, on three. One...two...three!"

One by one, the party glided like swans over the ice as the burly men ahead had already broken into the crumbling hut, reaching it quicker than their enemy would have liked.

Pul, at the back of the line, heard a woman scream and shut his eyes at the sound.

"You okay buddy?"

Munta had stayed behind with Pul, not moving since Angelica cried. The big man rubbed the boy's back rough, pounding his iron hand against bone and air, releasing a hallow sound they both felt. Though he wouldn't admit it, he couldn't stomach the sound of screaming either, not since the Eleventh Day, and would rather be dead himself than endure those agonizing wails again.

Pul shook off his nerves and gathered himself, repositioning the small knife he held dear on his side. The pair walked in unison, crunching the same untouched snow at the same time, until they meet a part of their crew still surveying outside.

They both breathed in deep before opening the door. The rest of the party were in the middle of tying up the other men, whose fur were of wild cats, sandy with flashes of color.

Jusceanous, with his powerful eyes fixed on Angelica sat across her, trying to calm her down.

"Now miss, we didn't want to frighten or harm you," he said with his palms out towards her. "We only want to know who sent you to hurt us."

"Please let me go!" she sobbed. "I did what I was told!"

Munta tightened his jaw and left the hut quickly. He couldn't see those tears again.

How can I survive in a world full of them? he thought.

He closed his eyes and the many faces of his friends and family he cut down to save stared back, grief stricken. He would never forget them. His badge of honor. And his life-long burden.

"Who told you to do this?"

Jusceanous leaned in close, nose to nose with the girl. His strong hands gripping the chair's arms, making a creaking sound as he squeezed.

"I can't. I really can't."

She turned her head to avoid him but his words still found her ears.

"If you won't, we'll have to beat it out of one of your partners. Linka, that one."

Jusceanous pointed to an Umeki man she looked to frequently, bound with rope, and the man he commanded took him up roughly and dragged him to the door. The girl screamed and Linka stopped in his tracks.

"Please n-n-no. No more... My h-h-husband's father... it was his idea."

"Why on all the nine realms would he do that?" said a member of the party to himself, out loud—certain no one could hear him. How he would glare at Pul for no reason—the boy couldn't understand. Not all armymen were friendly but he seemed...darker, somehow.

"B-because there's a b-b—" she blubbered, "Bounty! There's a bounty for the man and kid, alive, for a lot of dubels."

Pul's eyes went wide, and he shook his head in disbelief.

"Me?! What did I do?!

"Eh." answered Jusceanous. "Nothing, probably. It would seem our 'guardians' wish to possess the Prophezier before any of the other powers of the land can."

This wasn't the first time Pul had heard himself mentioned alongside the Propheizer. And when he visited the mountains, it was put on him then too, but that didn't go very well either.

"They must be looking for someone else! I thought you were cool!" he screamed, sneering at the girl.

He smashed through the flimsy door and embraced the cold with open arms. He staggered to be by Munta whose face was littered with icy tears, and as he cried and his tears turned to ice, he stared into the Sun and his age washed away, revealing a scared boy alone in the world.

Pul watched and said nothing. Rather, he placed his arm around the giant's waist and squeezed like any brother would. Munta felt the warmth and eased in, turning away from the Sun to face his closest friend. Hesitantly, he placed a weak arm in turn over the boy's shoulders, and they stayed close until his tears finally stopped, and both could rejoin their party, placing the tied up men and girl on the sled before whipping the dogs to scatter, pulling the tired Umeki into the icy nothing.

CHAPTER 6

Pul waited patiently outside the cave his party choose to sleep in for the night as his comrades had a meeting without him. He didn't see why he couldn't be included but didn't care either. He was ready to be done with this mission. He would have stayed in Allsingdale where he was training to be in the army, enjoying himself like he never had before if Marcello hadn't insisted. And Munta had already made plans to go back home for a while before he too was stopped. It was Captain Jusceanous who took the two aside and fully explained to them how much their lives and the lives of their families were at risk. They would have no choice but to go with him and his men as they searched for the enemy, where they would be the safest.

He picked up a handful of snow and tried molding it in his Dovin-made gloves but they quickly became soaked. He threw the melted ball in the air and didn't bother catching it. He grabbed at the mound near him, picking out small clumps just to flick them into the invisible winds surrounding him. It was in moments like these he nearly forgot he wasn't alone in the middle of nowhere.

Pul heard Munta growl from within and jumped a little. He didn't want to see his friend hurt or in despair, and worse, angry. He had seen him stand by the training lines, seeing him become a man, with such love and reverence yet never let the gloom of Venlet leave his face. He felt guilty his friend couldn't go back home, not even to visit. At least not yet. But he had no desire to, even after all this time.

The burly blacksmith charged out of the cave and grabbed Pul by the arms.

"Let's go!" he said.

"W-w-wait a minute!" Pul pushed against him, but it was useless. "The warm, cozy cave is that way!"

"They want to use you as bait. Not happening!"

Munta picked the now twelve-year-old boy and hoisted him over his shoulder.

"Can we at least discuss this?" asked Pul.

From behind them came a scurry of desperate steps, trying their best to keep up.

"Munta, please my good man! He'll be fine!"

The easy and warm voice of Jusceanous was enough to make the giant stop.

"How do you know that?" he asked as he let the boy down. "How do you know he'll be safe? How dare any of you suggest such a thing knowing what he's been through!"

Pul stood tall.

"I can speak for myself Munta. If it's safe, what the problem?"

Munta turned, his face a fireball in the blizzard.

"You are much too valuable to be playing games, boy!"

Pul ran back to the cave and got in before the lumbering one could stop him.

Munta and Pul shot terrified looks at one another as they sat awkwardly on the box of the horse drawn carriage, moving forward down the endless path before them. Odd, animal sounds fell through the trees, above and below them, and they saw none of what they heard. Their creaking wheels were hypnotizing, keeling their vision and mind to imagine all sorts of horrors that could be awaiting beyond the white sheet surrounding them. And all it would take is one breath too big. And so, they breathed shallow and short. And their eyes hardly stayed off one another, each other's expression of discomfort making the other's worse.

They agreed to this, though Munta tried to get them out of it. They were to drive the carriage through the snow and not stop for any reason. They were told a man would be wandering on foot and he was paid to get them, and that at his revelation, the pair would signal the party to come to their rescue and hope they make it to them in time.

Pul elbowed Munta who stiffened.

"Why'd you get so weird earlier?"

Munta sighed and relaxed again.

"Because...you're special and others don't consider that when making stupid decisions, like this."

He peered into the white veil, certain his eyes caught Jusceanous' green ones.

"I'm definitely not the Propheizer. There's no way."

"That isn't what makes you special, boy. How about your willpower and big heart? Just to name a few. Unmatched by anyone else in Zel, I'm sure of it!"

"But what about my friends?"

Munta's eyes shot into another part of the nothing.

"I completely forgot about them. When was the last time we visited?" He asked as he reigned in the horses to slow down.

"Last summer. We stopped in for the feast and left—"

"Oh! I remember! You wanted to leave so you could train. Your friends made you cakes and presents, and you left early—without seeing them!" Munta shook his head. "Why do you do that?"

Pul hung his head.

"I'm sorry, big guy. I didn't mean anything by it. Your friends are special, just like you. You should spend more time with them. They accept you just the way you are, just like I do."

"Are you sure about that?"

Pul's face was filled with an anger Munta hadn't seen since the wreckage. He sat back and kept his eyes on the horses.

It happened suddenly. From just left of the carriage, where Munta sat, came the outline of a man fitting the description of the one they were looking for. His black hat made of fine, stallion leather and his long, black cape—blacker than his polished hat was covered in snowfall. Munta seeing this spoke to the horses, and they sped up.

Jusceanous, by Pul's side, stared in disbelief.

"That braindead oaf is gonna mess this up."

"You want me to get a little closer?" asked another armyman whose terrible eyes were never off the boy.

"No," Jusceanous said with a grim smile, "Naton will take care of it. We'll jump in when the coast is clear."

The two nodded before sliding back with the rest of the group, surveying the scene as Munta slowed the carriage to walk alongside the weary, traveling man who could keep up with two horses twice his size. And they appeared to be having a conversation.

The armyman who seethed at the very sight of Pul looked to Jusceanous whose eyes flickered with fear. Munta's big hand fell to shake the walking traveler and with little effort lifted him onto the carriage.

"What the…"

The strange army man reeled back in horror as the man he paid to kill Munta and steal the boy sat alongside them, laughing and carrying on like old friends would. He looked to where Jusceanous had been, but he was gone. He turned in a circle and, to his dismay, was alone. He whipped around to see the carriage and it too had disappeared.

Footsteps crunched on soft snow around him. The earth was moving, or so it seemed as he fell backwards, terrified of what was to come. He screamed for help as he heard laughter from above. He closed his eyes until faster, smaller snow crunches came close to his head. He glared upward, hoping to find a familiar face, and saw the boy—his slightly scarred one, filled with his Venoxem features made his blood boil.

"You!" He screamed as he reached for him but was held down by many arms.

He whipped his head like a snake as he searched for his friends, men he spent the past several moons traveling with, and saw them among those holding him down like some criminal.

"Mr. Cagorion Fisenus, you are hereby arrested for the assassination of our leader…"

"No!" he screamed as his comrades tied his hands together and lifted him high above their head.

After many words and formality, Jusceanous continued,

"It is decided—you shall be sent to our Mother's Heart to be judged by her Righteous, Miracon the Wise."

None of the men showed their feelings and were as cold as their icy beards as they carried the screaming prisoner into the abyss.

"I did it for us—our people!" Cagorion screamed. "Those filthy slaves brought the Order to us. They don't deserve to be Prophezier! They don't deserve to live!"

He bit at the air as they threw him into the carriage and three of the military men sat with him, the fresh sounds of slapping clipped the wind ever so often.

Jusceanous walked to a smug Pul and proud Munta.

"Well, well boys! You did it!" He looked back to the carriage and shook his head. "I never would have suspected him. If it weren't for you two, we'd be dead by trips end."

"And here was where he wanted me ta' bury you lot," said the man in black, older than he had appeared on the road, pointing to a nearby cluster of snow-covered evergreens off their path. "He paid forty thousand dubels just for tha'!" He smiled at Munta and patted Pul on the shoulder. "If it weren't for me a-knowing Munta here, the best blacksmith tha' ever lived, I'd probably have killed you all."

Jusceanous took a step back at the man's honesty, and Munta laughed.

"Thank you for your services. You can keep the dubels he gave you, courtesy of the Army of Miracon!" said Jusceanous.

"I wasn't going to give it back anyway..."

The man in black turned and winked at Munta who waved in return as he walked into the snowy oblivion, as mysteriously as he appeared.

"I told you!" said Pul, jumping in place. "I told you he was a freak! 'Fucking slaves!.. Meh'"

"Hey, don't you swear!"

"I'm already a man Munta—get over it!"

As Pul walked off, Munta watched him and felt his whole world come crashing down.

"Already a man?"

"Come on, you big lug!" said Jusceanous, taking Munta by the shoulders. "We've got our own reward to collect."

IT WAS NEARLY Malkeevs when Mal Three and their group of military men left the terrain of the Tel-nequri with their prisoner subdued and their trip took less than a moon cycle. They sent a letter ahead with their fastest rider, no longer trusting the easily caught birds with the much-desired news of their victory. No doubt Miracon would be satisfied.

The prisoner, known as the Walksman, a fugitive once caught but escaped, who attacked travelers on the road from Venlet to Allsingdale and took their valuables before slitting their throats, draining them of their proud Oxem blood was apprehended. He had slithered through the woods and survived and convinced smaller villages to join him in his violent escapades. It wasn't until the Lord of the Land openly invited those from the Valley of Venoxem to live in Allisingdale that Cagorion decided to emerge from the shadows to make his mark on Zel. He stole, murdered, and tortured his way from the gates of the great oceanic city to Wolton, the last northern city to believe in the Seven Golden Gods. There, he found his way to Mal Three, pretending to be an armyman, and on numerous occasions attempted to murder Pul. Every which way he tried, he failed. He eventually gave up doing it himself and instead hired the deadly Dothnur—a man, perhaps, who could kill anything—if the price was high enough.

The group of armymen, while entering the green and fertile plains before Allsingdale were brimming with happiness for the cold drifts of the north were well behind them and the sun-kissed ocean city was well within their sights. When they finally arrived, they were met like lords and treated as such. Women threw themselves at the side of their horses, even at Pul's but Munta gladly refused their services on his behalf. Mothers and fathers, with bags under their eyes and stains on their work aprons, thanked them by throwing rice and barley on their path as they marched to Miracon's temple—the most holy place in her realm. No other tower in this realm but Osirs was as tall, and no one had ever taken the Long Walk to the top of the tower and survived. It had been white once, or so it had been told to Munta and Pul when they first saw it, but the sea had changed it into the color of sand, like the shore if one could touch it, and it sparkled spontaneously from hidden gems fastened by storms with waves that could drown a city. Those gems were the heralds to ships and creatures, welcoming them to its doors where anyone could visit.

True followers of the goddess and frequent visitors to her temple knew she dwelled under the tower, deep in the ocean below where she swam with her children for centuries before ever breaking the surface. But since the dawn of Man, her time in the water was less.

At the temples front gates, many priests stood waiting, their long robes of orange and maroon come together by their hands locked and held in prayer. They ordered their stable hands to take the horses and led the party through the doors.

The first chamber, which was also where they entered, was shaped like the moon when full and its walls were a dark graphite. Windows all the way around let through the gray light from outside and shimmers of the close ocean's tides newly hit by the Hiding Sun.

The priests were swift as they dodged the many followers coming and going, leading the party to the goddess' chambers, and to Pul's surprise, they used a similar form of transportation as the Imagi's in the Mountains of the Predicated to travel to such depths. Munta, who hated the magic, held on to dear life, pressing the priest maneuvering the descent with his eyes.

"So, you guys do this too?!" He asked.

"Haha. Yes. Mistacles has given the goddess many good things, hmm?"

Munta shook his head at the answer as Pul jumped and slammed his feet into the moving ground, causing it to descend faster.

"Will you quit it!" screamed Munta.

Before the boy could answer, the priests remarked, "we're here," as absent of warmth as any cold-blooded animal.

They were told they were lucky, though they hardly felt it, for the goddess was present and in her main chamber. And she was excited to meet them—particularly the boy.

Pul followed terrified, unsure how to feel about the meeting soon to come. He kept his head down and trailed behind Munta who walked at a snail's pace. When the big man stopped moving, Pul didn't. He fell after the blow, hitting his bottom hard against the floor, causing a rolling echo of metal on stone to resonate for a moment. A subtle cough jostled him to his feet, and he ran to stand beside his friend who was red from holding back laughter.

From the back of the temple came an echoey voice.

"*Dauke suo neof nheh ukita...*"

Pul's arm hairs stood on end as it came to him like a hymn and seeped into his ears. He felt drained and confused, as nauseous as any on a teetering boat. The singing continued and grew louder much to everyone's distress.

"*Dauke suo neof nheh ukita!!*"

His blood turned cold, and he wished to run away and promised to never look back.

"*Dauke suo neof nheh ukita!*"

Like lightning, he was pulled by his shoulders and wiped around. A beautiful woman with long black hair greeted him, laughing in his face with a candor unknown to him, with a force that almost made him jump out of his skin. He searched the room and found his comrades—their faces full of fear, much like his own he imagined.

He turned to meet her again and saw her eyes were not of this world. They moved like water and were a strange combination of turquoise, black, and rust. Further into her gaze he saw the Sun setting, of shadowed apricots and oranges, of lavender breathes and gray memories. And they moved with the churning tide, the end of which he was sure was a black tempest—of terrible leviathans and drowning waves. He did not blink once, afraid he'd be trapped in that dark place if he did. And he was wiser than most for it.

She ruffled his hair.

"My, my—you are a strong boy, aren't you?"

She walked away then and he could see her dress—long layers of stilled sea foam that shimmered as she walked, a flow followed from the entrance to her modest waste; her bodice laced and intricate, like spider webs and deep-sea sponges made of the blackest ink. He looked back at the door and then her and wondered how he hadn't noticed.

And then he thought, *how can such a dress shimmer in a sunless room?*

"Lady Miracon—"

Pul gasped at Jusceanous, having forgotten what human voices sounded like.

"We've brought you the murderous fiend you requested."

He bowed quickly and stood up. She bowed slightly back at him. He squinted at the faint gesture but made no other expression Pul could see.

"Very good, Jusceanous. You are worthy to be in my council and call upon me or my seeress whenever you are in need. Now, if you would forgive me, I would like nothing more than to see the murderer."

Three of the military men held up a wiggling sack, barely able to keep it still. At Miracon's gesture, they dropped it on the stone floor and from it came a sorrowful groan. Jusceanous was rough when he opened the sack's mouth, pulling Cagorion out by his hair, throwing him on the floor where he groaned again.

Miracon shook her head.

"Jusceanous, you must be gentle. Though we know he is the murderer, we mustn't judge those as false until they are proven to be false. We shouldn't be so used to using violence at first thought."

She floated to the very bruised Cagorion and held his face in her long hands, free of rings and bracelets and as bare and pale as a corpse on a slab. He cried at her touch. Pul stood awkward, unsure of what to do or how to feel.

She lifted him gracefully and led him to her throne, like a mother would a sick child to bed. He wept with every step. At the feet of her holy chair was a hole built to let in the ocean whenever the goddess so pleased. She patted his back as he stood over it, breathing heavily.

"I'm...sorry... my lady!" he cried.

He let his head rest on her long, pointy shoulder and she rubbed his arms. After much consoling, she left his side to peer into the ocean where she could see many things— past, present, and future.

"Cagorion," she shook her head, "I see all the unspeakable things you've done and all you would have if not stopped."

She waved her hand, and he looked into the water, seeing his life in the waves unfold. He saw those he hurt and those who hurt him. He saw his mother and father beat him black and blue. He saw the Order of Garatos take all he owned from his caravan and throw it on the ground, like filth. He saw the children of Venlet laugh at him as he walked through the cold, alone and destitute. He saw his anger and hate unravel when he killed his Lord for letting Venoxem's live there, free from the Order knocking at their door again.

He turned to Miracon and smiled.

"I'm ready," he said.

She smiled back. The temple then shook as black tentacles, like the limbs of willow trees but a thousand times its master came up from the hole and swung around the room wickedly, above heads, missing them deliberately—all except Cagorions. He screamed as the barbed, slimy suckers of its odious feelers latched to his back and drug him into the hole where he was never to be seen again.

The goddess chuckled to herself before turning back to her guests. And their faces were pale.

"Sorry you had to see that! Now, we can start the festivities!"

She clapped her long hands and the terrified group jumped. An army of peasants dressed in a similar blue dress seemingly made by one fabric emerged from hidden rooms at the call and levitated to meet Mal Three, taking their clothes from them where they stood and replacing them with new ones. Their hands were too fast for Munta who tried pushing them away with two more replacing the one he managed to remove.

The dark, stone floor was being hammered on like horse hooves which hurt the poor boys' ears. The chamber had become an ant's nest with every worker holding a tunic or building a table, carrying with them food and shoes to be placed in the sea of even more of the same. And it stopped as instantaneously as it started, and the room was left much different than what the party had seen previous. The dank, death room had become a theatre of tables and chairs with food and deserts too exquisite to eat while carefree people danced around the death hole to music Pul couldn't stand. It felt like a dream. Even if he could move, he didn't want to out of fear of running into her.

And just as strange as the mayhem just passed, Jusceanous had been given a letter by one of the workers and had read it in full before the procession had ended.

"Pul, my friend," he said which woke the boy from his daze, "I have a message for you, from the mountains. It appears some 'child' has gone missing, and you, me, and Munta must go and provide aid!"

"Chil is missing?" he ran for the door but was stopped short by Munta.

"What is it now?" asked the big man.

"I just told him, I was gonna tell you. There's a kid

missing in the mountains, and they need us to get some supplies for... some reason..." answered Jusceanous.

"It's Chil!"

Pul felt his eyes water as he was desperate for a way back to the horses through the many valiant armymen invited into the chamber, excited to enjoy the fruits of their labor.

"We need to get there, like, now!" said Jusceanous just starting to panic as Pul swam through the crowd.

"Maybe I can help," said Miracon with a voice as warm as the bottom of the ocean.

CHAPTER 7

The Child stirred in her sleep as an incredible wind rushed over her. Awakened, she turned over and smiled as the familiar scent of Dad stayed with her. It was something of freshly burnt wood and mint; perfect for the cold season well on its way. She fell back asleep and dreamt well as she had every night she had been away. The night terrors that never ceased had ceased. What had watched her and found a way to her every night for years stopped suddenly, as if the Darkness knew better than to be known near the dragon.

Her dreams for once were sweet and wonderful. On one of her nights away, she dreamt she and her mother were with Tane and her mother, and they were dancing in the robust fields outside of Venlet, where the crops grew tallest, around a decorated, towering wooden post as the Sun skirted the sky a collage of pastels—pink, blue, green, and purple. Her mother even picked her up and kissed her which she never had. They were happy and full of love like how she wanted all along. When the time came to wake, her heart raced. She reached for them, still dancing, but was pulled away too fast to grab hold of them. She hated this part, when a dream was too good to ever leave, and would have cried if not for the dragon who sat waiting to hear all about it, tears and all.

As she sat up, her nose itched a little. On her hands she felt many petals as soft as her palms, moving with the opening and closing of them. She looked down where clusters of beautiful lilies with dew still on them rested, heads hung low like the ones her people left as tributes on the burial mounds of those loved and lost. She took to playing with them, expecting the petals to wilt and for the smell to disappear, but they did not.

Suddenly, the flowers disappeared, and the world turned to black. Her body lifted in the air, like when her and the dragon cruised the skies, but the wind wasn't as harsh as usual and blew with her instead of against. It was as if she were sailing through the waterless sea, finally—like one of those great wooden boats on the pier of Glenloch, sitting as regal as any duck on a pond.

She opened her arms, expecting the mountains but was given the ocean below and the stars above. And she was among them, bright and hot like raving coals in a cast iron oven. The farthest stars were like tiny ornaments she could hold in her hand and felt colder than those closest to the Sun, whose warmth made her hands tingle.

She looked down again and the weight of the sky came upon her as she fell back to Zel, so slowly she could see the whole world from one end to the other; the molten, rock land of Zavai as well as the girth of the ocean so vast it could swallow the land entirely. It was incredible. As the Mountains of the Predicated came close in her view, she felt homesick. Before she could hit the jagged rock face, she woke up.

It was before sunrise, like when her and Mistacles snuck onto the greenery together. The dragon's smell was gone. The waterfalls' rushing waters were gone.

She sat up confused and looked around. It took her a few blinking moments to know where she was and though she felt overjoyed, she wished to be with the dragon still. She slowly got to her feet and sprinted past the flower patch and onto the turf where a giant boulder guarded the way in.

She sighed and said the magic words she heard Mistactles say though soft so she wouldn't hear: "In evening's eyes most grandeur awaits, whomever enters Yexour's gate."

The boulder moved, and she walked in, but not before taking in the beauty of the sky once more.

"I'M CONFUSED. What makes the mountains impenetrable? Is it some sort of magic?" asked Reine, stuffing hot soup in his mouth.

"Don't you know the story? I guess in Miracon's country, Garaton and his tales aren't mentioned as much. Well, there were once ancient spirits born from the earth who lived here peacefully. They were the ones who, when coming together, created Man and animals and creatures and such...

"They were very powerful—the only beings more powerful were the Seven Gold Gods, of course, whom they despised more than I do. And that's saying a lot!

"The gods, in particular Garaton, interfered in these ancient spirits' affairs with Man, poisoning their minds to think their gentle protectors were the evil ones. As the gods forced their believers to build their palaces and elaborate cities from the corpses of the fallen spirits, forcing them out of their homes to be slaughtered at will, the spirits banded together and fought back. Eventually, they took the gods to war and fought well, for a time.

"This beautiful spirit," Mistacles continued, patting gently an exposed side of the mountain in his office, "was Yexour, and he was a great protector of this realm since it's creation. He was their great hope in defeating the gods and fought against Garaton one on one. But he, like many others, lost."

He rubbed the spot again.

"Poor creature. It was tall enough to reach into the sky and move the stars if he so pleased. And when he was slain, he fell in this very spot where his skin, which was already rock, hardened more and thus became the Mountains of the Predicated. It's one of the most important stories of this world Reine—come on, you should know this!"

"Yeah, I think I've heard of it, but from what I remember, the big guy caused it by rebuking the gods, refusing to negotiate peacefully with Garaton who pummeled him. I didn't know he was fighting for his land and his own kind and all that," Reine said with wet food falling out of his mouth.

Mistacles grimaced.

"So, to answer your question—the mountains are magical. Probably the most powerful natural magic around. It forbids the gods and, at least used to forbid their own offspring from entering."

"Uh, maybe the Child being here is a sign the magic's worn off," Reine said, slurping down his bowl.

"I don't know about that. It's a complicated spirit. Even

while dead he still decides who comes and goes. He's a very old and finicky mountain!"

Mistacles rubbed his face and continued. "It appears the years have battered him in some places and those bastards have been weeding them out all this time, more invested since the arrival of the godkin. I will try to contact Yexour to see where he is most vulnerable, but he may still be too weak to speak. Get your men to survey the hole and area the trespasser came from. I think that's a good place to start."

"Oh!" Reine rubbed a napkin over his face and gulped down the last bit of food before saying, "by the way. We've heard back from Marcello. He's been on a hunt, tracking a very special person of interest who could get us to the heart of Gilton City, or so he says."

"Hmm..."

Before another word was spoken, Maggie whipped open the door.

"Sir! Come quick!"

SHE WAS sure not to wake anyone when she crawled into bed. She found Tane holding a stuffed animal with her thumb in her mouth, and Care lying half-out of his bed—all was normal. She worried if they had missed her. No one seemed to be looking for her. Even as she followed the path home, copying Mistacles even as she found a way down treacherous heights, through the musty, pungent alleys not fit for a child, no one seemed to care.

She thought on her long walk home the first and only time she tried to leave the dragon and left the oasis successfully, how frantic he became. He called for her and threw massive rocks, looking under them to find her. And when he did, she was crying, having gotten stuck on a rock with nowhere to go. They were happy to have the other then and she enjoyed her stay much more after. She snuggled under the covers and fell asleep again, thinking nothing of what may have happened while she was gone.

As dawn came upon the valley and entered the mountain through its mighty eye, the attendants entered in as usual with breakfast and clothes, surrounding the beds of Tane and Care, who resisted and tried to stay in. But they had to be up early, requested by Mistacles himself, for a reason the attendants refused to give.

As the attendants brushed Tane's wild and matted hair, she noticed. She was the first to notice. Her mouth opened wide, and her strange reaction made everyone else follow her gaze. It was then the Child moved in her bed to face them, still asleep and completely unaware.

"CHIL!" screamed Tane as she leapt onto her bed and squeezed her half to death.

Care walked over, smiling and relieved, and climbed on top of the small dog pile squishing the Child. The attendants gawked at one another in disbelief and then at Maggie who ran out of the room.

Tane wouldn't stop holding her face and Care kept playing with her hair as if it had changed somehow since she was gone.

"Why didn't you wake me when you came home?" asked Tane through slobbery words.

"I didn't want to bother you. Besides, you'd see me when you woke up! And you did!"

The children laughed and held one another for a bit. Then suddenly, the door abruptly open and in walked Mistacles, reddened and out of breath. He stared at the Child, eyes wide with excitement and fear.

"Oh, my girl, please stop trying to give me a heart attack. Oh, my sweet, little child!"

He fell on the bed and held the Child as the others held her hands and feet. She didn't expect this. She had no idea while gone for those few days her family had gone crazy looking for her and were in fear of the worst. Her family. She cried some more at the realization.

After many more moments of hugging and crying, Tane began to bombard her with questions on where she had been, and the Child opened her mouth to answer but couldn't.

"Not yet, sweetie. We can ask her later, okay?"

For once, Tane agreed with Mistacles and the group with the attendants went to the dining hall where every living person in the mountain cheered for the triumphant arrival of the lost girl they all cared for so much.

He flapped his wings though he didn't need to.

He was angry—furious. He had spent so long making sure the lines of his power—of his family's power—were never blurred and could never be crossed.

He skimmed over the mountains surface, feeling its rough touch scratch his scales.

"Nice try, old friend," he said as he flew high enough to see the world better. He stayed at this high point, acknowledging all he owned.

He smiled before frowning at the wasted gold that was Glenloch.

His daughter told him of their crimes; of what his grandsons allowed happen and he was embarrassed. An eternal flame grew in his chest as his undying spirit grew hot with rage.

"My son—," he said to himself in anguish, "my grandson, did not perish for this!" He looked to Gilton City no more than a night's flight from Glenloch. "So, which one should I burn first, old friend?" he asked as he set one clawed foot, pointed towards the peer city on the mountain that burned at his touch. "Glenloch it is then!"

The great golden dragon used his burning foot to jump off and plummet into a great speed in the direction of the great white city. He peered down as the trees turned into a blurry ripple under him and he remembered how much more fun it was to fly as a bird.

He arrived before nightfall and hid in the nearby woods his dreadful enemy, the Dark God, called his domain. But all the dragon saw was his, and nothing could ever take that from him. Perhaps a human or godkin will try, but they will fail, like all the others before them.

He thought back on the years since he started the celebration, remembering them well, but couldn't recall when it was to happen.

"Today?... Tomorrow?..."

Curious, he took the shape of a young worker boy dressed in filthy, tattered clothes and walked into the city, seemingly unnoticed. He came across an Order of Garatos soldier and approached him without hesitation.

"Excuse me, sir," he asked in his child voice, "is today or tomorrow the Eleventh Day?"

The soldier eyed the meek boy before smiling. "Does it matter boy?" he asked before he grabbed at his shirt.

Another voice approaching told him to let him go.

"It ain't till tomorrow. Better wait to have fun 'till then or you'll get in trouble."

At his peer's words, the soldier let go of the boy who smiled something awful in return.

His stomach shifted. When he turned to tell his peer what he had seen, a strangeness in the boy's eyes, like an eerie, empty hole of cold and silver, like a well with no bottom but at its core a fire that left his eyes burning even as he looked away, the boy walked back to the woods where he would wait until night took the sky.

CHAPTER 8

When the children first came to the mountains, they rested far past the healing of their bodies for their minds were slow to mend. Mistacles, who took them in as his own, sat beside their beds and got to know them and their life in Venlet, and it was soon revealed to him, and to his horror, they were students of the streets, taught basic skills at the whims of their parents with Care's mother being the exception. They were behind in every way and would remain as such if nothing changed. After much thought, Mistacles took the mantle as their guardian and decided to train them in the ways of the Imagi—the only way he knew. But this road would be long and would require patience for it didn't start with magic and power, but with books. And the Child couldn't read.

She sat content and comfortable at a beautifully crafted table made of the finest spruce on the mountain, gifted to the small room by a local artisan as many attendants cleaned around her, sweeping the already clean floor. She fiddled her fingers, knowing good and well the other two would be rushing in at any moment.

The big, jolly Imagi marched in with several tomes in hand, and behind him were several Magi's with many more. They were careful in setting them down on the fine table, lifting their graceful fingers from the brittle covers as if any wrong move could remove history all together.

He smiled with the new twinkle of thankfulness in his eyes as he spoke to his little girl, radiating a light she hadn't before.

"It's nice to see at least one of you here, ready to learn. How well did you sleep?"

"Great!" she said brighter than usual. "I could've slept for longer but..."

"You know, we could have taken the day off, since you got back home yesterday and all..."

"Nope. I don't mind!"

"And what about the night terrors? How are they?"

Before she could answer, a stomping so loud, turtans would hide came from the doorway. The Child had no time to see their maker but felt their shoving on the table. They rushed to their seats, ripping off their uniquely made surcoats, valuable beyond their comprehension as they got comfortable to everyone else's silence.

"Ah! Now that we are all here, it is time to start our lesson!" Mistacles declared, watching Tane and Care reach into their pockets for anything to write with. "And where is your graphite?"

"Uh..." Care was without words and Tane ignored the question all together. The Child took another of her own and broke it in two, giving one to each of them. Tane, irritated and in a terrible mood stuck her tongue at her who stuck it back.

"Children—" Mistacles threw a giant tome on the table, wincing after the thud, "are we ready? Good! Today's study will be on the Ultiquans and their time here among us."

"What the heck's an *Ulta-kwen*?" asked Tane as she stuck a pretty bobble in her hair. She fluffed the sides of the uncontrollable curls she could see but ignored a massive clump of matted grain growing in the back—the bane of Maggie's existence.

"It's Ultiquan. They are the spirits of this world who preceded us. Let me read you an excerpt from the *Elasveiser Romantica* and we'll discuss this further:

"After the making of Zel, the First One—Father of Fathers grew from its own breasts its own people—entities made entirely of his skin, of various elements valuable and rich, and of his own energy.

They were not made of flesh nor bone and were as dense as rock and as wispy as air. They were small and they were enormous. They lived everywhere and in anything from Zel.

It was through them the first of Man came. The earth spirit and water spirit, in love, came together as one and created the body of Man. The air spirit, their honest friend then breathed life into the body and thus became the soul. They were unlike beasts and other thoughtless creatures who missed the Great Breath.

They were the protectors and bearers of Man, who loved them more than our Father of Fathers.

"Now, children, what have we gathered from this most ancient text?"

"Um, there were these spirits that came in all shapes and sizes, and they made us?" Care asked, hesitant his answer was correct.

A gracious smile from Mistacles raised his confidence and he sat back smug.

"I didn't come from a spirit. I came from my parents."

Tane had somehow found a piece of candy and was smacking it in her mouth. Mistacles, with the grace of the sea, ignored her attempts to ruffle him and instead looked to the Child who looked back, without words.

"What's the matter Chil?" he asked.

"The, uh, book says we come from them, and they help us, but how does one know if they've been helped by them if they are so much like the earth?"

Her mind wondered back to that moment in the woods with Ganguen and his men and her experience with the otherworldly animal. She hadn't spoken of it to anyone, but its appearance had left a mark on her, and she felt it deep in her soul.

"Oh, sweetie, that won't happen. They've all been destroyed. What's left are their bodies and some of their essence alive in the waterfalls we plunder and the mountains we occupy. But, that's it! There is an ancient rumor few survived and went far west but I highly doubt it to be true."

"What destroyed them?" asked Care.

"Garaton, you dummy!"

"Tane, please behave just this once! This is an important lesson!"

"Did you say they make up our waterfalls?" asked the Child whose sudden fascination sparked a curiosity in the old Imagi.

"Some do, but not all. And what do you know of waterfalls, sweetie? Have you seen them in your grandmothers' books?"

"No," the Child smiled downward, bashful having to tell her tales with the dragon again, "I mean, yeah—we've heard of them, but I was taken to one, by the dragon, and it was such a wonderful one, too!"

Tane's eyebrows went upward.

"I think Chil has lost her mind, Mr. Mistacles. Maybe we should lock her up and tickle her for more answers!"

She looked to him with playful eyes, like a child who knows more than they should.

"Alright, enough of this. Back to the Ultiquans! They were a kind bunch who wanted all creatures to live freely, so long as they respected their homes. It was they who tried to stop the godkin, numerous then, from taking slaves, but failed miserably. Some became slaves themselves and birthed abominations unimaginable, who would have ended our world if they hadn't been slain."

"So, why do we care?" asked Tane playing with her hair again.

"Because, children, to truly live in this mountain, we must understand how it came to be and how it still protects us to this day. And, we must learn to respect those lost to us for their sacrifice is what gave us the freedom we have today. Now, I will keep reciting words from the book. I suggest you all take notes as I will ask questions after. Graphite and paper at the ready?"

Before Care could ask, the Child passed two papers to Tane who took one and gave him the other. They nodded at Mistacles who then began the rest of the history of the lost race. Care scribbled notes the best he could but forgot how certain letters were drawn and wasn't sure how the sentence in his head could be written out. Tane took the once in a lifetime chance to learn from an Imagi to draw pictures of what she thought the Ultiquans looked like. As Mistacles went over the battle between Garaton and Yexour, she drew a big man next to a big mountain with the Garaton caricature having sharp teeth and black eyes.

The Child tried to write but, like Care, couldn't remember how certain words were spelt. She would cry when no one was watching, frustrated with how hard it was for her, regardless of Mistacles' efforts. She pretended to write then, drawing simple figures she could recall from Tom's book, and listened to Mistacles words, careful not to miss anything, knowing well she would never forget it:

"...and with his great and mighty sword Fengorson, he smote the lofty creature whose fall broke river systems and cracked the earth to its core. Hestha, the beautiful and lush island, once an Ultiquan herself, transformed into a lava field, and all who lived there perished..."

As the story went on, the Child again fell back into her memories with the dragon, blissfully lost wherever her mind settled.

Hestha...

The games they played there, like how Pul played with his dad. And Tane hers.

Her eyes remained on her parchment as she drew the dragon's very own without thought, smiling wickedly to herself.

"Chil?"

She shot up.

"Are you alright?"

The room turned to her, all staring and concerned. She had learned to play it cool and pretend to be happy to avoid the many questions she had few answers to. How was she to know why she daydreamed about an event so short-lived? Or how her mother's beautiful face was almost lost in her mind, but other faces, from those horrid in Glenloch and peaceful in the mountains she can see so vividly? She didn't know much, but for the first time in a long time, she felt the outside world and missed it very much.

"Yes, I'm okay!" she said smiling.

Mistacles, unconvinced, continued with the epic as the children grew restless in their seats. When the lesson did end, Tane and Care leapt from their seats and escaped, leaving their papers where they sat.

Before the Child could get up and do the same, she heard the all too familiar—*Chil, can you stay a moment?*—and fell back, leaving the table as slow as a slug, dragging her feet to yet another discussion.

"Where are all your notes?" Mistacles asked, rummaging through her drawings, finding little to no writing.

"I got lost."

"Why didn't you say so? I would have slowed down."

Her eyes shifted downwards, and he understood why.

"I'm sorry, sweetie. It can sometimes take longer to learn—not everyone's the same. Care struggles too. There is no pressure to get better right away!"

"But I just can't do it! I want to but I can't!" she cried into him, wrapping her arms around his round belly.

"You are too young to worry about something so trifle. You will read. And you will write. All of you will, if it's my last will to this world, you will. It would be nice if Tane would help you."

"It's okay," she said, wiping her eyes. "Maybe I can watch the next time you read us a bedtime story?" she asked, her big eyes shining into his.

He noticed their change since she was returned by that unsightly dragon. They had grown purple hues and were dazzling, especially when she spoke of the creature. The abductor.

"Say, why don't you tell me more about your dragon friend?" he asked, biting his tongue.

He had spoken unwell of the monster, and she shut down, refusing to speak for the rest of the night. He learned then to get the answers he needed he'd have to play nice.

"I don't know..."

"It's okay. I promise I won't get mad. He was kind to you, brought you back home, you had fun—why would I be angry?"

"Well, he took me high into the sky and we dropped down through the clouds." Mistacles winced at the thought. "And we landed in an area surrounded by rocks, like the ones here in the mountains, and there was a big waterfall! Huge!"

Her eyes lit up again at the memory, but Mistacles' had turned dark.

His eyes went dark as he grabbed Tane and Care's drawings.

"Sounds fun, sweetie!" he said through gritted teeth.

"Yeah, and I jumped off it and swam in it's pool! It was so deep!" she said, laughing and jumping around the room.

Mistacles examined Tane's expert drawing with cynicism until he noticed Garaton with razors for teeth and sharp claws. His eyes widened, and he tried his best to hide his panic.

"Hey, sweetie, I forgot—I need to go and see Mr. Hisousen, to invite him over for dinner. Can we talk more about this later?"

She nodded and kissed his cheek, giving him a hug before saying goodbye and leaving the room.

He left soon after in a huff and didn't stop until he reached Hisousen's tent where the lieutenant sat casually at his desk, legs up and crossed.

"I know where they found a way in! The mountain is strange, indeed!.. You see—some areas get warm, even during these wintred months! Of course, they would follow it, but how did they know when and where?.." He shouted his words, rambling like a mad man as he ran to the desk and forced Hiousens feet down.

"Get up, you fool! We need to move with great haste!"

"Whoa, whoa! I thought you were teaching the kids this morning?"

"I did, and now I'm here!"

"Relax, old friend. Before you start, we just got word from Marcello and Mal Three. They are on their way here. I sent a group to meet them near the site you marked on the map where the supplies should be. We're talking days until they're mission's complete!"

Hisousen grinned at the reddened man and lost it when his demeanor didn't change with the news. "I take it your news is better?"

"We'll need to send them another message!" Mistacles screamed.

CHAPTER 9

T he night was the only time the hooded figure could cover ground undetected. Cloaked by darkness, he crawled over dried leaves, eager to lessen the distance between himself and his prey. He had been following a small party of men on a mayhem spree since they left the forests near Huntington, east of the mountains, having lost them months before and was determined to never let it happen again.

It was him alone who had found them. It became clear his men were what kept the criminals out of reach, for the more he traveled with, the less hidden he was. Eventually, he ordered his men to go opposite his path and watched nonstop the sinister duo.

When he finally reached Beningdul, a neutral city where servicemen from both the Order and Miracon's Army were stationed, he gave word to his side's commander to inform Mistacles of his position and further intentions with the two men he pursued. He hadn't bathed nor ate proper food for a long while and took the time in waiting in the old, dusty city to do just that. Though their fish wasn't his favorite, he engulfed three servings of Alabaster bass in a small shack near where he rested—homesick, wishing his skin was closer to the sea.

After he freshened up to his liking, he returned to the commander's office and waited for a response. A bird of bright blues and marigold wings flew from the center of the wall with a white light tailing behind it. The parchment it held was full joy for Marcello, the Shining Knight, for making it through the rough woods alive. It also instructed the agile warrior to meet Mal Three near a part of the mountain a days' ride from where he was, this courtesy from Mistacles and him alone. But the letter wasn't from Mistacles. Rather, it was from Lieutenant Hisousen whom Marcello despised. He took the letter and scrunched it in his hands, throwing it on the ground.

He left the room and waited outside. Nearly the night passed before the commander would speak with him again. The armymen searching the streets for the bamboozling pair found no such men, and Marcello was asked to pursue them once more. It didn't take him long to find the pair, his already diminished faith in the city dwindled into near nothing. He found them, pissing in a pond near a small patch of homes where most were asleep and unawares. He then watched them enter small tavern after small tavern, his eyes as dark as a neglected eagle's as they threw plates and ale at those who served them, leaving without paying and threatening to harm those who tried to stop them. They seemed to be celebrating, singing drunken songs of Marcello and his army, of their impotence and lack of morals, losing them leagues ago to a whore in a broken-down caravan. Their boldness, their audacity made the hardened man's blood boil.

He inevitably made the call to inform his fellow

armymen in the last tavern in the city of his rank, and that a certain party were to be charged with treason and conspiracy to commit kidnapping, and it was to be done immediately. He made sure the two were still patrons and scowled as they joked like foul leeches at a feeble table at the other end of the room, throwing their tankards like young men at their first drinking. But he knew it was all a part of their act. They were masters of illusion and capable of tricking even those trained to spot them for who they really are.

As the armymen approached the table, he moved to the bar where many innocents sat unprotected. He pulled down his hood, his hair freshly cut and again the very bald he felt most comfortable in.

"Excuse me sirs. It is our authority, under the laws of this land and under the mercy of Miracon..."

As a confident, young armyman spoke the arresting lines to the disorderly men, the one with black hair and all-knowing blue eyes mocked him and put his fingers in his ears while the other, with long, white-blonde hair and similarly blue eyes laughed hysterically.

"Oy! You had better listen boys!" said an older army-man, knocking the black-haired man hard on the head. He was slow to look back but when he did, he had death in his eyes. For a moment, Marcello reached for his saber but relented when the malice went from his gaze and a light-ness returned as he blew raspberries into the armymans' faces.

"Are you gonna arrest us, or not?" asked the blonde one.

He looked to Marcello and winked which troubled him. As the men were arrested, half the room stared amazed the two rowdy punks, appearing no older than the youngest armyman there, were taken without incident. But their continued laughter made lifelong patrons leave their tankards half-full even as they were escorted out of the dry tavern.

Marcello choose to stay behind the prisoners as two guards held them up, walking on a path dimly lit by side lanterns.

"So, you finally got the nerve to catch us, ol' saber-gut! We've been waiting since Jostletown!" the black-haired one gloated.

Marcello faced the blonde one and spoke harshly.

"Ganguen, you're lucky we got you before your brothers. Maybe Lady Miracon will have mercy on you too, but I doubt that."

"What did I do?" asked the black-haired one as cheerful as a child.

"What didn't you do?" retorted Ganguen and they both laughed so hard they fell to their knees and stopped the traveling party.

The armymen guarding their sides kicked them while they were down and brought them back to their feet as they mockingly oohed and aahed.

"You've got some strong men," said Ganguen. "They'd probably have more fun on my brother's team!"

"Shut up!" screamed an armyman near the front.

"Don't listen to him," Marcello responded. "Do not listen for they will confuse you. They are not here; keep walking and do not say a word back to them!"

There was a moment of silence before the black-haired one spoke.

"Wow, that was a little harsh, don't you think? I mean, we didn't do or say anything wrong!"

"Be quiet," said Ganguen, "or they'll hurt us!"

They both laughed again and continued to rattle the

armymen even as they reached the jail, a sad sight compared to the monolith stone labyrinth in Gilton City or its High Guardian's lair, whose own prison only one had ever escaped.

"Oh wow! Do you really think a being such as I can't break out of here?" asked Ganguen.

"They obviously don't see you as a threat pal," said the other.

They were rushed into their cell and thrown in together though Marcello protested. Ten armymen stood over the bars with halberds aimed to kill. The pair sat against the stone wall, unamused, and started to whistle.

"Ganguen, son of Gilton and brother of Gargo and Girgo —you are hereby charged with the attempted murder and taking of one of the godkin, and for other crimes too numerous to say. You are to sit here and rot, for your safety, until I return and take you to Allsingdale, to be judged by her most high, goddess Miracon. Any questions?"

Marcello stood tall, relaxed for the first time since he started the journey to find them. It hadn't gone how he would have liked but the reward would be better than he could ever imagine. If only there was another way to Gilton City.

"Why are you so mean to us? And why are we being charged with stealing a person? When did that ever happen?" Ganguen put a hand to his chest as the other laughed impiously.

Marcello didn't say another word but instead left the jail as the two abrasive men screamed at his back, beckoning his return. He bid the commander farewell and wished to give him advice on the two, but he wouldn't hear it.

He wasted no time leaving the city, taking a horse until the horse could go no further but was thankful to be abandoned so close to the location. He followed Hisousen's directions to the pathway on foot the best he could, but memory didn't serve him well and foliage blocked his vision everywhere he turned. At his wits end, he cut through the overwhelming forest with his saber and came across the entrance at last.

The modest trail seemed long, bending with the curve of the mountain as it got higher. He shuddered. At the trailhead he flicked his hood up and tied his cloak tighter around his chest—the hike would be long. As he progressed, he was careful and checked where he walked, knowing better than any his chances against a bear were slim. And he tried to take the path out of many where the wind blew lightest but found there was no spot safe from the tundra's wicked tongue. What should have taken two days took three as a large family of elk crossed his path ever so slowly and he hadn't the energy to outrun them.

When he finally arrived at the destination, a human icicle, a small tent barely visible until close swayed in the storm, on its ropes, nearly flying away with every gust. He walked in before making his presence known. Inside sat a pale Captain Jusceanous with Munta and Pul close besides, the very faces he had been longing to see for ages. He shook their hands in sincere brotherhood and knelt close to the fire, his head frozen for which he cursed having cut his hair so soon.

"So, why are we here?" he asked through chittered teeth.

"Pul, get the man something warm to put on!" said Munta, biting on a chunk of hard jerky. Pul took from a large sack a massive fur hide and threw it over the spit recently warm from a burnt fox. The men watched him and he sneered in response.

"Mistscles needs some plants and fruits and shit for a spell or... I can't remember anymore!"

Jusceanous eyes were half open, tired by the unending cold around them. Munta moved to slap him across the face, but Jusceanous moved as if by memory.

"We need kettle's breath, snow drips, a petal from an ice beak flower, and..." Munta looked up to remember, "two elk tines."

"Damn!" said Marcello. "I just saw a heard a day ago downwind. It would be like hell to go back then up again!"

"There's more up here! We've already gotten the kettle's breath—lucky break, I guess, and we grabbed a sh —I mean *crap* ton of it. The only thing not in sight is the ice beak."

Pul seemed cheerful for being in the eye of a blizzard. When his body was covered in achy flame, the cold was soothing, and still was in some ways even when most of the pain had gone without reclaim.

"Well, what are we waiting for. Let's get it and go!"

"We also need to find the hole the trespasser made and the waterfall."

"Trespasser? Waterfall?!" Marcello's angry, cold stare turned to concern.

"Yeah... A lot has happened while we were gone, my friend. We just got word of this trespasser who attempted to steal Chil but was stopped by Hisousen. Everyone's safe and sound, but the hole is still open somewhere on this side."

"What hole? And what do you mean somewhere?!" Marcello looked to Jusceanous whose sad eyes said it all. "We need more help with this!"

"It is what it is, my friend. Mistacles sent a siren bird down the hole, and it should be loud enough to hear over the cold when close enough. We'll be leaving soon to find it. One of us will have to crawl in and examine it for clues. And there's more." Munta said clearing his throat. "Apparently, a dragon took the same girl and brought her back unharmed. For this, we are to check the surrounding area for a waterfall and report back to Mistacles if we find anything."

"What has gone on?!" Marcello wrapped in the bear hide accepted his fate and rested as they waited for the storm to calm.

GANGUEN GAZED upon his foot as he rolled it on the heel, bored but pleased with how things turned out. The armymen who swore to see him dragged into the ocean lowered their halberds just hours after Marcello left—no magic needed.

He kept his eyes on his black-haired friend who was playing cards with a few young armymen, beating them with each hand even after they checked his for cheating. He had hated him for years, as was expected of him, but after he saved him from forever prison and kept him free from the many arms of his brothers, his hate had grown into familial affection—they were family, after all.

Dreqtaton waved a hand behind him which made the cards in his other change.

Ganguen chuckled.

"So, what can you tell us about your brother?" asked an armyman, half drunk and eyes half shut.

A short burst of excitement erupted as many wanted to know about the Guardians of Zel.

"Uh, there not much to tell. I mean it, really!"

The crowd then threw chicken bones and bits of trash his way until he spoke again.

"Okay, okay. I'll tell you a few things. They are worse than what the stories say. They don't care about anyone outside of their palace walls. And they didn't do anything about the child murders and enslavement in Glenloch just a few years back. And what is worse," he looked to Dreqtaton whose eyes had changed again, "is they hired the assassin who took your leader and meant to take the life of the Prophezier which..." he rubbed his chin as he felt the air in the room change, "would have meant the end of the world, really. Without him, the Darkness would eat us whole."

"Weren't you the one who took those kids too?" asked an armyman in the back which caused the others to turn on him, but his demeanor didn't change.

"I saved them from the city and was punished for it. But it is no matter."

He looked again at his friend who tilted his head, listening to something unheard of in another room. He could hear it too. From several rooms away, the commander and his men discussed Marcello.

"*... I just love some hot-shot can come barging in and force prisoners on us. And he had the balls to keep from me where he was going? As if I wasn't going to find out!..*"

More talking continued until they heard, "*... and why on Zel would they send him up the mountain, like that? He'll end up in the middle of nowhere if he follows this foolish map! And he wanted to take some of you with him?! Over my dead body!*"

At the end of his words, the mood changed entirely. With a snap of the fingers, Dreqtaton was gone—disappeared, and Ganguen laughed as the armymen searched, befuddled by the trick.

From outside his cell, he heard guards and women scream from the hall. Most were wise enough to leave him —god revealed—alone. One armyman remained near the cell, and held his halberd the best he could even while his hands shook it into a dance.

"It's okay, son," Ganguen said, moving the bars with his hands before walking around the weapon. "It's already over. There's nothing to win here."

And he walked past the boy who dropped to his knees, broken, who crawled to an empty corner to hide. Other armymen hid as well as Ganguen walked casually among them.

He walked through the prison's halls, giving no notice to those squabbling below him, begging for mercy. When he reached the commander's chamber, he entered.

Near the dark-wood desk, at the helm of the room, he stood motionless with the map tightly held in his hands. Dreqtaton, still in the form of a young man searched around the man's grasping hand, hardly able to discern it's ink-stained coordinates.

"Does this look at all familiar to you?" asked Dreqtaton with a grin.

"Ugh," Ganguen reached for the hand, "I'll always hate you for that. And for taking the girl from me."

He smiled. "She is not ours to take—not yet, anyways. But retribution is ours to give. And I am eager to give."

The commander's eye went wide, and his fist was unrelenting to the commanding force of the Dark god.

"I don't want to harm you, tubby!" he said laughing.

Eventually, the commander's hand gave out and he dropped the paper into Dreqtaton's very own.

"Thank you for your accommodations!" said Ganguen as Dreqtaton took the Army's magical transportation bird meant for the mountains with a message of Marcello's arrival and instead sent it to Tel-nequri postmarked to no one.

They left the commander frozen and made their leave through the turret's window, landing gracefully on the earth below.

"Man—I am proud of us." said Ganguen. "We didn't kill a single person today. Not one."

"Well..." Dreqtaton said somewhat concealing, "the armyman from the bar received a little gift from me after we left.

"You didn't?.. I thought you said we need to keep it clean, as to not get discovered?"

Dreqtaton laughed.

"It's nothing. His wife will smack him across the head with a cast iron pan, and he'll be better for it. If he lives, he lives."

"But won't he hurt her if he does?!"

"No, he's not that kind of man. Interesting...you care so much about humans. They would love to watch you bleed just to see if it's like theirs. I would know."

The two then walked upside the mountain, following the same careless and amateurishly-made path left by Marcello.

CHAPTER 10

It was early morning and Tane was the least of all tired. She sat on the cold rock floor and watched as hundreds of armymen scrambled from one end of the hall to the other, doing this and that which she couldn't understand. They had come in droves to occupy the mountain and its streets, and more were coming in by the hour. They were preparing for something, but she had no idea what.

"Isn't it fun how they run around, working like busy bees?" asked the Child next to her, sitting legs fluttering in the shape of a butterfly's wings.

Tane peeled her grave attention to the bouncy girl—and she was beaming.

"What's got you all chipper today?" she asked pinching her on the arm.

"I don't know. I'm just happy, you know?"

But Tane didn't understand.

"Okay. I haven't had any night terrors since I got back from my trip, and I just found out Pul is somewhere near the mountains. Those are great reasons to be happy!"

"Trip? Did you forget you were stolen by one of those monsters in the sky who works for the very people who are trying to kill you?"

"Kill me?!"

The Child realized she hadn't thought about what would happen if she ever fell into the Order's hands again, but it was clear Tane had.

"Yes! You said yourself it was gonna take you to them. I wonder what changed its mind? Maybe it wanted to eat you whole but thought you'd taste nasty!"

"Tane Venal!" Mistacles voice shot through the crowd and hit the kids like a smack on the face. "Come here!"

She jumped and ran but not before giving her friend a sympathetic look. Just one said pages worth. They had seen each other's eyes and knew them better than anyone else could. Sisters in ways unknown to some real sisters who could hardly acknowledge they share the same eyes. And these two didn't. And it wasn't just in the eyes but also in the small gestures, the moving of their hair and the way they spoke—all said so much. It was as if, the smallest change was evident, by experience alone, that Tane could see in the Child and the Child could see in her. And she could tell by the distance in her eyes she had gone too far. The colors did change but she cared little for that—it was when her eyes were brown she knew her friend was truly there, listening, and not away in some made up place in her mind.

Her head felt like stone as she sauntered to Mistacles, waiting with arms crossed.

"This is not the time to play your horrid games, sweetie. You need to be close to her and... Oh gracious!" He glanced at the empty place Care was meant to be and nearly lost his mind. "Do you kids have any regard for me at all?" he screamed before escaping to Lieutenant Hisousen's tent.

The Child reached Tane as she flexed outward her right hand, waiting for the gentle touch of her sweet sister. They turned to each other and nodded before going their separate ways—hands cold again.

Tane, like a hawk, flew through the crowds en route to the northern outskirts of the small mountain city, Grumwell, as the Child did the same but south. They had known Care to escape to these places where only stalagmite and empty holes leading nowhere lived, and where no one could find him. They knew the farther from Grumwell they went, the more likely he would be.

Tane came to many stops and grunted as tall adults walked by unassuming. She scuttled past small stations thriving in the newly thinning streets at the city's edge. She waved at many sword-smiths whose area was in disarray, filled with carts full of iron strewn where anyone less nimble could easily fall and hurt themselves. But Tane was more than nimble—she was light as a feather. And she cursed at oblivious tanners who tore their eyes from their work to see who made the gesture but saw what was left of her dust. She did love watching the women weave and sew fresh fabrics and wool that provided a warmth seemingly lost everywhere else.

She could recall then, walking slowly now, how nice they were treated when they first came. So many mothers who had lost children and some grandchildren of their very own rocked her asleep some nights and told them stories, just like her mother would. And the men kept their distance and bowed at her and the Child as they walked by, as if they were the daughters of lords. They loved them and she knew that.

But there were those who weren't so welcoming. The leaders of the mountain, many there were, had talked at good length about such an arrival to an otherwise restful and discreet hideaway. Mistacles was one of these leaders but even his power and influence couldn't turn the power of all of them combined. There were those who were against keeping fugitives of the guardians from the guardians, and more importantly, they hated the idea of having the potential child of their most loathsome god. Many doubted her paternity, if not for her being a girl, simply due to her being able to roam freely in the mountain without harm. They figured the blood work had been wrong, but Mistacles was determined to keep her safe, nonetheless.

There were a few times when trusted members of their society, known to the close colony for a millennia or more, tried to capture the children and throw them back to the wolves. Regardless of how they felt of the Child's blood, the kidnapping of such small children was unacceptable, and they were thrown out of the mountain, into the cold as they would have the small, defenseless children.

Tane hated their faces and saw them sometimes in the black passageways naked to the light. She remembered how they tried to lure her and her friends into dark alley ways and into the darker places Care went freely but always alone.

At the thought, she hastened her pace and booked it to where she knew the little guy would be.

There were plenty of armymen who roamed the twilight tunnels leading from one area to the other and so few places were even remotely uninhabited anymore. But she knew of one hidden behind a distorted rock face as two young armymen speaking of politics, ale, and women passed by unawares. She used the strange rock face to climb up its sides and hoisted herself carefully as it was practically black and the step could be an endless one if not careful. Mistacles almost had a heart attack when he found the three playing near these endless, mouse-size caves and forbade them from entering them. But they didn't listen. Though he tried to explain to her the terrible things that could have happened, she didn't listen and instead tried to find a way out of it, yet again.

She slithered like a snake across the giant rock's back, careful to keep her hand near the surface where she can jump out and be free again.

"Care!" she whispered adamantly. "Care, are you in there?"

She heard the twitches of rats and figured her friend wasn't there, at least not yet. She considered waiting in the event he made his rounds. He would no doubt creep the same way she had gone and she could catch him before he ran off again.

But from the depths of the black came a low rumble that shook her from her thought. It was impossible to know if it was the movement of the mountain or something unnatural. She waited, still in frightful suspense as the low rumbles continued in succession.

She then thought she heard laughter, but the voice was unpleasant. She bravely looked into the dark and felt something approach. Before she could slip in, she stopped as a light from above illuminated her.

"H-h-hello?" she asked. She turned to her left and heard more rumbling, but it sounded too much like scrap metal on a smithy. She got lost in its sound and didn't notice the figure crawl next to her.

"What are you doing here?" Care asked.

Tane dropped her hold on the light and fell into the dark. She fell on a slab where her feet had been. Care desperately grabbed her hand as the slab, wet and slimy, allowed her body to slide off. In the nick of time, he took her and with a strength of a man lifted his friend above him. She grabbed hold of the distorted rock face's crown, too scared to move again once safe.

The scrapping sound grew louder just after and the two, like jack rabbits, jumped out of that small space and ran into the city streets screaming. As Care waved down an armyman to come help, Tane turned to the dark. In the space they left were two yellow eyes, squinting joyously at the sight of her. A low cackle, like that of an old lady came from it. Care took her hand and ran to the city center before she could say another word.

The Child didn't make it far on her adventure south before armymen stopped her and took her back to the dining hall where she pouted and felt helpless as her two friends remained missing. After a long time in wait, a running Care and Tane came to her, and their grave expression told her they saw something terrible.

"Oh guys, I'm so glad to see you are okay!" she said, hugging them as they tried to push her off.

"We need to get Mistacles!" said Tane frantic and covered in old dirt.

From in the distance an armyman screamed—WE'RE UNDER ATTACK—and at his words, all chaos broke lose. From above them, through all the screaming, Tane caught wisps of dust fall from the ceiling which were beautiful across the natural light. But above the sheer veil of light reining on them was a side of the mountain splitting in two.

Her eyes widened.

An arm picked her up and she was in flight. She saw the blurry motions of hundreds of armymen grabbing and reaching for their way out. She could smell wood burning and something awful, worse than iron being hit on the wheel. It made it hard for her to breath.

They entered a room and were thrown in with no explanation. They clawed at the lock, but it would not open. Care kicked at it and made a big crack down the middle. Something was keeping it shut no force could open. Not long after, the door opened, and Maggie and the attendants entered. And the door closed once more.

"Where's Mistacles?" cried Tane.

He had always been there, even when she pushed him away. She didn't want him to get hurt. She banged on the doors and cried for him only to be stopped by the Child who held her and they cried together.

Care kept kicking the door until an attendant begged him to stop. And he fell into the crying fits of his friends who wanted nothing more than to see their guardian again.

Time passed slowly before the door opened on its own. They hoped behind it was their jolly master but there was no one. The attendants, brave and wise, held the children close in the middle of them as they examined what used to be a part of their house, that Mistacles built many years before that was empty and cold before they all entered his life.

They picked up the children as they walked on rocks that came loose and twisted ankles. They eventually left the broken home and gasped at the mess around them. Half the city was covered in boulders and the opening that gave natural light and the air they breathed had caved in with a small hole left that shot a beam down as round but just as small as the moon in the sky.

Tane desperately looked around, prepared for the worst —to see more death like back home. She was prepared to see a person she loved dead and beyond recognition.

She believed she was ready until she saw him.

He stood under the giant space with his arms above him in the air. He was alive but exhausted. She continued to look around and found people walking, holding their arms and stomachs, but she saw no death.

Her eyes overflowed with tears of joy as she left the soft clutches of the attendants and stared into the eyes of the many dusty but only mildly hurt people she had grown to know over the years. And their eyes lit up at the sight of her and of her wellness intact.

She then ran to Mistacles but was stopped by Lieutenant Hisousen, equally as exhausted and bleeding from the brow.

"What's going on?" she asked painfully.

"He's trying to repair the mountain. He needs to open the air hole more otherwise we'll faint." he nodded to some of his armymen and whistled them over. "Do you need anything, sweetie?"

"Yeah, help him. Please?"

She searched his face for strength, but he was tired and defeated. Though they had stopped the siege from happening, the damage to the mountain was done.

Undeterred, she ran to the other Imagi's and their Magi and pulled on their tunics.

"You need to help Mistacles, now! He needs your help!"

"He said he can do it alone. We trust our leader and he has seldom been wrong!"

"Well, this is one of those times."

The rambunctious girl grabbed one of their staffs and ran over the debris like a pheasant as they pursued her. She ran close to the hypnotized Imagi and after seeing the deteriorating state of their master, the running Imagi's and Magi forgot all about the sneaky girl and jumped in to help. They pulled down the robs on their arms and shot them up at the hole, same as their master. Whiffs of smoke curled and danced from their shoulders to their fingertips aimed high. And when the smoke left their bodies, it pierced the air like a beam of light. Mistacles hadn't noticed them when his body became covered in that illuminated smoke now coming from his every pore.

Tane wanted to run and save him but stopped when she noticed the Child stand by herself, just as hypnotized as Mistacles—her eyes fixed on the ancient giant's side slowing moving in a way it shouldn't. Her eyes grew suddenly, and a chorus of loud gasps made Tane look to the mountain's opening once more, and it was as big as it was that morning.

A vibration filled the entire mountain, making some fall into sick slumber as Yexour straighten his spine and all was how it should be. The Imagis and Magi fell on their backs at the end of it all and all came to pick them up.

The children ran to Mistacles, climbing over rocks and dirt to find him motionless on the ground. Tane shook him violently until a gentle snore came from him and she fell back herself, relieved but spent.

She looked to the Child who turned away at her gaze. Her eyes were moving in circles, not stopping even after closing them, certainly a color she can't explain. As the attendants with armymen picked up Mistacles, she ran ahead to the broken house, not wanting to be seen.

.   .   .

THEY CHILDREN HELPED the attendants pick up the bits of debris that dirtied their already dirty room. They spent too much time waiting for Mistacles to get enough rest and were better off helping clean things up.

As they were making their beds, Tane went to the Child who was silent and all too much to herself.

"What's wrong Chil?" she asked warmly.

"There's just...so much going on. Why can't it all slow down? I just want things to go back to normal" she said through mumbles.

"Nah-uh. What did Mister Mistacles say about mumbling?"

The Child smiled.

"And who do you think you are?" she asked.

"Assistant teacher, and I am also to teach you to read, but this time I can't let you trick me like before."

"Trick you, I never!"

"You might be able to fool them, but you can't fool me! I remember when you convinced Glat's daughter you were from the Isle of Merka and your parents were fairies. And for two moons she ran away from you because you kept hissing at her!"

The girls laughed like maniacs as the attendants shook their heads like usual.

"No, this time I will not read the story to you first. I forget you remember everything!" she said finally as she kissed her on the head.

"Can I tell you something?" asked the Child scurrying them far from the ears of their attendants. "When they were working on the mountain, I heard a voice."

Tane couldn't believe what she was hearing.

"I did too. But it was right before. Was it a woman? Was she laughing?"

"Not sure, but it told me to want the mountain to feel better. And so, I did. What did she say to you?"

"She laughed and wouldn't stop. It was right before the mountain caved in. And when I looked to where it came, I saw two yellow eyes!"

The Child stared in astonishment.

"I've seen two yellow eyes before. Should we tell Mistacles?"

Tane looked to his room where he still rested.

"Not now, maybe later."

And they went back to cleaning before teasing Care about his jump-kicks at the door nearly off its hinges.

CHAPTER II

From the blackened forest came a great golden beast with eyes as red as his breath. He had been waiting for hours to show himself at the first sounds of fear and despair brought on by his special day, his scales rustling at the sensation.

He had grown to monolithic proportions; an enemy to the dragon who picked up his child—the memory, small and fleeting, added to this passionate rage, fueling his want for past reverence, long-gone from his years of neglect in every part of his life. But he would get it tonight.

Glenloch would be frightened to near death by end of day.

The earth cried at his force as he pounced into the free air, taking it again as his own, and the winds remained still, too terrified to be noticed by the harsh creature. For a short while, he remained in his isolated throne—free from all eyes in the dark skies except for the Moon and his stars, surely praying they weren't the targets this time. Ready and blood-thirsty, he fell back to earth and hovered above giant buildings made in his honor, eyeing like a vulture the mangy beggars and whores scrambling the streets for any place to hid.

But not from him—they had no idea he was there, at least not yet.

He surveyed the city until the giant pavilion was well within sight. At his approach, the sound of children in pain, defeated and miserable, homesick and abused, rang like the inside of the most sacred Celestine Bell, her cries the laments of the long-dead and saved from years of unimaginable torment in Reicher's Realm.

The roof broke and crumbled as he landed and the walls that never faltered cracked beneath his odious weight. There, he waited like a bored snake for those inside to fumble out, perched to meet them but without a hint of worry in his monstrous eyes. And they did fall and onto their knees and cried as they witnessed his menace, his glory in the flesh for the first time in a generation.

"My children—"

His voice hit like thunder and resonated into every home, into the dark depths of the all-knowing sea, pulling from the shore at his appearance.

"Do you enjoy mocking me? Your savior? Your god?"

He took a black, poisonous claw and ripped into the side of a stone pillar as if it were made of sand.

"What am I to do with you?" he asked, pointing the sharp end at the hundreds gathered who cowered and covered their bodies at the expression.

Many prayed in gibberish and many more, poor and rich, threw dubels, bloodied in his great eyes, which to their dismay didn't improve his grim disposition.

"Please, spare us your grace!" said one of many who begged for his mercy.

He listened and sighed, nonchalantly resting his glove of swords under his horned chin to think on it clearly.

"Tell me, then, those who claim to be my people—who were they who harmed the children of Zel?"

Shaking and afraid, all with hands pointed at the pavilion nearly collapsing.

He grunted before lifting his giant snout in the air. Like an old oak in a terrible storm, he waved it slightly before taking a deep breath.

"I can smell those monsters in this blasphemous crowd now! Step forward and, perhaps, you will be shown mercy."

Some men and women in white robes stepped forward, their ensemble clean but covered in their filth and lies no other could sense but the great dragon. And he showed it by revealing his teeth, long blades for giants or so it seemed, nostrils open and as big as a well.

He knew there were more, many more in fact and waited till he couldn't. As if it were nothing at all, he lifted a lazy arm and snapped his claws and those who stepped forward fell to their death. Those who hadn't began to panic.

The realization that the great dragon before them wasn't just a beast but their god made all who could make an attempt to run away. Men and women, teens and children were thrust into the air where they lingered in agony while those who stood by their side moved away from the hole they left, afraid their treason was contagious. They clawed at the air as the great dragon, wiggling his very own in the air laughed as he brought them closer to that dreaded pavilion.

"Oh where, oh where..."

From the side of the building came the bustling open of

a door where the cries of children could be heard loudest of all.

"These children will be sent back to their lands, and you will protect them from this point forward. If another one is harmed here, I will melt this city into the earth. And no one will ever know you existed. Did I make myself clear?"

A flurry of tired mothers ran to the children and tried speaking with them to find out where they came from. The dragon watched amused and left his prisoners hanging; no doubt in pain until his elephant stomach howled. Those who were still in the air waited for their death, of his chomping and tearing of their skin, cleverly eating them so they would stay alive longer. He asked for no one to enter the pavilion as he roasted it from the inside out, using its flames to keep warm his food.

THE DEBUSSE MIKA WAS PETRIFIED, in near tears from what he just witnessed—Garaton, his god and savior took to form a golden dragon and ate his officials, burning down his best place of business in the process. He moved but hesitantly after the dragon finally left after hours of flaying and burning many to death. He watched the Moon be consumed by smoke, costing all the city to be without its night light.

He turned to sit back at his desk when he saw him, standing where his grandson had years before. To any other, a simple farm boy would hardly cause them to lose their bowels, but Mika knew better.

"My lord—" he said falling to his knees to grovel, "oh my lord! You are so wise, my lord!"

"That's enough," said Garaton, sauntering towards the

desk, his devious eyes smirking. "I need to ask you something."

"Anything, Great Golden Knight."

"My child—you've heard of her. Everyone in the Nine Realms but I have. An amazing creature...she was here. Tell me everything you know about it."

"Oh, your grace, how on Zel can I remember? So many kids come from all over and get mixed together after their examinations..."

"Ganguen intervened, didn't he?"

Garaton smelled the air, a sign for the gluttonous Debusse to tell the truth.

"Yes."

A simple look, like a boy at an insignificant ant destined to meet his shoe, came from the god and it burned Mika like fire.

"YES! Um... it was my worst Telvreias! How could I forget! He stopped the Eleventh day in the early hours stating..."

He paused to think on his words carefully.

"The practices were done outside of the day and were crimes against children which are outlawed, of course."

"So, you knew?"

The terrifying boy stepped slowly towards the Debusse, shaking his head like a madman.

"You knew and..." he sniffed the air again, "why do I smell... a giant and a kiln full of bones?!"

He showed his pretty, white teeth then and the Debusse knew his end was near.

"I-I-I... I can work for you and help get more information! No one else knows what I know!"

"I think I can sniff out the rest."

"Wait! I remember! Yes, a strange little girl, had black

hair and wasn't examined—that I am sure of! She hit her head and worked at the bar before Ganguen bought time with her. I can have my assistant find which areas brought in children that day if..."

Garaton breathed in.

"You want to live? After all you've done?!"

THE WINDS RAVED at Mal Three and Marcello as they tried desperately to climb along the mountainside completely unprepared, their backs heavy from their entire lives heaved in bags made in the warm, tropical climate of Allsingdale and not suitable for temperatures such as these. They heard a rumble from under them and held onto dear life as what felt like an earthquake separated rock before putting it back together again. They kept the ingredients close to their chests as they waited far from the waterfall turned frozen museum, having gotten closer and nearly suffered frost bite from it, for another team to meet them and bring them into the warmth. They didn't bother questioning the bird sent after the mountain had shifted but were alarmed it hadn't been from Mistacles.

They moved as quickly as their bodies could, having to cover ground already covered, walking over the mountains spine not long after it had opened into an absolute deathfall.

"How much longer?" asked Marcello whose bearskin was barely enough to keep his toes from shrinking.

"Soon, baldman. And we'll have ale and women for days!"

Pul winked at Munta whose words were slanderous but lost in the snow.

"Maybe we should try and find a way in ourselves," Pul said walking away from the group.

They grabbed at his jacket, but he pulled away. He meant to jump over a rock wall in his way but stopped when he saw, not far from where they were, a group of men not wearing the colors of Miracon, chipping at the mountains' skin. He turned back and sprinted as low to the ground as he could.

"Guys! There are men over there, beyond that rock wall!" Pul screamed.

"Whoa, whoa—what men?!"

Jusceanous walked to meet him and was pulled to the ledge where the working men could be seen. He pushed the boy down and they ducked for cover, crawling back to the others.

"Guys, there're Order men breaking into the fucking mountain!"

"What?" Munta asked. "Say it a little louder so all the creatures up here can hear you!"

"How many are there?" asked Marcello instantly warm and ready to fight.

Jusceanous caught his breath and spoke.

"At least ten but only five can fight. It appears they've found a soft part in the mountain and are taking turns cutting into it. They're almost through!"

Munta gawked at his fellow men and winked before stomping threw the thick snow, running like a warlong deep in hunt at the trespassers with his axe ready like tusks. And Pul went to run behind him but was dragged back to safety first by Jusceanous, then Marcello. He walked as the others ran, dismayed he would miss out on a battle yet again.

Munta knocked into the largest man with a long sword

on his belt, having the hazy winds at his advantage, catching the soldier off guard. Jusceanous smacked and stabbed the other soldiers who ran at him, feeble in the snow and not much of a fight and saved the workers who begged hands up for mercy. By the end of the melee lasting only moments, one Order soldier remained, and he was doing whatever he could to be slain.

"You filthy mongrels, nasty slave monkeys—"

Pul smacked the man in the face and the others laughed.

"That's about all you'll deserve, sad man," said Munta as he took him into his arms and walked to where they left their things.

As they returned to their bags, from the whipping winds came their relief, armymen wading slowly through snow towards them—just as tired and showing signs of recent battle as well.

"What happened to you?" asked Marcello.

"We were under attack! Group after group of Order soldiers and their worker bees chipped at the mountain nonstop until the summit caved in. We heard the siren bird and went to investigate, and it was worse than we feared! They must have used some sort of weapon, a huge beast of a thing to break through! Thank the gods for Mistacles and his Imagis—without them, we'd all be rubble meat!"

Munta's eyebrows went up and Jusceanous rubbed his head. No other words were spoken as the group with their prisoners in toe and armymen at their sides waded to an entrance not far from their location, hidden expertly by winds and rocks. The dead were left dishonorably to be covered by the harsh tundra where they would remain forgotten.

Pul walked far behind, realizing he would be entering

the mountain again, and his friends would be waiting inside. The butterflies in his stomach flew and nearly made him puke. He hadn't changed much since they last seen him, but he felt different. And he wasn't sure they'd like him anymore.

So lost in thought, he allowed time to pass and when looking around couldn't find his party. Frantic, he tightened his bag and readied to run until Jusceanous grabbed him by the shoulder and led him back to the others, closer than he realized but hidden by the blocking winds.

"You know, kid, if it weren't for you, we wouldn't have gotten this far."

"I don't think so."

"What?!" Jusceanous grabbed his shoulder and looked in his eyes. "Without you, we wouldn't have captured Cagrion, and we wouldn't have the Blessing of Miracon from the goddess herself."

"She thinks I'm the Prophezier."

"You are, bud. It's a blessing and a curse, you know. But that's not why I love ya!" Jusceanous said as he ruffled the boy's hair from under his cap.

They followed the army men as they entered a small embankment where behind hid a small trap door rattling in the wind. He held his breath as they entered the mountain and descended, bracing for the inevitable magic that warped his body to travel such distances he couldn't fathom walking on his own. But besides the sensation of limb leaving bone and skin turning into mud, the worst feeling was in his chest for in a matter of moments he would be with his friends, his sisters again—his biggest wish and fear.

CHAPTER 12

Hisousen sat casually in Mistacles chair, caring little for the posture of his position. He had requested the children be brought to the Imagi's office but wasn't prepared to see their somber faces—at least without Mistacles present. He had hardly spoken to his own and had no clue where to start. But he started just the same.

"I understand a lot has gone on and it might be a lot to deal with right now. I may not be your first choice but if you need anyone to talk to, I'm here," he said as he pointed to himself.

Tane revolted as if on reflex and looked to the Child who reacted the same.

"I heard we have visitors, but no one knows who!" she whispered to the Child as she tried to listen to the babbling lieutenant.

"What was that Tane? So, you've heard we have visitors? Yes, we do."

He stood up.

"In the other room is your dear friend, Pul, along with a

few of our good men. They're dying to see each of you. They wait only for my signal."

The Child's mind went blank. Not even when the dragon took her and flew her through the air did she want to escape as badly as she had now. Her heart sank at the realization it was going to happen. With great effort she forced her mind to remain empty, just like Mistacles had told her, as memories of valleys and waterfalls flew into view. After many trials with his steady guidance, she found a way to stop from falling back into the Otherworld and hadn't taken the voyage in over a year.

But it was calling to her.

She resisted the urge to fall back where she felt most comfortable as her Otherself knocked softly on the cherry-oaken door of her mind.

"Chil? Hey Chil, you there? Or is it the other you?"

She looked into Tane's eyes and regained her focus.

"Nope, it's still me. I think she wants to see Pul, just as much as we do! I can't believe he's here!" the Child said hopping on her feet, taking her friends' hands in hers.

Tane yanked hers away.

"Oh, what makes you think I want to see him, hmm? He's been close enough to see us many times, and many letters he has sent saying he'd be here and yet he hasn't come. Why would I want to see him now when he obviously doesn't want to see me?"

Tane's arms had crossed, and all present stared at her in awe. Such a young girl with such a spirit was hard to miss but Hisousen would not play this game with her, not this time. He ordered his men to open the door and they did so slowly, causing all waiting to enter and those anxious to receive them to nearly jump out of their skin in anticipation.

The Child held on to Hisousen's desk to keep herself from fainting. The first to walk in was a man called Jusceanous who smiled at them without ever opening his mouth. The next was Marcello, a man she had only seen once the first time Pul came to the mountains years before. He waved at the children, but the movement was not received in kind.

Soon after, grunts came from the other room, like angry bears scuffling, before Munta, the gentle, Venletian giant jumped through the door and ran for the small girl, picking her up as if she were made of feathers.

"My, my—you've grown so little! That Mistacles had better let you run your legs!"

He tickled her under arms, and she wriggled like bound fish.

"You are such a lovely girl!"

He squeezed her tight before putting her down. He did the same to the other two and the other adults watched, bright-faced and young again it seemed. The Child kept an eye on the door and was the first to see a nervous young man walk through. He had grown a finger's length or two since they last saw one another and was well on his way to becoming a man. His brown hair had blonde streaks in spots but kept its usual mousy shade at the tips and along his neck. It had grown longer than most boys his age allowed, and it covered his eyes, steely and wild like a horse nearing a terrifying impasse.

She didn't stare where his body should have had scars, and surely didn't when they first meet again in the mountains, rather, she observed his shoulders which were as wide as some of the armymen in his company.

When Pul felt her eyes examining him, his heart fell to his stomach, and he pulled down his sleeves in response.

When his moving eyes found her still, welcoming ones, they grew. And so did hers. She wanted to cry but chose to smile instead. She scuffed her feet as she ran to him, and they hugged as strongly as they used to, when time was on their side, before their lives were changed forever. And like before, neither wanted to let go.

"Oh my! Pul—your hair is so long!" she said pulling her fingers through, exposing his full face.

"It needs to be cut," he said smiling but looking down.

"And his voice!"

"Pul!" Munta screamed and by some hidden language the boy snapped into a firm posture, his shoulders forced back.

"I got you something," he said, pulling out a small box from his fur tippet, wrapped in pretty paper reminiscent of the sea-inspired silks of Allsingdale.

"What is it?"

"It's a surprise, and you can't open it until I leave!"

He smiled faintly as she took the box and set it on Mistacles' desk as if it were a baby. She came back to find Tane still arms crossed, staring daggers into the young boy. She took her place by her side and frowned.

Care took this time—of adults talking and his friend sulking—to speak with Pul about things the girls had no interest in. They had known each other from before when Pul and his brothers played with Cara and him, and any hard feelings he had for his friends' favorite, he kept well hidden. It would seem, like last time and the time before Pul only became comfortable after talking with Care about the many army things he'd seen since they last spoke, and he was more animated about it than ever before.

"—she did what?!" asked Care.

"She summoned some beast to kill the guy. It was seriously disturbing. And then when we came by the hole in the mountain, Munta killed, like, four guys!"

"I didn't kill them, boy, I *defended* myself, and you are an ungrateful shit for saying that!" said Munta.

He covered his mouth and excused his language, but the Child was already laughing.

Everyone was enjoying themselves, welcoming long-lost friends with food and drinks, catching up and sharing memories they'd cherish forever—everyone but Tane. Without saying a word, she uncrossed her arms and left the room. The Child made a *don't know* gesture at Pul before running to catch her.

When she opened the door, she found Tane sat outside Mistacles bedroom, crying on the floor, rocking back and forth.

"You okay Tanesy?"

"Don't call me that? Why does everyone call me that?" She cried into the Child who held her. "I keep doing this. Why?"

"Doing what?"

"Crying like a scared little girl!"

"But we are little girls!"

"I'm eleven, okay!" Tane said, pushing the Child away. "And he's twelve! And how many birthdays have we shared?! And he didn't bother once, not once to let us throw him a party! It's a joke, this whole thing is a joke!"

She sobbed into her folded legs as Pul entered the hall. The Child noticed finally how differently he walked, like Marcello and the other armymen. She stared down, defeated.

"Okay, Tansey Lion, are you going to always throw a fit when I'm here?" His words made the golden-haired typhoon jump to her feet faster than eyes could allow and she hollered back like when they were younger which made him smile.

"You've got some nerve coming here, mister, 'I hang out with the army now so—I'm so cool!'"

"Get over it, Tane!"

"I don't want to!" she screamed so loud it could have shattered glass.

The door to Mistacles room opened and out he came, eyes red and fixed on the bewildered brat. Before he could raise his voice to scold her, he saw Pul and his face lit up.

"Ah, my boy, what fresh eyes for an old bat such as I!"

The girls gawked at one another confused by his words as he patted Pul on the back. "Are these hooligans bothering you?" he asked.

"Hooligans?" asked Tane hurt by his words.

Maybe Mistacles didn't catch it or maybe he knew and said what he said on purpose. Whatever the case, Tane fell into despair as he took Pul back into the room where the others were—where everyone was having a good time.

Tane shuffled to her feet and walked to his room and the Child followed. She closed the door and the two girls laid in his bed and stared at the ceiling.

"He can't be twelve. There's no way!" said Tane.

"I'm afraid he is. And it seems he doesn't need us anymore."

"I think you're right," Tane said as she held the Child's hand. "Is it okay if I'm mad about it?"

"I don't know. Maybe don't show it so much, you know? They'll think we're crazy."

"Not you, Chil. They think you are *amazing!* I am the crazy one."

The two laid in the room for hours as the others did gods know elsewhere. Eventually Mistacles came back to his room to grab something and barely noticed the girls still lying there.

"Girls! This is getting ridiculous!" he said as he pulled the covers off the bed. Tane threw a pillow at him, and he ducked. "You begged for years for him to come. He's here. Why are you acting like this?"

"It's hard to explain, Mistacles," said the Child. "I thought you'd understand." The aged man looked at the girls and sighed, defeated.

"It's not fair!" sobbed Tane into the sheets.

Mistacles got up to pat her on the back. The overwhelming sense that no matter what the Child did, her past life could never be made the same again, and that the old Pul indeed was gone forever made her pass her breaking point. Without warning, her mind turned to black, and she fell into the never-ending realm of her Otherworld.

THINGS HAD CHANGED a lot since the Dark One destroyed nearly everything in her Otherworld. Her old house full of her mother's things had fallen and a giant cave took its place. Small creatures she had no memory of creating lived and worked there, digging constantly into the ground, as silent as a mouse. And when she tried speaking with them, they stayed mute and continued to dig.

Her Otherself remained hidden, in the shadows of those creatures, refusing to reveal herself even after the Child asked. It had been Mistacles' idea, put upon her to ask, and he didn't seem surprised nothing came of her inquiry.

"I don't think you've fully made her in your mind," he had said, softly. "Perhaps you don't know what you look like. Do you ever look at your face in mirrors?"

"No."

Water that stared back at her she splashed to avoid the truth. A quick glance at its rippling waves was enough for her to know she was still there, but all else was unknown. Mirrors were completely out of the question.

"You need to—there's nothing to be afraid of. Let me ask you this: are you afraid you won't look like your mother, or are you afraid you will?"

She had no answer to give. She thought on it for so long but couldn't decide which. A part of her felt relieved she forgot a lot of her mother's face so she wouldn't have to know one way or the other. But the other part lived in constant confusion.

She stood across a moving bush where her Otherself, having jumped along the dirtied path of newly sprung trees amongst the dead ones, avoided the many questions aimed for her.

"Why am I here?" she asked, hands into fists.

"Because your friends are acting dumb," her Otherself finally answered.

"They're not acting dumb! How—"

She searched the ground for something to throw.

"Here—," from the bush rolled a rock, "throw this at me."

"I don't want to hurt you," the Child said rock in hand.

"Sure you do, but if you hurt me, you hurt you, too. What happened to you?"

The Child snarled like a dog as she threw the rock into the bush. She instantly felt a sharp pain in her head as the world flipped on her.

She closed her eyes and waited patiently to open them until she was back in Mistacles' bed where she found herself alone. She was slow to leave the room and staggered into the hall where no attendant lingered. She opened the door to the office and closed it when she found it empty. She left the hall and walked until she was outside where a mass of her people were enjoying themselves.

"There you are!" said Munta, leaving the crowd, picking her up again. "You okay there, Musta?"

"Musta?" she asked.

"Yeah, that was my grandmothers name, and now it's yours!"

She giggled as the red-bearded fellow threw her over his shoulder so she could see over everyone else. The big man meandered around the party, talking to the armymen with tankards in their hands.

She peeked over the crowd and saw Tane and Pul talking calmly to one another. She nodded and then he. They shook hands before they gave each other a hug—long overdue.

The Child smiled warmly and kicked Munta hard in the shoulder.

"Let me down!"

"Now that's the girl I remember from back in the village!"

He set her down as gentle as a midwife a baby in a basket. She thought about what he said as she went to join her friends tussling a few groups of people away.

Munta gazed at some of the last children of his people's blood with both peace in sadness in his heart. They had changed more than they could ever know.

He sighed at the memory of the feisty and cunning child without a name, who could outrun a horse and scare any man walking home alone at night. She had been a survivor, always. But something changed her. She was a shell of her former self.

He watched as she politely walked through the crowd and went to stand by her friend's wrestling. They pulled her in, and she hardly fought back. Her eyes were like that of a frightened mouse, anxious and pained.

He sighed.

"Big man, when are the two of you heading to Venlet?" asked a drunk armyman from the bubbling crowd.

"What are you talking about?" Munta asked, confused and a little drunk himself.

"Didn't you hear? A dragon burned down part of Glenloch, and some child slaves from your village were found. I thought you knew? Everybody does!"

Munta dropped his drink and ran screaming for Marcello. By the time he reached him, the news had spread, and he too was equally as frantic to find him. He looked over at the children playing and his heart sank as they stood shocked and upset amongst one another.

The serviceman who told Munta the news had also told every person he saw. He held the ale in his hand with no intention of drinking it. As the news spread and the many interested people rushed to one another for more information, he slid back into the hole in the wall he came from. In the dark his bright blue eyes were brighter than ever.

Ganguen sat uncomfortable in the in-between—cold from the outside yet warm from the many fires lit nearby.

"What's going on out there?" he asked through chattery teeth.

"They had no idea what Garaton had done. Now they do. The girl's in there and she's protected from all sides. And the fat man was somewhere else."

Ganguen rolled his eyes. "Then go find him."

"Later. For now, we rest. Maybe you should go in and find yourself some company."

Ganguen pointed at himself and motioned up and down. "Unlike you, Dreqy-poo, I can't change my form."

"Whose gonna know what you look like besides those kids and Marcello, hmm?"

Ganguen rubbed his chin before leaving, and the young serviceman with brimming blue eyes took his place. The strange fellow, whose eyes moved like air, sneered as the runt of the litter tripped over rock and clumsily made it to the party, and he chortled for his plans were slowly falling into place.

"Soon, Yexour...soon."

CHAPTER 13

She ran her thin fingers through the baby blue sheets she hung to dry, dreamily recalling a memory she never had. Her dark hair blew in the wind like ribbon as she held a small, beautiful shirt close to her face.

She breathed it in, hoping the smell of her daughter, unknown to her, would caress her nose with the same softness of a baby's hand. She imagined her child would have smelt of lavender and mint. She breathed in the shirt once more, but stale peat greeted her.

She held back a sob, a startling gasp in the back of her throat. She hardly gave her daughter anything and what was left of her burned with the house.

"Parity! Parity, dear where are you!"

She shook her head and looked to the house where her mother, waving frantic beckoned her to the door.

She ran to meet her, shivering at the breeze turned cold at her leave.

"Ugh, mother. I can't get over this weather. By this time new moon, we'll have more snow than air!"

Agatha scoffed.

"I guess I had better leave now before the way back closes up again."

"So soon?"

Agatha walked to her sweet daughter who was young and fruitful and more beautiful than she could have ever hoped for and nodded.

"Your father's knee isn't doing too well and the 'clucks have been cawing for me, apparently!"

"Well, maybe you could send dad to keep me company. Then I can take care of him too!"

Agatha eyed her, suspicious.

"More like you want someone to cook for you!"

The two laughed as they finished tidying up the home, singing and whistling while they worked.

It was nearing the end of day when a familiar face came trudging up Parity's walkway and she beamed at the sight of him. She ran down her steps and gave him a warm embrace.

"Oh Unta—am I happy to see you!" she radiated.

"And I you, Ms. Hollon. I see you and Agatha are ready for the children."

He hadn't changed much over the years but in his eyes —small, dark specters that caught everything and hardly stayed still. They bothered most, but not her.

"How are the boys?" she asked, hands on hips.

"I have no idea. You should take the trip, you know, and see your daughter sometime!"

He bit his tongue as the vibrant lady's spark diminished.

"Maybe.... I'll go with you!"

"No, you won't! You'll never leave this place, ever!" Her spark returned, and his heart again felt at ease.

"Well, I know you planned to leave for Holfenya last

year. I would be lying If I said I wasn't pleased to see you've stayed—"

"For one more year!" said Agatha from behind them, smiling impishly.

"Don't listen to her! Come on up and visit with us for a moment!"

"I can't. I only stopped by to let you know the children will be here within the hour, and there are about a dozen of them. They're not all from our village. The Order destroyed their people, and they are the last of their kind, so…"

"Perfect! I'll take five!" Parity answered, dancing near her gate. "Oh! I should get dressed!"

"Parity, my dear, this isn't a performance—it's children!" said Agatha as the gazelle of a woman pranced past her and closed the door.

She took this moment to come close to the red-haired man.

"How's my granddaughter?" she asked.

"She seems to be doing fine. From what Mistacles sent me, her night terrors have stopped but she still can't read. Something may have happened, but he didn't say. They're expecting my brother and Pul soon. Hopefully they'll send a letter; I haven't heard from them in months!"

"Is Munta angry with you?" she asked sincerely.

He laughed. "No, he's been in hiding with Pul. They seem to be having the time of their life. I'm afraid, though, if he ever were to die—I would never find out!"

Agatha spat on the ground next to him and snarled. "Don't say such words! For a Venletian, you are not superstitious!"

Before he could respond, the feathery Parity took him by the arm, dragging him towards the village center.

"You coming mom?"

Agatha declined. She shook her head as the two spoke and laughed like young ones, walking the short walk to the village center. Merchant carts were packing up, ready to go home or settle in at the recently revived Inn that, though not as glorious as before, had the same amenities it once had. Even the loose women of the village now newly sprouted stood outside where their predecessors had, and business resumed as normal.

She glowered at the odd travelers—tourists with arms waving and fingers pointing for their companions to *go-see* the scorch marks on the strong buildings that survived and to the blackened fields they came all the way from their land to witness.

Like some traveling side-show, she thought as she wrinkled her nose and spat at one come close to the steps.

She closed the newly crafted garden gate and turned back to her daughter's home where she watched from the window people crowd the streets, desperate for a peek at the carriage as it entered. She cared little for all the hullabaloo. Rather, she fixed the cushion on the chair she claimed near the kitchen and took a book from one of the excellent bookshelves left undamaged. So much of the house remained as it had before.

She massaged her chair's leather surface with her hands and closed her eyes. Instantly, she was back in time, five years or so. She was sat outside Parity's home with her granddaughter in her lap. It was an unremarkable moment but she cherished it more than the others. It was the last time she read to her.

With tears in her eyes, she opened the book and read it out loud.

· · ·

Munta banged on Mistacles desk as the Imagi rubbed his still weary head.

"What do you mean there were survivors? You knew?!"

"Munta, I'll explain. Just please—no more banging?"

The big man stepped away from the desk and folded his arms as Mistacles continued.

"We've known since the children first arrived. As you can recall, most were burned to death or thrown from windows to be feed for the dogs. That is all true. There were some with clients when the pavilion's staff panicked over the uprising and sent those poor children to their death. The survivors were placed back in the room, and it eventually filled with more kids. It's the worst possible thing to have ever happened, and it has kept me up many of nights. I'm sorry you had to find out this way."

"Why didn't we do something?" Munta asked, and his voice broke.

The other men in the room watched him, dreading seeing such a man cry.

"We tried, for two years. I lost half of my Imagis, and I can't lose anymore. We caused such a commotion the Order pursued this course of action, to chip away at the heathen mountains impenetrable until nothing of it is left, further escalated by the fact we have the godkin and still do."

Mistacles sighed and sat in silence before speaking again.

"It is a blessing, I think."

"Are you sure about that?" asked Marcello who sat in a corner, listening with words always on his lips. "I've heard whispers of Gilton City sending a legion to wipe us out. They think we burned down Glenloch."

Mistacles laughed and held his head after.

"That is the most absurd thing I've ever heard. If they

said it was a dragon, then it was. No one can control such a beast!"

He stopped and with a look of horror stared into Hisousen's face who shared a similar visage.

Eventually, Hisousen spoke.

"Several nights passed, the Child was taken by a dragon but brought back unharmed. By Mistacles own speculation, he believes it was Garaton in one of his crazy forms. If she told him what happened..."

"But wouldn't he have already known?" asked Reine, playing with an apple.

"No," said Mistacles standing up. "It's been years since he's been in Zel. Someone, or something must have told him about the Child, and she in turn told him what happened. No doubt the twins would be too embarrassed to admit—"

"Their grandpa broke their toy?" asked Munta in a dry voice.

"We're gonna need Miracon's help if they intend to send their legion. And we'll need to armor up as many of the villages along the way."

"Or," said another armyman near the doorway, "we could bring all the people in their direct line of fire here, for safety."

Mistacles paused at the thought and shook his head. He then paused again and stared at a wall near the back of his office.

"Maybe. Just maybe."

"First, I think we should fortify the mountain again. It's falling apart everywhere."

"You're right," said Mistacles, "and maybe we should send some correspondence to those horrid twins."

"They'll want something," said Marcello. "And I know

just what. Right before I came here, I caught Ganguen and one of his lacky's traveling through Beningdul after they spent three moons polluting every hamlet and city on their path with their presence. Crimes were committed. I arrested them and they await my return at the Beningdul stronghold. We could offer Ganguen in a parley; it may save lives. And, if necessary, I can be the one to speak for us."

Munta shook his head. "Why didn't you tell us? We could have helped!"

Marcello laughed.

"Oh, and inform the already treacherous Cagorion of my plans? He may have been in league with them, one way or the other. No, I had to keep it to myself until they were captured."

Suddenly, the door burst opened and an attendant came crashing in.

"That girl!" he said and Mistacles jumped.

The Imagi noticed the armymen in the room stiffen and he gestured for them to relax. He spoke with the attendant in private who left their interaction in a huff. He returned to his desk with all eyes on him.

"My friends, I'll be at the entrance of Mother Summit at high-moon tonight. The Imagi's who helped during the collapse will be performing their own rituals on different peaks as well. I'll need those ingredients then and a few volunteers to help plant them at my command." He looked to Munta and Jusceanous who avoided his eyes.

"Damnit!" said Jusceanous. "I just got used to the warmth!"

"And we'll bring Pul."

"But it'll be in the middle of the night!" exclaimed Mistacles who, for a moment, was the only one who remembered he was just a boy.

"He's used to it. Loves it. We'll be there tonight, big man!"

Mistacles remained in his office after all his comrades had gone, staring at the wall in the back of the room with an intention he couldn't quite grasp. Anxious, he rummaged through one of his many drawers and found a giant map of Zel. Amused, he stuck it to the empty wall with great force. From memory he thoughtfully pushed in pins of blue and red on locations he knew were occupied before stepping back. And to his dismay, a typhoon of red pins surrounded his side of the mountain.

The Child watched as the many men she had grown to trust left Mistacles' office one by one. The last of them seemed odd in some way. When she stared a little longer, he looked back. His eyes were ablaze of blue and she knew instantly who it was.

He grinned and waved at her and she returned the gesture.

"What's going on Chil?" asked Pul with his eyes following hers, hoping to see what she sees.

"Nothing, just one of the armymen who helped us before saying hello."

"Nice. I wish I was there to help."

"Are you kidding me," she said with a smile. "You would have been too loud and fought back way too much. They'd have killed ya' on day one!"

"No way, I'm not that stupid!"

"No, but you are that hot-headed!" she laughed, and he warmly took it in.

He leaned back on the bench where the two observed the small city overwhelmed by armymen and innocents. He searched the sea of blue and found Tane trying to sneak into a kitchen and relaxed a little. He cracked his back against the soft wood and listened as his friend spoke, and it was like music to his ears.

CHAPTER 14

The carriage arrived in Venlet just as the Sun left the sky. From Unta's memory, the old rickety wagon was more regal than the one that took their children the first time.

He scoffed bitterly.

He watched as the driver, a handsome man from the Army of Miracon, known well to the untrusting villagers jumped down from his post, grinning as if a mirror to the many friendly faces among him.

Unta had received a message on gold letter head, on gold-lined paper, that the Order soldiers who brought the caravan from Glenloch abandoned it close to where the Army waited and would be there the following day. And all went as planned.

There were more Venletians who survived the Eleventh Day than they could have imagined. Many left the night before, secretly in the night and fled to the hills and forbidden paths in the mostly open space of the valley and returned moons later to the near shunning of those who remained. Tension was still high between those who endured and those who fled, but all were would agree— the few children who were soon to approach were more important, and all past grievances could be dealt with later.

Unta stood close to Parity and prepared to grab her if she chose to run. It had been made clear by her actions of the past she could be unpredictable when pushed to her limits.

He wrapped his arm around her waist, and she blushed.

"So, are you to be the daddy and me the mommy?" she asked.

He pulled his arm away and his face flushed red.

"If you feel upset about seeing them, I'm here for you," he answered. She made a silly face before pinching him.

The armymen who stood jovial next to the handsome one took their time to open the caravan doors. The audience of hundreds turned silent as its creaking caught them. From where he stood, Unta could hear the soft words of the armyman, asking the children to come to them.

"Don't be afraid. It's okay. You're home now!"

He watched as men took in their arms small and dirty children with hair ravaged like that of a rabid animal. Armymen knelt to their level and allowed the tired and hungry children to rest on them as they stared into the silently depressed audience, unsure of what to do.

A brave armyman patted one on the back and said, "Alright, my son, are you hungry? Would you like something to eat?"

A woman from deep in the crowd screamed, "I've made rum cakes and buttered warlong if you want some!"

"And we've got turkey and maple pie!"

Soon, everyone clamored to their homes and towards the children very frightened but amazed by what was happening. Unta, noticing this was swift and reached them first.

"Bring them to my home. We don't want to display them like cattle, do we?"

The young armymen whispered to the children, and they quickly ran to Unta's newly modeled home, fortified to last another hundred sieges while he stayed with the crowd, wrangling them to a calm.

"Listen, my friends and cousins—they are tired and frightened. The Council will meet tonight to decide which of you will take a child if not two."

"I'll take three!" a sweet, aged woman said bouncing like a child herself, bidding on a toy.

"That's nice Lina! Everyone who would like to foster one of these wonderful kids will need to speak with Plea Eric and he will take down your name. Alright! You'll be informed in the morning if you've been chosen! You're welcome to stop by and bring food, but please not too many at one time? Thank you!"

Unta felt the ground under him move, their many feet rushing home to finish food and clothes and toy preparations made special for their new kin.

He was slow to return home, unprepared for his quiet space to be filled with noise again. He approached the door and could hear laughter from inside. He breathed in before opening it.

Past the staircase was a living space where the laughter became many, and he intended to go upstairs but stopped upon hearing Parity's own voice.

"So, you're her momma?" asked a child with chubby cheeks and patches of hair missing. She spoke like a toddler but was nearer to eight and taller than ten.

"Mhm! What kind of crazy things did you guys do

together in Glenloch?" asked Parity and before the confused children could answer, Unta took her by the arm and led her out of the room.

"What do you think you're doing?" he asked as he squeezed.

"Hey, that hurts! What's the problem?"

"They were abused, Parity. In the most unimaginable ways. For years. The last thing they need is your reminder of them being left behind."

"She didn't leave them behind. She had no choice!"

Unta gave her a cold look.

"Just—not yet Parity. For the gods' sake, not yet!"

He let her go and left her there, entering the living space where the same armymen from the carriage put their nice socks on their hands and played puppets, making the children laugh—all but one.

He felt pulled to the young man whose dark hair and angry eyes told him to stay away. He would have ignored the tall boy if it weren't for the seething green from his glare—reminiscent of a child whose tale should never have been true. A small knot firm in his stomach emerged at the revelation.

"Sarty—is your name Sarty, by chance?" He asked as he approached. The boy's eyes changed, and he looked at Unta with a similar sadness as the other children. "We've been looking for you for a long time."

Unta motioned for the boy to follow and he did, away from the vivacious room with a haste he rarely showed. As they walked through the cool night, Unta noticed his muscular body move like that of a lion fresh from the hunt. What he thought was a young boy had indeed been a young man. He couldn't help but stare.

"Wow, son, you are strong for your age. Are you twelve, thirteen?"

"Something like that."

His voice was low and raspy, much like Untas brother's whose strength and future stature showed young.

They continued to walk in silence as they came closer to the newly built hut where Plea Eric resided. Unta was the first to enter as Plea Eric watered his nightfall flowers—a clever present from the great Imagi Mistacles for his hard work in rebuilding the village after Plea Marcus Daniels' passing. He was the first of the Grand Eunichs to keep their hair—a sandy blonde that didn't blend well with his skin nor his terrible robes made of a brown, itchy wool.

"Oh, my days! Friend, come in—have a seat!" said Plea Eric. "And your friend, too. Would either of you like anything to eat... drink?"

Unta noticed the young man's indifference and declined for them both. "We're here about the children."

"Ah, yes! They've come home at last! Are you one of them?"

The boy gave the Plea his harsh eyes and Unta spoke for him. "He is, but different. I need you to send an urgent message to Mistacles."

"Oh, you mean like right now?" asked Plea Eric who slapped his knee at his own words. "Yeah, you mean right now. Give me a moment. What is it you would like to say?"

He grabbed a quill and piece of papyrus and held them in anticipation.

"We have found the long-lost Sarty, and he is in Venlet. Please send for him."

"Well, that was short and simple. I'll send it as soon as..."

"Now, Eric—it's important."

Plea Eric sighed before taking the paper and calling in his dark bird. It came in like smoke and grabbed the paper from his hand before flying into the wall.

"Well, that's all. You'll be expecting a lot of visitors this night in regards to the other children and their future home."

Unta left before Plea Eric could say anything.

He led Sarty back to his house where he heard Parity in the living space once more. He ran for the door, prepared to berate the woman again, but stopped as Sarty grabbed a sword left on a neighbor's door and prepared to use it on him. Unta, shocked but undeterred, reached for the blade and Sarty swung and scowled in response.

"I'm not going back to Glenloch. I don't care what any of you say!"

"No one wants you to go back. You're home now!"

"This isn't my home; I don't have one!"

With sword in hand, he stomped into the darkness, down the path headed south with Unta hot on his tail.

"You can't just leave—you haven't eaten yet! And what about your clothes!"

But the boy kept going—past the south entrance of Venlet, past the carriage soon to return to its owners with no sign of slowing down.

Unta bolted back to his house and slammed into the door, calling for Parity who ran to him, a hint of guilt badly hidden on her face.

"I'm sorry. I should have..."

"No time. The boy, Sarty, has left, and I need you to bring him back!"

"What! Why me?" she asked as he pulled her arm again and led her outside.

"I'll be close. Just trust me on this! Go now!"

He released his hold on her and she was deep into the darkness before he could blink, taking the path he very badly pointed out. At her footfalls he crept behind buildings adjacent, prepared to take the boy by surprise if necessary.

It wasn't long before she came upon the young man's silhouette, a tree among trees, making strides down the dirt path. She ran as fast as she could to greet him, feeling the dirt lift from behind her.

"Hey! Hey you! I need to talk to you!"

"Forget it!"

She jogged in place besides him and spoke softly.

"Hey, I made you something. Come back and I'll show ya!"

"Made me something? You don't even know me; how did you make me something?" he said, half-laughing and irritated she could keep up with him.

Parity stopped.

"Did you know my daughter?"

Her question made his hulking frame come to a halt.

"Did you know a little girl with long, black hair and deep, color-changing eyes? She would have been small and not well taken care of...hair matted. I would tell you her name, but she had none."

Her words were like a cup of cold, mountain water on the hottest of the warmer days. She gasped as her soul lightened and shook away tears unseen in the dark.

"That doesn't make it any easier. Everyone was like that there."

He had a warmness in his voice and eyes as he approached her in kind.

"There was once a girl, here, who I saw at the Inn. She was a wild one in a civilized place. I did see her in Glenloch but she was one of the many taken to the kiln. I'm sorry, mam!" he said before turning to leave.

"Wait! She didn't die! She lived."

"Really?!" He spun on his feet, nearly knocking her over. "Please take me to her!"

"She's in the Mountains of the Predicated, protected by the Imagi's and the Army of Miracon stationed there. Her and a few others."

"Imagi's? But they're not real."

He swatted at her before continuing his path.

"You're a crazy broad, you know that?"

"Come back, please. Don't do it for me, do it for the others who came with you. They spoke so highly of you. You gave them strength on the journey here. Please!"

Parity felt the years she fought taming her inner demons come to an end and closed her eyes, unsure if she could hold back her sea of unforgiving emotions.

A breeze like those come tumbling from Mother Summit herself to the groveling peasants below moved her and she opened her eyes. The blur of Sarty running back to the village caused her heart to crash against her chest. From an unassuming building came a lurching Unta, lunging for him but falling short a stride or two. Parity was slow to pick him up, laughing as he groaned to his feet.

"That boy—ugh—is a titan!"

"Yes, and he's returned home. You better get up, he's probably hungry!"

MISTACLES SAT HIS IN BEDROOM, holding the scroll in his hands—an aged papyrus with a distant fragrance of his home long lost. He examined it with severe caution; the ends already ripped to near extinction. But all remained intact as he read it in full. Plea Eric was the author, and his news was unexpected and wonderful. Overwhelmed by the revelations, the Imagi fell into a laughing fit, his sides hurting in a pleasant way.

"Of course, of all things to happen now!"

As he shouted, a curious Care came in and jumped on the bed.

"What's up?" the young boy asked, searching the room ever curiously.

"I just received a letter from Venlet. They found survivors in Glenloch and they've arrived home today. One of them being Sarty—the other Prophezier, who was stuck in that horrible place. What wonderful news at such a terrible time!"

Cares eyes widened.

"Do you think Cara's with them?"

Mistacles' mood shifted and he reached for the boy who pulled away.

"It takes time to get over..."

"I'm sick of hearing that! I don't care what I said before, she's alive and I'm going home, too!" he screamed, running back to his room.

Mistacles flung the priceless paper on his bed and ran after the boy.

CHAPTER 15

It was well into the night and Care couldn't sleep to save himself. If they had windows, surely he'd look out and see the Moon moving through of the night sky by now. How he'd like to see such a thing. And with Cara.

He slowly sat up, back sore from his hours of waiting. He found the girls—both sleeping in Tane's bed, just as it should be. They had hoped Pul would sleep with them that night, the Child's empty bed left empty for him, but he chose to sleep with the other armymen in their poorly made barracks much to their dismay.

Care glared at the empty bed and felt a pit of disdain grow in his stomach, like the hammer claws of dragons, ripping and tearing from the inside out. Red bumps grew on his arms since the arrival of the Prophezier—or Pul as he had always been known—and they grew harsher the more he scratched them. It had been this way since Glenloch; Pul was all they ever talked about. The day could only get better or worse at his mention, and far more harrowing the odds when one of his nonchalant letters came. And how they searched the parchment for any real trace of him though the words written grew smaller each time. The worst affected was Tane who hadn't gone a day without uttering his name and whose very memory could send her into a fit.

He fell back on his pillow and moved his spindly legs which ached. He needed to get out of here—he often explored the caves deeper than he'd ever admit to his guardian, but no matter how far he searched, there was always a block—a boulder, a door, a mountain. He would never be free at this rate. He once thought he could stay here forever, like the others who lived so unaffected by the outside world, but his new, safe home had turned to ruin and now anyone could get in. With a clarity that hurt, he knew the only way he could ever feel peace again was to leave and never come back.

Before yesterday, he was willing to wait until he was old enough to be free, until Mistacles used enough resources to teach him what he needed, stealing those kept from him. That would have been a good enough life, he supposed, but knowing the other survivors came back home, he knew where he needed to be, whether it made sense to anyone else or not.

He didn't want to hate him—the man who saved their lives and gave them a better experience in life they would have never had if not. The only adult who could touch them without hurting them, whose words were like medicine even when he was mad. Care didn't want his love for him to turn to hate, but everyday he was forced to live in a place he never asked for, living like a prisoner without bars. The closest he ever felt to feeling free was as the mountain was collapsing—his true feelings he could never say out loud.

He left his bed quietly, tiptoeing over hardwood less

creaky, stepping to the door, opening it slightly. From the beginning the attendants found out the hard way how eager the young, sunshine boy was to fly away. Through patches of adults unaware of his movements, beneath their legs and under tables, Care had made it successfully to the path of Mother Summit, a climb so steep only a fool would take it by foot, within his first year but couldn't go further without magical transportation. Undeterred, he leapt over a black, gaping hole, reaching for a ledge only a deer could reach and was caught midair by an attendant who, from then on, left traps outside his room at night with little exception. He spent years figuring them out, tripping more than he could count and causing unnecessary scars, much to Mistacles chagrin.

To his right was the kitchen, illuminated by candles and magic light he found so wondrous. There, three attendants played cards at a table just in view, two faced away from him. He looked ahead at Mistacles' door directly across from his. He opened it just enough to squeeze through and stopped midway when he saw the wire. He gained his footing and squinted downwards, where handfuls of flour laid in waiting for him.

He giggled as he slowly stepped outside the wire and flour, pivoting to skip backwards so he could see their handiwork. The stickiest goo imaginable, the same stuff the attendants used to hang heavy things to the cave's wet rock-face, hung from above his door, linked to the tight wire he nearly nicked.

He kneeled down and reached in front of him, into a space nearest the walls from the attendant's light. This trap was the hardest to figure out. The attendants with the help of Mistacles made invisible a small board with wheels, so if he were to step on it, fall and scream, the attendants could snatch him up and put him back to bed. He found the board with little shuffling and moved it out of his way, rocking it slowly out of view as to not make a sound.

He got up and slithered into Mistacles room and was shocked by how cold it was. His teeth jittered but he paid it no attention. He watched amazed as the big man laid on his back with his covers clear across the room, belly heaving as if he were in desperate need of air. He was sweating and shifting a great deal in his sleep.

For a moment, Care changed his mind and felt a strong urge to go back to his room—no harm done. But his plan hurdled these feelings in his heart, and he felt he had no greater loyalty to Mistacles than it. In the fight for his life, he bit his lip and continued forward.

He searched high and low for the big man's famous belt known second to his robust laugh. He opened drawers and searched blind through clothes soft to the touch but found nothing. Same with the closest, in disarray before he even opened its doors. Puzzled, he sat awhile and, by chance, looked up. On a sheet fastened like a hammock was the belt, dangling as the cloth swayed gently at a cool breeze following the room.

He laughed. The Imagi knew of all Care's restrictions, his height was one he could hardly overcome. He lingered in that moment, already missing the simple whims they shared he might not ever again.

He wiggled out of his funk and went for Mistacles' big chair sat alone in the corner, nearly as bloated as the sleeping man. With little effort, he picked it up and thrust it near the center of the room, in front of the bed. As the chair landed, it rattled in place, and he was quick to hold it down. But he feared it was too late.

He peered above the chair's long back to the bed and

exhaled as the already sleeping Mistacles stayed as such. Exhilarated, he wasted no time crawling up the chair to stand awkwardly on its buoyant base.

It was subtle the first time he jumped, eyes never leaving the bed, but after a few more, he felt light and got higher. On his fifth, he caught the tail end of the belt, pulling it down with the same power as his falling. And it whipped back and hit him in the face.

He rubbed the spot already puffy and wanted to cry. He looked down at his small hands in the dark and remembered, then, who he was and where he was again. There was still a chance to stop and go back to bed. He knew this but he couldn't let it go.

He crawled down and stopped, the overwhelming reality of not knowing what to do next hit him like a ton of bricks. He ran to the door and froze on the handle, afraid once more.

He poked his head out of the door frame and squinted at the kitchen.

"Damn, they're still there!" he whispered as the attendants sat calm at the table, still.

He gripped the handle harder, angry they assumed he would leave again—an assumption proved right.

The front door was too risky—the attendants' quarters were there, and they awoke at any sound. He remembered then another door that led out the back through the kitchen. He would have to sneak past the few awake, somehow, to get to it.

He opened the door, smug, and braced to run. He reached down for the invisible board and picked it up, holding its moving wheels against his chest. He braced the wall closest to the sitting attendants and breathed heavy. He quickly glanced around the bend and noted the exit door had no lock. With a bravery unknown to his age, young Care sent the small board zipping down the hall where the front door led, past his room, and the calm attendants bolted by him, unaware, showing a dread unusual for their tiring station. As the last one skittered by, Care skirted the wall before sprinting through his exit as alarm bells were rung.

He was halfway through the city when he finally heard them, the eerie wails of Tier birds whose song sounded like a woman falling to her death. With every home he passed so did their candles become alive as if by his presence alone.

He dodged the barracks still smelling of freshly cut pine as young men rumbled out of their sleep, grabbing for their weapons in great haste for a reason they need not know for the alarm had been sounded. He ran to that part of the cave where only he could fit and snuggled in, barely able to breath.

He held the bag in his hands and smiled, victorious finally. He weighed it casually and was surprised by how light it was. He opened it and a foul odor filled his hole. He closed it and coughed louder than he intended to. He covered his mouth and hoped no one had heard.

"Hello little boy. I suppose you don't remember me, do you?" said a low voice deep within the cave.

Care jumped at the sound, dropping the bag in his lap. His breathing quickened.

"Don't you remember? I was the one who saved you from that horrible man and brought you here."

"Dreqtaton?" he whispered.

"Yes, my son."

He didn't hear the god move but felt him settle nearby, small rocks falling into an abyss under him.

"What are you doing in the dark?"

"Uh... hiding."

More birds sang and screaming men yelled for him from above, and he started to shake.

"Are you cold, Care? I can help you, you know."

"I'm trying to get out of here!"

"Ha! You and me both kid!" Dreqtaton paused and the air grew warmer to Care's surprise. "You've got my powder, I see."

"I need it to get home!" Care said holding it close to his chest. "Don't try and take it from me, or I'll dump the whole damn thing!"

"Wow, such rage, my son! I'll help you use it if you give me half?"

"No way, I earned this puppy all by myself. How about you show me, or I'll tell the guards you're here?"

Dreqtaton laughed and Care prepared himself to leave.

"I could take it from you without effort, my son."

As the god spoke, a loud crack like the falling of a great oak could be felt from underneath and Care knew his options were limited.

"You promise you'll show me and not trick me like you tricked the guy in this?"

Dreqtaton laughed again.

"What's so funny?" asked Care.

"I didn't trick anyone. I never have. Never will. He wanted to live forever and he does. Who in their right mind makes deals with powerful beings without defining them first?"

"Okay, how should I define mine?" the boy asked, and the endless god grumbled, satisfied by his whit.

"You're very smart and for that I will help you. It is important when asking you clearly state what it is you want. You want to go home? Be sure you say alive. You want to use the powder? Make sure you state where, when you want to get there, and that you do so in the way you left. You don't want me to trick you? Speak honestly and ask clearly. It's the simple things, like that, that ruin people..."

As the god grumbled some more, Care cleared his throat.

"But you control what happens. You know what they really want, so why make them clarify?"

"Clarify? That's a big word for a baby!"

"I'm not a baby; I'm nine years old, just recently so."

"Very good. It is important to be clear. From my perspective, you are younger than what you are. Why allow me to decide what you deserve when you can just tell me. I get SICK and TIRED of humans expecting me to know what will make them happy. I've lived longer than Time and her judgment ever should have allowed—I chose to never again guess what you lot mean. You ask what you wish, and I allow the energy to do the rest. Then, it's not my problem!"

Care sat deep in thought.

"You are not evil then?"

"Evil doesn't exist, my son. Well, not until my brother killed Yexour and gave you humans authority over these lands, if you mean what I think you mean. The Darkness that wanders the eons is just an echo. But humans—your people and their people far removed—choose to harm, willingly. I don't do that."

Care took the bag and opened it.

"Okay, here it goes: my name is Care and I am from Venlet. I am nine years old and haven't seen my homeland in four years. I believe my sister may be alive and in Venlet—"

Dreqtaton tried to speak but was cut off.

"I would like for you to show me how this powder works so I can return to Venlet in present time in one piece just as I left, and in return I will give you half of what is in this bag and all our debts will be paid thereafter. Do we have a deal?"

A hand came from the black below and shook Care's reluctant one. He then emptied as good as half as he could measure into the odd hand, and it slowly pulled away.

"You know, I had no idea things would turn out this way, and I am happy for it—less for me to do later. To use the powder, one must speak in a tongue impossible for any human, let alone a boy like you. If you were to try this spell, you would fail and be sent to Reicher's Realm, more likely, or wherever has the strength to pull your soul and body into it. You would not go to Venlet, and if you were to make it there, you'd land in pieces no matter our bargain. I'm sorry, my son, you cannot use this powder and that is the truth."

"You tricked me!" Care cried.

"No, Care. I could have but I didn't. Now, listen carefully. Go to Mistacles office and open his desk drawer. Inside should be a bag full of magical pebbles." He stopped to allow Care to calm down. "This is very important. Take one pebble—just one—and say 'Venlet'. Then, throw it against the wall. A portal will open, and you can walk right through. This is much safer—I don't know why in all the nine realms you'd ever want this heinous powder. Did you hear me, boy?"

As Dreqtaton spoke, a large crowd of armymen aimed their focus on the small hideaway.

"Yes."

"Do that before he puts them away tonight. And you'll go home. Now, our debt has been paid."

Care felt an armyman's hand pull on his shoulder and he fought back as he was yanked out crudely. He quickly pulled the draw strings of the bag together so none of the powder could leak. He held it to his chest and looked into the dark for any semblance of a face as he was escorted back to the thermopolia.

People in long robes and night tunics stood at their door with their hands at their waist as the boy sat still on an armyman's neck. He saw their thankful smiles and waved and was not hurt when they didn't return the gesture.

After a quick look-over by Hisousen, the boy was sent to Mistacles' office—his eyes cast down in humiliation. The big man sat at his desk—gritting his teeth and ripping paper as the party approached.

"I don't know what I did to make you hate me, Care," he said as the armymen left them alone.

He looked up at Mistacles whose sad eyes were hard to hate.

"I love you, like a son. Maybe I've been too hard, or maybe I should have let you guys do more—I don't know. But I never meant to make you so...angry."

"Why does everyone say I'm angry?" Care said clenching his teeth.

"Listen, your running away caused a big stir. The people here love you—"

Care with the powder in his hands began to cry and Mistacles sighed. He came to the collapsing boys' side and took him into his arms, cradling him like a baby.

"There, there, my son—it'll be okay. I'm not mad at you. It will all be okay—you'll see."

"I miss her."

"I know you do," Mistacles said as he sat at his desk

with Care's arms around his neck. "Why don't you tell me all about her?"

"Well," he sniffled and sobbed, "she had hair like me but was...*sniff*... taller. She was really smart, like my mom...*sniff*... She had blue eyes and liked to run outside and..."

He went on, telling Mistacles all he remembered about Cara and the big man never left his side. They talked and laughed well into the morning and were jostled out of their conversation when Hisousen walked in unannounced.

"Oh, there's our little escapee! Please stop doing—it breaks our hearts every time, you know!" Hisousen said smiling at the boy. "Mistacles, you got a minute?"

"Yeah. Excuse me, young man, but I have important business to attend to," he said which made the boy laugh. "Wait here. I'll be right back."

Care's eyes followed the two as they left the room, feeling his way to the drawer. As the door shut, his eyes shifted to the bag of pebbles resting just as Dreqtaton had said. He carefully looked around the room before putting one in his pocket. He wasn't going to leave that day, but he figured he might need it eventually.

CHAPTER 16

It was several days until the start of Malkeevs—the Festival of the Stars, when winter takes it's throne over the land, and Mistacles was on his feet, attending to this thing and that, as if nothing had happened. But in reality, It had been a whirl wind of a past few days—Care escaped yet again and successfully stole and lost half of his special powder; Mal Three arrived with the supplies but with the dire news that Order infantry men and laborers were cutting away slowly at the mountain in parts where the auspicious dragon was last seen; his precious girl, Chil, was returned by a terrible dragon who he believes to be her father who, in turn, melted the abhorrent pavilion of Glenloch into the white, gold streets; and the mountains nearly caved in, nearly killing all inside, and were in a dire state of repair. And what was worse—his children by all things but blood were falling apart at the seams as the safe world he cultivated for them all these years was crumbling away. And it could never be repaired—this he knew.

He sighed as every sad face, every sobbing mother and

father from the Eleventh Day crossed his mind as armyman after armyman and attendant after paisan came to him with further news, questions, or deeds asked to be done—as if they couldn't see the anguish on his face. His heart raced—it was fear. He quickly took to work on a small cottage near where the top of the mountain caved in and was badly beaten by giant boulders. Luckily, everyone inside survived but they needed their home back. With a flick of his hands, a young and ruddy armyman was sent to see to the problem. But he knew this simple solution was one of thousands and nothing would get done without him there. And he was preparing to leave.

It had come to his attention the other Prophezier, potentially, arrived to Venlet on the caravan with the other survivors and he felt as low as one could feel. He had thought for years the boy was in the company of the Army of Miracon until they couldn't find him and figured he must have perished with the other innocents. But he would make this wrong right, if he could ever get out of here!

He walked too fast for his aching feet, burning at the heels and under his arch. He loved his children, he knew this and thought on it often, but as the days pressed on and as they got older, he realized he couldn't care for them in the way they deserved, at least not anymore. He had kept them from the outside world but couldn't any longer. He had considered bringing others to the mountain for moons but couldn't bare seeing another prisoner tortured or his very own taken from him again. But it would seem, if not by fate of the First One then sheer coincidence, this would be his chance—before the storm of the Order of Garatos hit them and the children were too old and too far gone to ever listen regardless of the reason.

As he glided past moving forms in the thermopolia,

taken to pretending not to see them than admit he rudely ignored them, he sent the children who were chomping at his heels to do something, ANYTHING, and they chose to pack his luggage for him as he finished his duties. He wouldn't be gone longer than a few days but knew his leaving would leave them the most vulnerable.

He briskly walked to Hisousen's tent where Munta was briefed and red in the face as he entered.

"What seems to be the matter?" asked Mistacles as an enraged Munta turned to him.

"We are to leave as soon as you get back and go to a nearby mesa where a few of our men found a large encampment full of Order soldiers. While the spell is being prepared, we'll divert as many of them as possible. Upon your arrival, it would be most important if you would do it as soon as you arrive."

Hisousen showed a disdain that made Mistacles frustration grow larger.

"Lieutenant, this is the only time I could do this since the spell takes time to manifest. I asked you moons ago for the supplies and was put off. What, did you think all magic and powers of the Imagi were instantaneous? We are only human after all! And let me make this clear—if anything were to happen to those children while I'm gone..."

Mistacles lifted his right and most powerful hand to meet the horizon of Hisousen's eyes.

"You've got my word, friend."

The two stared in silence before Munta spoke up.

"Am I to accompany you, sir?" he asked.

Mistacles turned and shifted his face. "I would love for you too—this boy might be a lot to handle but you must stay here and keep everyone safe."

Munta smiled.

"He'll make an excellent addition to the family."

He walked out, leaving the two men stuck in an invisible tug of wars of the eyes.

"You are lucky I haven't lost any of my men," Hisousen said coldly.

"And you are lucky we saved the mountain. Maybe after this is done, you should leave and never return!"

Mistacles closed the tent and walked back to his room as hundreds of hands waved for his attention. He walked through the front door to several concerned eyes carrying his every step, their usual fast movements slowed to a snail's crawl. Maggie with his associates had their hands in his drawers, picking out his clothes as if they would never do it again.

"Where did the children go?! Oh, stop that! Pick anything! That'll do! Just—throw it in!"

He touched hands with Maggie and squeezed them before leaving the room and entering his office.

He sighed, relieved four of his favorite children sat around his desk but were as solemn as everyone else. The first to notice him was Pul who shot up at attention with an apology written on his face. The other three saw this and mocked him, blowing raspberries at him and the old Imagi.

"Do you have no pity for me children?" he asked as he picked up Care and Tane from his chair and set them on the ground.

"Do you have to go?" asked Tane whose hardened glare had miraculously softened.

"Yes, sweetie, but only for a few days. I'll be bringing back another child, hopefully."

"Why so many kids?" she asked.

"Can Cara come, if she's there?" Care asked behind his long lashes.

"Of course, my son. Everyone is welcome."

"Can Pul stay here, too?" the Child asked, whose gaze at her friend turned his downward. She looked away.

"Well," said Mistacles, turning to him, "it's completely up to him. But you don't have to, my boy. You can always come here whenever you want too, like on holidays, for the summer, and what not."

"So, he can come and go but we can't?" asked Care with Tane besides him.

"Well," Mistacles' body was turning inward already, and he couldn't handle much more of this, "you three were exposed to evil men who would stop at nothing to find you. And," he pointed to the Child, "she will never be safe, anywhere in the world, ever again. I suppose you could all go but she must stay here for as long as possible."

The Child's eyes widened.

She had been told this before but brushed it off, like being told to bathe often or to be safe when walking about or else. It was important to know but seemed asinine as her life in the mountains had been uneventful for the most part. She figured she'd have to deal with this when she got older, when she would get more freedom like how it had been in the mountains so far, but she never thought she'd never really be free again.

She turned her back to her friends and stared down at the desk, playing with the scraps of paper no one had cleaned up.

Pul walked to that end of the desk and bent so he could look up to her.

"You'll always be safe with me, Chil. And I'll be here whenever you need me, okay?"

She smiled half-heartedly and he gave her a hug. Mistacles could feel his spine bend under the pressure and acid rise in his throat.

He wondered, deep down, how much longer he could do this—other parents made it seem so easy.

He got up and apologized to the Child, but his words had already done its job. The lightness she had just achieved from her brief affair with freedom had disappeared and the girl he had known well, the quiet, small one he wished she'd outgrow had returned in full force.

He gave his goodbyes to his wards, each with large embraces and tears.

"What'll we do if anything happens?" asked Care.

Tane, standing farthest from the Imagi, held the Child in her arms.

"We'll wait for the mountain to fall down again and have to figure it out ourselves!"

He ignored Tane and bent his knee, cracking as he got down to Care's level. He winked at the young boy stared back, shocked.

"You'll know what to do," he said as he pointed to Care's chest.

As he slowly got up, Care put his hand to his front pocket, breathing heavily at the revelation.

Mistacles walked to his door and swung it wide.

"It's time to go children. I will be back, and you will see me again. Have a good night sleep and listen to Maggie, for the love of the gods—listen to him!"

He closed the door at their leaving and fell on it. He was near sleep, exhausted from a day of endless work. He lifted himself from despair and went to bed and slept for a few hours, awaking in the middle of the night, every night, since the first incident happened.

He put on his best traveling clothes—a wool, green

shirt, brown pants, and darker green cape. His shoes were thick and padded, ready for long walks through Venletian terrain. He said his goodbyes to his attendants who held on to him. He pushed them away.

"The other Imagis will be done with the spell in a few days' time. If they need access to my chambers, let them in. Take care of them all, please."

He grabbed his luggage and headed back to his office.

He gazed upon his wide map once more and frowned at the many more red pegs planted recently. Troubled but energized, he threw a pebble at the wall, and it caved in, revealing an open space before a bunch of trees and lush green grass with the Sun's colors entering the dark sky.

He breathed deep the fine air and walked through. The wall behind him returned to normal—the map again untouched, and the mountains were left without its greatest defense.

SARTY SAT resolute as he examined the room Unta had given him with severe criticism. It was said to have belonged to many damaged on the Eleventh Day, but he felt no kin to them—their problems were theirs, and that was that. And he'd rather sit in the dark, oaken rocking chair than rest in the bed Pul, the other Prophezier, laid in and bled. At least the well-loved Venletian boy had a soft place to rest his head, rather than stone and white gold, and blankets to keep him warm if not from his own body still hot from a hard day of laboring. The tales of the Prophezier had been told to Sarty since he was little but if he knew he would be one, potentially, he would have given it up, for his family to be spared.

Never were there two destined for such a horrible fate.

He reached for the bed's covers, woven in the intricate Holfenyan way but shot back at the feeling, not welcome to such luxuries. He was always sent to the horses pen and would steal his time of sleep there for the Block, where most slaves were allowed to roam, had little room for him.

He loved horses, remembering fondly how well his sisters would parade them and treat them no less than family. He hadn't gotten a job working with them until his second year as a slave and after many painful long days of hauling fish and wares from faraway ships which was well worth the cost of getting such a position. He knew he was one of the lucky ones.

Everyone in Glenloch knew the horrible things that happened to the kids who weren't laborers, including Sarty. From the start, those white robed, child-robbers spoke so nicely about these positions—how easy it was and the nice presents they were given for doing practically nothing. And they spoke to the kids who didn't want to slave away collecting cotton; cooking hot, molten sugars; or clam-catching in the heavily tentactacon filled ocean. Instead, they could take the easy, white-gold road to the pavilion and keep people company.

Sarty almost fell for it, his bones near breaking and his heart longing for a bed, until a fellow slave boy years ahead of him told him the truth. He often wondered why the kids who took the offer were never brought back and was horrified hearing about the giant kiln at the pavilions center, deep underground, having seen the girl taken there unaware of what was to meet her. It was a cruel and monstrous end. And it was all the Order of Garatos and the guardians doing.

He squeezed his large hands together, the callouses and their dry husks no longer hurting him. He remembered first toiling over a grassy knoll, collecting whatever the slave master wanted that day. He remembered how his hands and knees and his back ached, and how he felt he would die at any moment. But those feelings never went away, and he became accustomed to them.

Because of the journey to Venlet he hadn't worked for a month and his body made it clear it was angry with him. His ankles ached and his thighs screamed as if they too knew a striking whip could come if they stopped. He would go and run into the river nearby but feared that crazy woman would follow him again so didn't.

He moved to the floor and rubbed his legs, tensing at nothing when the door suddenly opened.

"How did I know you'd be awake?" asked Unta with a bowl of warm water and a towel.

He dropped it lightly on the nightstand before sitting on the bed.

"You people are annoying," he answered, taking the towel and ringing it expertly over the bowl before applying it to his legs.

"You've done this before, haven't you?"

"Well, they didn't much care for the weak ones and threw them to the dogs when they messed up. But the hard workers, like me and my friends, were treated like ring fighters and given whatever they wanted after the work was done and before new work began."

Unta watched in misery how hard the boy pressed against his muscles, as if his own existence caused his body to erupt and convulse if not pushed to their limits. He remembered Munta doing much or less the same thing when first learning to smithy, but he never was this ruthless. And his brother worked for a few hours a day. Sarty always worked, from the moment his eyes opened until they were closed.

"You speak pretty well for being there for so long."

Sarty's face hardened.

"I'm not an idiot."

"No! I never said you were!"

"My mother was smart and taught me everything she knew before they killed her. I know how to count, read, write—everything most here don't, and they were never slaves!"

A rage was in the boy and Unta felt it.

"I see. Sorry to have upset you. You don't have to worry about defending yourself here, okay?"

"Why are you really here, bothering me?"

"Well, uh..." Unta scratched the top of his head, "a friend of mine, and a friend of the Army of Miracon has arrived to Venlet. He wishes to speak with you."

"If I don't, are you gonna run after me again? Because that was annoying too."

"No, but he's an Imagi and very powerful—much more powerful than the men you dealt with in Glenloch."

Sarty's eyes lit up and for the first time Unta saw a bit of pride in them. He would have felt betrayed had he not known the legacy such a title of Imagi kept with it. They were the ones who could work with the energy left by the Ultiquans without the help of Dreqtaton. They were but a few who could wield such magic and energy without being consumed by it. They were the only beings besides the gods who could move mountains and run dry oceans if they pleased. It would seem then, to Unta, the boy was much smarter than he could have ever imagined. And for the first time since meeting, felt an uneasiness showing the boy his back.

Sarty sprung from his chair and walked out, leaving Unta scrambling to keep up. He galloped downstairs and left a hard thud on the last step. He knew the other children had been taken in already, housed in warmth and no longer his concern. Whoever was waiting, he wanted them to know he was powerful too.

He marched into the living room like a well-seasoned fighter, where a round man sat with satchels and sacks hung on his waist. He was slow to notice the boy and smiled patiently. Sarty kneeled in a way most in the valley would never have, like the Blood of Oxem refused to many generations before.

"My son, what a surprise you know such a custom?"

"My mother's brother was a Magi and visited often. It is nice to meet you...sir?"

"Mistacles. And you are Sarty, correct?" Mistacles snuck his eyes to the doorway at an exasperated Unta, mad with fumes in his ears. And the boy nodded.

"My friend here, Unta—"

Mistacles motioned for him to come over, "has been so kind as to allow you here. I hope you've been treating him well."

"Well enough for a man who hasn't brought me proper clothes and fed me well after my food was cold."

Unta opened his mouth to yell but Mistacles' faint hand prompted him not to.

"I'll see to it you get what you need, brave, young man. Now, come and sit with me and tell me all about your time from Venlet to Glenloch."

As the two sat on the couch, Mistacles waved his hands in a circle and floating pillows, linen, and some of Unta's clothes went flying through the air.

Unta gave up glowering and grabbed the few pieces he could catch and set them lightly beside the talking two.

"How did you know I was in Venlet? It would seem everyone knows who I am!"

"Well, one of my wards seemed to have crossed your path. And she was very concerned for you and happy to know you were well."

"Ah, I remember her. She didn't say anything as I escaped. I think either way, I was destined for the cage. So, she lives with you?"

"Yes, her and two others who survived. There were so few who did, you know. And we are thankful you made it here alive."

Sarty laughed.

"I never gave up my life so I could see to it those who harmed my family harmed tenfold. That has been my driving force all these years. And still is. I worked along men and monsters—I know nothing of strength and survival. I know pain, suffering—and I know power when I see it!"

Mistacles studied the boy who moved like a warrior when he talked.

"How would you feel about coming to the Mountains of the Predicated with me to see the Army and the girl?"

"I would gladly be anywhere but here."

"Venlet or the Valley of Venoxem?"

At Mistacles' question, the boy didn't answer.

"You have my word you'll be safe. We'll leave tomorrow afternoon. I need to take care of a few things first. You should get some rest before then, hm?"

Sarty smiled and got up to bow again before leaving the room with his fresh clothes on his arm. He gave Unta a snarky scowl as he passed, and the gingery man stomped to Mistalces still fuming.

"What the hell was that? That kid is a monster!" Unta whispered but with such intensity he might as well shouted.

"Just relax, Unta, it is not what it seems."

"Oh, and how is that? He thinks he's better, stronger, smarter than everyone here, except you. How is that a good thing?"

"It isn't."

Mistacles hand went up to grab a floating cup of tea and Unta rolled his eyes.

"He doesn't really think this way. He has learned to never show weakness and has persevered in the face of death because of it. He only knows of me in the way he's been told, and it probably wasn't so nice, but he still honors me because of my power. Power to him is absolute—no matter the way in which it is received... or taken. So, please, Unta, pay his attitude no mind. He's still just a kid, after all."

Unta shook his head, dizzy from the heat leaving him so quickly.

"I can't believe I've been yelling at him. He just seems so unaffected by it. It drives me crazy! How do you deal with all of this?"

"I don't. When the three first came to me, I was shocked by how well behaved they were—except the Child who was uncontrollable. It would seem Care has taken that mantle now. It wasn't until my attendants informed me of Tane's bed wetting I became concerned for their REAL state of mind. The reality of what happened to each of them hit them separately with Tane and Care having the worst of it. Care wouldn't let anyone change him or be alone with any adult for the first few years. And Tane would jump at any loud sound, and still does but tries to hide it. We used to have dogs, but their barking would send her into a frenzy. It hasn't been easy...

"And my poor child, the one with no name, has been haunted by a dark entity since it found a way in. It harms her while she dreams. She's lost so much sleep her eyes have worsened into near blindness. I can't tell how you many spells I've done to correct them. And she has refused to really learn to read because of her fear of it—and of everything else for that matter! She was such a lively, strong girl and now... what we see is her shell.

"Not a single moment of this has been easy. But it has been worth it. I love them more than life itself and I would like to return to them sooner rather than later. Please, inform Plea Eric I would like to see him in the morning. Also, I would like to see Plea Marcus Daniel's grave. He was an old friend of mine. Ugh...I have so much business to attend to..."

Mistacles looked into Unta's eyes, and they were like navy sails in a sullen storm.

"One more thing. That Parity woman, I would like to see her at some point as well. Not for very long though. I can only stomach so much bull-honkey!"

"She isn't a bad person anymore!" Unta shouted.

"That remains to be seen. I will go to my room some-where, hm."

Mistacles looked up and found one in his mind.

"Yes, that one will do, and I will not be awakened by anyone but myself. See you then, Mr. Unta!"

The big Imagi got up gracefully and walked up the stairs, leaving Unta slumped on his couch.

CHAPTER 17

From above, where the heavens of Santioch meet Zel's forest fingers and mountain face, no city has ever been built so perfectly as Gilton City—the heart of Zel. Its very name impassioned those who were thankful for the god, whose namesake it was given, who did what no other god had done before. And the Sun often shined upon it, accentuating the perfect marksmanship of slaves and their predecessors; free people but serfs to the real royalty of the land—the High Guardians.

Through stringy clouds its golden peaks and glassy finishes beamed like the very rays of the Sun himself—a feature made possible by the hands of men and men alone.

The great ocean Amebac—also known as the Red Sea—was at its largest, higher than anywhere else where all with eyes could see. Its waves, leagues of life, its source as great as the core at the center of the earth burst against the dusty shores, dreadful to all those ported there but dared go no further onto land for unseen treaties were made and could not easily be unmade.

Beyond the great city was the blue, hazy, distant but so

very close mountains that served as a monument to the gods victory over Zel until recently, whose purpose for existing was proving to be more trouble than some trifle reminder to those wishing to rebel was worth. And it would rattle the earth from time to time, making small cracks where few could see but have since grown into massive schisms at indirect points on the globe to the growing irritation of the High Guardians whose claim over Zel included this secret and mystical place.

To travel through the city was to travel through time—ancient, stone homes greet you but they change, as if Time herself moved her children, wisps of memories long forgotten to those long dead along as you walked—iron replaced stone, iron became silver, and building after building, home after home grew taller and bigger the more north one went, the tallest at its most northern point. This was the tower of Osir—the Eye of Zel, a sister to Ozerith. No human had ever been up its tallest heights and neither had the current High Guardians who called this their home, where they ruled over every Lord and person alive on this earth.

With a massive stroke of his wings, the great, gold dragon flew faster, passing through dark clouds to gaze upon his city with a love and admiration he hadn't felt since The Great Sacrifice. For years he stayed away, avoiding this once sacred place his sons grew up and played in, well before they became gods of their own and turned their blood ties to bloody rivalry. Every stone, in the earth unseen with human eyes held their very memories—he could never forget them, even if he wanted to. Especially his Gilton.

He lightened his body and glided down the winding sides of Osir, prepared to change form and walk in with his human form when he heard her. Her light rattled in like a calamitous crack to the invisible sky and marked the side of the building his foot recently touched—a black, gaping scar on what had been unblemished since the beginning.

He flew far away then, faster than air could allow, from of the desperate grasps of this most odious creature he had little heart to speak to. And he was pleased his mighty wings breaking wind cut out her shrieking, but he could still feel her teeth on his spine, like small knives piercing his scales. Her breath was on him, but he was just out of reach. He clasped his golden jaw shut and, in a flash, disappeared.

Peasants and serfs minding their business stopped to look to the sky and fell on their backsides terrified the same horrible dragon who destroyed Glenloch was there to do the same. Still with eyes on the sky, their fear shifted to the horrific screams of light shone bright over the guardians palace, burning their eyes worse than heat from their humble fires ever could. Those who could help got those unable back to their feet and all business resumed though the languishing screams of their Goddess made them speak louder.

"Oy, what the hell was that? Did I see a dragon?" asked a laborer running past a woman returning to her milk churning.

"Yes," she yelled but calmly as the sky filled with more unsettling screams of anguish, "but it left. So..."

"Uh, I see. She had better be done before I get to sleep or so help me?"

The two nodded and went back to work. Siracon who was always watching looked down her nose upon them with contempt.

"WHY DID HE LEAVE?!" she screamed as her light glowed and then waned.

"Grandmother—," came a voice from a window below, "please come inside. We need your help in here!"

Her maddening light dimmed, and the echoes of her vocal lashings eventually evaporated into near silence. The Sun took back its place in the sky, though reluctantly as the goddess began to pull away. Her light then fell through the building, smacking floor to ceiling, floor to ceiling, until she was in the High Guardians new chamber room just below the clouds where they could breathe much easier. There, Gargo and Girgo sat poised and at attention, like two boys ready for a lecture as she took her human form right before their eyes.

Few had ever witnessed her as such and those working in the room knew best and turned away before she was totally unveiled. And it was a quick motion, as fast as one could blink, and there she was—a woman of beauty no realm could deny with skin that radiated and shimmered crystals, with locks of endlessly curly yellow, and eyes of a tiresome maroon and blue.

She turned to the window to see herself, examining every inch from one cheek to the other before nodding in approval.

"My children—" her voice was deep but playful like a little girls, "what are we to do?!"

"Uh... About what, mam?" asked Gargo, rubbing his stone hands together.

"Stop that!" she screamed, and he forced them under his thighs. "Oh, why do you make me yell! You know I hate that! Oh, poor babies! Your father would be so proud of all the work you've done for our people. Though ungrateful they can be at times. If only everywhere could be like Gilton City..."

"May I ask something?" Girgo lifted a finger as soft as milk in the air.

She nodded.

"How are we supposed to do that?"

"Simple—use the Order of Garatos and slay those who oppose your will. That's what your grandfather did, and your father to some degree."

She looked again in the window and noticed an unevenness from one side of her face to the other. She scratched at it until skin moved to the shape of her liking, much to the two guardian's horror.

"What about the kid?" asked Gargo.

"What about *it*? Some imposter who's trying to steal your grandfather from you? They've tried it before, but they were clever this time."

She laughed.

"A girl. As if the great of the gods would ever have a girl. If with anyone, it would have been with me!"

"So, what should we—"

"She is not a concern now. All you must do is continue your force on the mountains and do not yield. No matter the cost. It must be destroyed once and for all."

She walked the room, grabbing things and setting them back down again as loud as one can.

"I will need to rearrange things here, to suite my needs, of course. Eventually, when your grandfather comes home, we'll need to make it more comfortable for him too!"

As she called for staff and ordered them to do impossible things, like move immovable objects and clean pebbles off stone, Gargo leaned into Girgo.

"I'm gonna bloody scream if she doesn't leave!"

"Patience, Gargo. She is going to give us the world, we only have to listen to her shit until then."

"I don't know if I can wait that long. What would grandfather do?"

The bigger twin became a boy next to his younger brother, whose cold disposition changed little as he answered.

"I'll tell you what—he'd do whatever he wanted no matter what she said. Like he did just now. She could be useful to us, but we could easily be thrown aside at her whim. I say, let's keep our cards to our chest, brother. We have competition now."

"Oh, you're right. If that filth ever makes it to this palace, we'll be out on our asses like Ganguen!"

They both laughed as the unharmonious yelling of the goddess clung to walls.

"When I find him, I'm going to kill him."

"Not unless grandmother says so," Girgo said passively, rolling his eyes at the notion.

The twinkling woman whose own servants were reduced to the floor proudly walked back to the duo with fresh clothes full of gold and ingots in her arms. She handed them slowly to both godkin, as if they were made of feathers. But Girgo's hands trembled as they barely managed to keep them up.

"Grandmother," Gargo said through batted breaths as he struggled to hold his new tunic, "this is too heavy to wear."

"Then you must train. Call the captain of the guard and start now. If you need me, I'll be in my chambers."

She left before another word was spoken. Girgo rubbed his eyes as Gargo insisted he didn't need training to the captain whose men were pulling him off his throne.

"Don't fight it, Gargo. It'll only make it worse."

Girgo had already thrown his gift on the marble floor,

chipping a work of art already beaten down. His eyes cruised the small craters and scorch marks left long before him and his brother took up their role.

He shook his head.

He walked to the glass window, wider than most homes and squinted into the sky. The tiniest shimmer of gold from afar came into view.

He chuckled.

"I will wear your skin someday, Garaton. Just you wait."

PARITY AWOKE DAYS FROM MALKEEVS, trembling at an intruder wind in her room. She pulled on her dress and put on her shoes, modest but durable. She ran downstairs as the Moon was saying her goodbyes to the night.

All morning she prepared a great and hardy breakfast for the handful of kids she took for the night and thought to fix her hair at her own reflection—as if they would care. Unta had stopped by earlier than the Sun to tell her of Mistacles wanting to meet with her before he planned to leave that afternoon. And this was to be her big moment—to finally show the man who held her child she was a good mother.

As the children ate, coughing as they swallowed too much food at once, a knock at the front door made Parity drop her bowl of cookie dough and her flock laughed.

Plea Eric came through the front door mournfully, apologizing up and down for the mess.

"It's fine, Eric, really. What can I help you with?"

He got lost in her face and she noticed this. As if on instinct, she turned away so he could focus on anything but her.

"Oh, yes, um. We, uh, got in the votes for who would be

taking them in. I...didn't see your name in the pool—I figured that was an accident. So, I did it for you—I hope you don't mind."

She beamed a joy Plea Eric had hardly seen in his life and he nearly had a heart attack at her beauty, fresh on eyes.

"I didn't forget, dear friend. I... may need to go to the mountains to see my daughter. I didn't want to leave a child abandoned."

"Oh, that's too bad since... you were chosen as one of the fosters."

The children hearing this hoorayed for they had gotten to know the sunshine woman and wanted nothing more than to spend every night with her—reading bedtime stories, making forts, and eating chocolate cake like they had the night before.

"I am so honored!" she said, throwing her arms around the surprised man.

"If you need to see your kid, we'll look after the little one while you're gone. It won't be a problem Parity!"

As he said her name, the children laughed.

"Your name is Parity?! I thought it was Mrs. Wobblers!" said one kid as he spat his food on his plate.

"Yeah, Mrs. Wobblers who lost her teeth!"

The kids covered their teeth with their lips and shook, calling themselves Mrs. Wobbler in a very bizarre way.

Plea Eric giggled.

"What is this madness?"

"I'll tell you later. Do you know which child will be mine?"

"Yes, we'll let you know later today. Congratulations again!" he said, waving goodbye. But as he left, still eyeing the door as it closed on him, he turned and ran smack dab into Mistacles whose usual jolly face had turned grim.

"Sorry!... Oh! You must be Mistacles—the great Imagi! After all these years?! I'm so pleased to meet you!"

"And you," said the round man in such a short way.

"You've made it here so quickly!"

"Yes, well, time is limited for a man in charge of the sacred Mountains of the Predicated! While I'm here, I will be dealing with a few matters that have been left unattended for far too long. I was wondering if you could help me with that?"

"Whatever you need. Your name is spoken of well in this village, and I will do my best to make you feel at home while you're here."

The Plea reached to shake Mistacles hand, but was ignored.

"Where's his grave?"

"Who's grave?"

"Marcus—Plea Marcus Daniels. I would like to see it."

"Well, he was burned on a slab of pine from the forest over there, with wildflowers in the vale not far from here. Like all other Grand Eunichs before him."

Mistacles gave him a dry look and Plea Eric took up his legs and walked down the path outside the village, leading them onto a path less traveled recently.

"What a beautiful place. I'm sure it was prettier before the massacre—I can't seem to remember being this far into the valley before then."

"Yeah, well, we've recovered just fine. Us Pleas have gone over and beyond to make sure the people are safe and protected. And we'd gladly do it again."

"And what of your goddess?"

Plea Eric sighed. "

She's provided some aid over the years but has always been modest—she believes in her people and knows they can overcome it themselves. I was sent here by her will, called to serve her and those she loves, and I've seen the beautiful impact it's made on the community. It has been a privilege to serve this village. It is unfair so many think of her so unwell. She is a strong-willed goddess, yes, but she has always meant well."

Mistacles raised his brows.

"I think I can sense him nearby," he said under his breath.

"You can do that?!"

"Well, I knew him once before. We were close, like brothers. I could tell his energy from anyone else's."

"Okay, so what's next?"

"Well, Plea Eric. I thank you for taking me here. I would like a few minutes alone to say my last goodbye, if you don't mind. I will be at Unta's residence later this afternoon if you would like to bid me farewell. And please bring fair Parity with you!"

"Very well, it was nice meeting you!" said Plea Eric before leaving Mistacles alone in a smaller part of the great valley, full of endless green, of rolling hills and colorful flowers swaying to the wind in some ancient dance.

Not far, from the corner of his eye, he could see the area of black they used to burn the bodies.

He shook his head.

"Damn you, Siracon! Damn you and all you stand for!"

He lifted his hands towards the Sun, like a flower hungry for love. He closed his eyes and whispered in a tongue unknown to most humans alive. He growled and grumbled, his voice a hot wave seeping into every bone and muscle before entering the earth through his feet.

Behind his eyes he saw the world differently. Spirits of animals, Ultiquans, and humans zipped fast in clouds of smoke past him. He searched the many faces, like one did cards on a table, until he saw the stricken one of his old friend, who hadn't changed but for his lack of hair and growth of wrinkles. And his friend was stuck where he was.

His soul had been dragged into the goddess' realm, Eternie, where he was forced to stare at her light for forever—and it was blinding. Mistacles was close enough to reach him but was realms away—thousands upon thousands of worlds and years away.

He looked up at the light burning holes into the sockets of Marcus' eyes and made his decision. This wasn't his best moment—he had done similar things much more gracefully. But he knew an opportunity like this wouldn't happen again and his friend's soul was at stake. But he also knew doing this would lead to more problems and his escape would need to happen sooner than was intended.

He shrugged off his options and took up a proper stance for such rituals—legs apart with his weight evenly on both.

He snorted in deeply the air too clean for his mountain lungs and coughed up as hard as he could a force of energy at the malignant light. And on impact, the light spun in turns like the spinning of the world. In this simple moment of relief and in one seamless motion, he grabbed the soul of Marcus by the hand.

He spoke again in the unusual tongue and both men were jolted leagues from Eternie before the light stopped. Without prompting, they walked towards a different light—a sweet light before them, entering another afterlife—the one most unsworn to a god went to, and it was a peaceful place.

With a heavy heart, Mistacles released Marcus' hand

who in turn stared back, too astonished to move. At the speaking of further words, Mistacles fell back to Zel and into the realm of the living, but as he felt his soul reach his body once more, a faint whisper from a dry voice said—*thank you brother*—and his heavy heart became lighter and the weight of decades of guilt washed away.

As he regained his body, his legs trembled, and he fell on his bottom. He quickly got to his feet and ran towards the village as the sky once clear turned a dark, battled charcoal and thunder struck the ground with stinging death where he had stood.

CHAPTER 18

In the mountains' many chambers and cave systems, in the dead of night, came loud trumpets and soundly snares that awoke all who slept early that morning. The children rose from their beds, frightened but were calmed by the attendants to not worry. It would have appeared that it was nothing more than the sound of Yexour snoring again. But this time, it wasn't.

They couldn't sleep as the antagonizing sound came through the walls and the floors, slowly surrounding them. It finally came to a head when desperate cries came from outside, similar to the mountain caving in days before.

Pul, who choose to stay with them that night and slept on the floor, finally resembled the boy trapped in a crumbling inferno, calling for his father until his lungs filled with smoke. And his friends kept their eyes on him, with the growing reality of hopelessness realized as the stoic, young man showed them how real the end could be for all of them.

It was only a moment before he was back again—the man in the mirror; the fearless one. He reached for his belt and unveiled his saber like a chef did his knife and aimed to leave with every intent to do damage.

"No, you don't!" screamed Tane who put her body to the door.

"I have to help!" he cried jogging in place. More screams and horns rumbled the air, and they all looked up, petrified.

A great many bangs slammed on the heavy door and Tane stepped away, collapsing into a fit of sadness long forgotten. A thump and another thump made the door rock on its hinges. The Child stared intently at their only way out, forming a fist in hands that could do no more than give her friends time to escape. Care had found a place to hide behind his bed, bracing to run.

Pul hid besides a giant cabinet as the man entered violently, splicing the door in two. He glowered at the small children before him, helpless and afraid, and smiled.

"Which one of you is it, hmm?"

As the great and bloodied soldier stepped further in, a confident and strong Pul lunged his sword into the man's side and pushed him as hard as he could across the room, feet scuffling over rugs and wooden frames. As the man stood stuck and bleeding to the wall, Pul screamed for them to follow him and they did, leaving their room and the dying man without question.

Pul stopped in the hallway and the children did not pass him. He peered around the corner into the kitchen where the slain bodies of attendants without weapons lay lifeless and soldiers, pacing and also bloody, screamed at the few attendants still living. One of them saw the kids and Pul panicked, taking Care by the hand and the other two followed him into the only door left intact. He closed it shut and held the knob to stop it from turning. The three others under his silent command took the worn-out chair and moved it to cover the door. They had no time to think before their foe would be on them with nowhere left to run.

"W-w-what are we gonna do?" screamed Tane through scattered sobs. The Child searched the room, desperate for heavier items to bring to the door, wishing she had taken the time to look at the few artifacts cluttering the walls—how she wished that was this moment rather than what it really was.

Care tried his best to help Pul but neither were stronger than one man, not even with the two together. That was when he remembered. He stood up and released his hold as the knob was gaining way against them. Pul could hardly speak but his shocked face showed it all. Care smiled before running over to Mistacles desk and opened the front draw. The sack full of pebbles was gone.

He closed his eyes. He felt over his clothes and asked desperately to some invisible thing for it to be there. With no luck, he thought back to earlier that night and remembered—he moved it when he went to bed. He reached into the front pocket of his shirt and clenched it tight.

"Hey guys—look what I've got!"

He pulled back him arm and, in his mind, thought of the village he once called home, whispering its name as the house started to shack. He unleashed the pebble onto the hardened wall and fell forward from the force. Instantly, the wall became a mural of the green expanse that was the home of the Venoxems. The others, stunned, could hardly believe it.

Pul whose body was giving in to the harsh clamors of the soldiers opposite the door screamed, "Go!" and his frozen friends awoke from their stupor.

As Tane and Care ran through, the Child came to Pul and dragged him through the portal as the door caved in.

As the men fell through and pummeled to the ground, the portal began to fade back into a wall again. One man who had seen what it truly was ran to it with the intention of going through. His bones broke upon ancient rock. The others searched the room as a different sounding horn played through the mountain and their spirits fell.

THE CHILDREN LANDED hard on the grass outside a small house nearest the village. Care knew it well though it looked different from when he and his family lived there. Without thinking, he ran up the many steps as a beautiful woman walked out unawares.

When she noticed the children, she froze. She stared at the Child who squinted to try and remember how she knew such a face.

From behind them came a loud crash from the valley as a red faced Mistacles emerged into the village, unaware of the children either. But anyone who had ever met the Imagi could place him anywhere. Relieved, they ran screaming, even Care, calling his name, leaving the woman standing alone, speechless and crying.

Mistacles turned to face them, and his heart stopped.

"My children, what are you doing here?!"

"The mountain—It's under attack!" said Tane through short breaths.

The sky had been dark since they arrived but turned nearly to night from the overcast looming towards them at Mistacles' heels.

"We must get inside, children. Hurry!"

He pushed them towards Unta's home with a slow Parity meandering close but unseen.

The Child ran swiftly like any agile child would. As

quick as a heartbeat, she heard the loudest sound she ever had, like snapping wood or a tree falling from a great height, and it came from behind her. It made her ears ring and she wanted to cover them but couldn't waste her swinging arms. She looked to Mistacles and his face turned to her, or what was behind her, and it was tattooed with terror. A bright light crossed his face, and an even greater shadow covered the earth. The Child looked behind her and saw the blinding glow of a thunderbolt aimed for her back. She gawked for a moment before it became several.

She gasped as her eyes surveyed her village—or what was left of it. Everything had slowed to almost a stop as soon as she heard the thunder. She realized then she had time to get away but it was slowly running out. She carefully moved from the bolt's sharp edges an arm's length from her as it came closer but no faster than a snail. She could feel it's warmth—a radiation that burned through happiness; that seared through hope before it could be born. It was an agent of hate and disease, and it was determined to end her.

Very carefully, she took a very still and scared Care and moved him out of the path of the blast. And she did this with the others as the air grew hot and tendrils of light, veins of deadly poison, streamed towards them in a contagious, hateful way.

When they were all out of range, the Child readied herself and spoke into her mind—to Tom—that he could let time go. She took a deep breath in and began to run as time resumed and a stupefied Mistacles turned back to running while the others were too scared to ask any questions and did the same. She had put herself a good distance from her friends, choosing to run away from where they were going, as the lightning bolts struck at her feet and hers alone.

Mistacles screamed words not known to her and the sky rumbled some more. She noticed most of her friends had made it to the house as she turned quickly to run behind a home the great storm barreled through, striking it's wood —leaving a giant crack down it's side.

She closed her eyes and time stopped again. She ran again, against the stillness of time and was a few large gallops from the door when she heard a woman's voice bellow from the deep clouds above.

"*You dare live?!*"

The Child jumped onto the steps and into the still bodies of her friends who risked themselves to save her. And as she entered, time resumed. The door quickly closed, and a loud bang hit against the wood and it smoked from the inside.

All the children laid in a pile atop Mistacles who begged them to get off. He picked up the Child and squeezed her as hard as he could.

"Oh, you are such a wonderful girl—I didn't know you had powers!"

Before she could tell him the truth, he spoke again.

"Everyone, we need to get back to the mountains imme-diately."

Parity entered the room, taking the back door to meet them inside, and hid behind Unta who had been watching from the kitchen.

Sarty sat at the top of the stairs and glared at Pul whose burn marks gave him away though subtle they seemed compared to the stories he'd heard. Unta had told him everything about Pul, even about his recent mission with the Army of Miracon. But he looked barely strong enough to hold a sword.

Unta reached for Parity, to pull her into the light, but she resisted.

"Come on, go and talk to her."

"And say what?" she whispered as she peeked around him to see her charming, young girl. He took her arm and dragged her to the group talking amongst themselves.

"... and so, Care made a portal into the wall, and we escaped the Order by the hair on our heads!" said Pul, explaining with an arm over the Child's shoulders. "I had no idea it was this exciting in the mountains!"

"Yeah, I'm pretty sure he killed a guy!" said Tane poking him in the side.

Mistacles gave Care a wink.

"We'll talk about this later," he whispered to the boy.

The group turned to Unta and Parity as they approached, and the air still ripe from the thunder got thicker. Both Tane and Pul remembered the woman well and Pul made a rude smirk as she glanced at him nervously. But the Child could hardly remember her but knew she had to know her from somewhere.

"Children—this is Unta, Munta's older brother. And this is Parity, she's—"

"I'm her mom," she said, pointing to the Child whose bright eyes widened. "I am so happy to see you."

Everyone waited for a response from the Child, but she didn't give one.

She smiled and nodded and Tane spoke up first.

"Are we ready to go now, Mr. Mistacles?"

"Yes! Children, let us go! Unta, I'll come back for my things later. Sarty! We're leaving!"

The Child looked up at the stairs and stared at the young man who was bigger than most men.

He noticed her eyes and, for the first time since being there, smiled and waved.

"I guess we have time to chat when we get to the mountains," he said to her, seemingly no different than her Care or her Pul. But Pul saw the difference and glared at the boy as he approached.

"Okay, let's go guys!"

Mistacles reached into his bag and took out a pebble and threw it against the wall. More thunder offended outside that no one dared open the door to see. Mistacles walked through first as they entered the tent of Lieutenant Hisousen.

As the children walked forward, a tired and curious Care stood behind as a sneaky Parity walked through in his place. Before Mistacles could notice the subtle swap, it was too late.

Unta stood speechless as the little boy smiled at him. He jumped up and down and ran up the stairs, screaming for someone named Cara.

"Son, what have you done?" Unta asked as he ran his hands through his hair.

"Take me to them, please! I want to see my sister!"

LIEUTENANT HISOUSEN HAD BEEN in serious contemplation when the Order of Garatos made their great strike. Ten thousand men with their beasts found passage into their part of mountain and made it effortlessly without so much as an alarm. It would later be discovered the Army of Miracon's post in Belingdale had been compromised after

Ganguen escaped and there was no one there to alert them of the giant legion following their secret route.

The mountain's military with the Army of Miracon were no more than a thousand and their only ally was their knowledge of the harsh terrain. Hisousen spent most of his morning keeping the enemy lines from entering the major parts of the city in which the Child, no doubt their main objective, would be. The Imagi's hadn't finished the spell and Mistacles was away. It was the perfect time to strike. But how could they have known unless they were told by someone trusted in their group.

Hisousen was in his tent later that morning, attending to his wounds and helping those surviving when a portal opened from behind him. He almost stabbed Mistacles as he walked through but hugged him instead. He was surprised to see the children trail the big man and had been upset thinking they had been taken all that time.

"Oh, what a blessing! Thank you Miracon!" he said through tears with his arms folded over his chest. "Where's the little one?"

"Care?" asked Mistacles. "'Too long of a story. But in short—he is alive but not in the mountains with us. Now, take me to the Imagi's immediately and keep the little ones protected."

Mistacles followed Hisousen, leaving the children and Parity alone in the tent with a small group of armymen to guard them from outside.

"So, what happened?" asked Mistacles as they walked through crowds of armymen gathering weapons and armor, smelling of whiskey and weeks old stink. Those huddled nearest the tents were either healing themselves or preparing for battle—half-restful and half-lively. Steel hitting steel was not far enough away for Mistacles to be at ease.

"They came in from the central cave, in the twilight zone—all of 'em through there," he said as he pointed toward the heart of the battle. "Not the brightest of their plans, but I think they intended to catch us by surprise. I don't think they knew how many of us were here or how slender these caves can be. You Imagis were able to trap most of them but too many got through and a fair amount of damage has been dealt."

"And the spell?"

"All the Imagi's and their Magi are working on the Order. We were helpless until you arrived, old friend. I will forever be in your debt."

"Don't loan me your life until I've successfully saved it, old friend. I'll need access to where the spell must take place. If the supplies are still there, I'll be done by tonight...hopefully."

The two men walked well into the city turned battle-field, where large planks of wood and slabs of rock were put in places to help block aerial attacks and give shielding to armymen from the unavoidable melee coming for them at any time.

Mistacles breathed in deeply and took the long road leading into the icy tundra, to the top of Mother Summit, sprinting at a brilliant speed to finish the spell.

CHAPTER 19

The children with Parity were left in the tent as the other adults ran off to defend the post. All stood stunned except for Sarty who quickly looked for a sword and found a jagged saber hidden besides Hisousen's desk.

"I didn't know you were a thief!" said Pul with disdain.

His arms were crossed, and his muscles were showing though it did little to stop Sarty, who peered from under furrowed brows as he smiled and motioned him to follow.

"Don't do this. You'll get hurt!" said the Child who had kept her back to her mother since they arrived home and didn't want to be left alone with her, though what she said she also meant.

"I'll be fine."

Sarty waved to the Child before looking again at Pul.

"If your gonna stay, you might as well defend yourself."

He threw the sword and Pul caught it by the handle. Parity gasped at the move.

Sarty left the tent from the back where no armymen were stationed and snuck by those near the front. He hid besides a cluster of crates full of long, jagged sabers much to his giddy surprise. He grabbed the least rusty one and crouched along the running people in chaos for the second time in less than a cycle, blending in seamlessly in a crowd of other lost, young men.

He found the front line where most of the Army of Miracon had overpowered the less skilled and younger Order of Garatos. He looked down upon the faces of those fallen and saw boys not much older than he.

He scoffed.

Had he been in those front lines, he would have died killing as many as he could, not cower into a ball, or so he thought.

Distant yelling took him from his terrible thoughts and he searched the are, finding Hisousen pained to see him there, motioning for him to come over and he jogged to meet him.

"What are you doing boy?! Go back! The next wave is soon to come!"

And as he spoke, a low hum of nearby screaming grew as those running across from them drew near. They were soon to approach with axes and swords and other manor of weapons expertly held. The armymen took to poise and waited for further command. As a loud superior spoke words Sarty didn't understand, the first of the line twisted their bodies and moved to parry the attack from the upcoming menace. And they did so successfully.

The few armymen who died fell in every way—forward, back, and sideways. Their closest friends had no time to grieve and had to act faster than their mind could allow. And they did. Another command rang through the air as the second and third linemen parried then stabbed, throttling the oncoming attack with even fewer casualties on their end.

Where Sarty stood was nearest the end of the many lines which started to move from front to back like a giant wave. Men moved along with one another so their blows were more impactful and their defense was doubled upon doubled what it would have been alone.

He marveled until he too had to move.

He took a step back as the men in front of him pushed roughly into his chest and Hisousen stared at him incredulously for not moving a muscle, not even to save himself, a feat no armyman would ever do without training.

Another scream came through. It was from the enemy's end and their words were just as commanding and their actions suggested a change in their strategy much to Hisousen's satisfaction.

From behind Sarty came the hollering voice of a man scratchy and low. He turned around to see the giant of Venlet with his mouth wide, screaming at the many men preparing for battle. Sarty stepped back and waded through the endless people to get to the boy next to him who stood in a trance besides the big man—as he had just moments before.

They stared at each other with such a hollowness few who had not seen what they had would feel sorry for. But they knew better.

They smiled at one another and Pul handed Sarty a smaller sword.

"Here, this'll be easier to swing."

Sarty noticed on Pul's belt a small hatchet. He raised a brow.

"You'll see in a minute why I need this. Consider it in the future—if you live!"

And after Pul's words, the many linemen ahead of them who survived the oncoming attack ran forward, together like a herd of wasps and their screams were just as frightening. Pul and the man with him, Munta, ran past Sarty and he threw down the larger saber and ran with the lighter sword, screaming as he entered his first battle.

TANE HID BESIDE HER FRIEND, her wandering eyes looking for a way at the woman. She couldn't help herself—she couldn't keep her eyes off Parity. She had never seen her up close and was curious to find similarities between her and Chil, though try as she would few could be found.

When the Child noticed this—her looking at her than up, and over again—she hit her in the side.

"Ouch, what the hell was that for?" asked Tane readying a wallop of her own.

"Excuse me?" The two girls turned to the only adult, confused and intimidated by her tone. "That is no way for a lady to speak."

"Oh," said Tane, staring down at her torn up sandals before laughing.

The Child tried not to follow but couldn't help but burst into a fit herself.

Parity walked to the front of the tent and opened the flaps. The children were without words as she commanded to speak to whoever was in charge. They laughed some more which made her angrier.

"Alright, alright—that is enough!"

She stomped to them with her finger in their faces but dropped the attitude when she looked into her daughter's, who stared down at the floor in response. She caught a glimpse of her brilliant eyes and smiled. They were like that even when she was a baby—like purple silk and brown gold, married and entwined. She told no one this but wore those colors when she could, choosing to pay more for these uncommon colors than for her own food at times. And much to everyone's disbelief, she did hold her and would stare at her, imagining she was Bart's and they were all in Holfenya, married and entwined. It was when the colors would change, to unknown blues and terrifying yellows her mood would as well, and her mother would have to take the baby for her own safety.

She walked away and sat down at the desk, observing the many grooves in its skin.

The girls whispered and Tane continued her research regardless of how the other two felt. Parity thought it would be easier to be around her daughter again, now since they've both grown. But it would seem the old wounds she gave her daughter were hardly healed enough and she wasn't sure what to do about it.

A commotion—words amongst men could be heard from outside the tent before the flaps opened wide. In walked a young man with maddeningly blue eyes whose gaze went straight to the Child.

"I think it's time to go, Doe," he said with his hand out to her.

"Uh, excuse me but who the hell are you?" asked Parity jumping to her feet. The man stared at her with so much hate she almost vomited.

Tane walked in front of her friend and started to speak in tongues.

"What is this?" the man said jovial and laughing.

The Child seemed confused but didn't seem frightened by the stranger with them. As he reached for the girl again, an angry Tane took his gloved hand and bit into the gauntlet as hard as she could. She pulled back and held her mouth and the Child hugged her. Parity took her shoe and started to hit the man who held up his arm in defense. He continued to only reach for the Child and nodded for her to follow him. When she shook her head no, he reached for her anyway.

Before he got hold of her arm, he stared up at some unseen force before bolting from the tent. Parity followed him and ran past the two armymen stationed in the front who were out cold. She tried to find him in the dark and crumbling cave where he ran but gave up when her eyes started to hurt. She ran back inside and took Tane by the face.

"You poor thing. Where does it hurt?" Tane pointed to her front tooth that wiggled in place.

Parity sighed.

"You'll be alright. It's gonna fall out but it's only a late baby tooth. You're lucky at your age to still have those. A new one will grow back. When everything is settled, I'll make you some tea that'll help with the pain, okay?"

Tane gave the woman an unexpected hug and she hugged her back. When she let go of the girl, the Child walked up with arms open and filled the space her friend left. And Parity was without words. She carefully embraced her child as to not scare her away, and when she realized she wanted to be there, she hugged her as tight as she could and took a deep breath of her wind-wrapped hair.

"Oh, my sweet Lilith—my sweet, little girl!"

Mistacles shook at the malignant winds aimed to harm him. He imagined it to be the work of those horrid twins in the city who had their own masters of magic, who could do some of what he could, but their attempts to stop him were futile—the ingredients had gone into the mountain and were accepted by Yexour. The ritual was all that remained and he wouldn't be stopped.

He sat on the cold snow, sticking to his cape like porcupine balls. He closed his eyes, gathering himself and his energy on short supply. He could feel it flow out of him, like a slow stream.

It's not enough! He said with a sigh.

He moved his legs and got comfortable once more. He breathed deeply, reaching into his mind where knowledge found nowhere else spiraled infinitely, waiting to be picked. With his eventual death, so much of the past will go, unless he can give it to his children. But they were younger than him when he first learned the ways of magic, and his teacher, who was older than Yexour, shared with him little. With his death was not just the morning of one of the first of Man but the death of all things unshared.

Mistacles shook his head, shrinking from these memories and swam through his lessons with the ancient man.

"You must calm the mind and think of someplace nice. It'll be there, you'll see. Then, you grab it!" His master's voice sung in his mind, leading him through the depths of his concentration.

As his head became cleared, free of the usual upsets and stresses of life, with the current cold outside the slowest to leave, his memories came through in flashing lights, moving too fast to stay and enjoy. When the memories did stop, he opened his eyes.

It was a beautiful springen day on the summit, mountain birds sang their peace and the flowers recently bloomed swayed gently in the soft breeze. It reminded him of a time when he was a young man, and he and Marcus played with the wildflowers, changing their colors much to the dissatisfaction of their teacher.

He could see Marcus as he was back then—his head full of copper hair and his heart full of life. His mind then switched to what he looked like before his death —miserable.

He smiled at his friend and noticed his very own hands were no longer young.

Marcus stared in return, tired but relieved.

"Old friend, I've made a mess of things," he said.

"Oh, no you haven't, brother. You've helped so many people and saved so many lives."

Mistacles reached to touch his arm, but his hand went through.

"Well, if it's okay with you, I plan to stay on this mountain."

Marcus gave an understanding, teary-eyed smile to his friend who nodded.

"Until I see you again," said Mistacles as he reached into Marcus' chest and grabbed hold of a very white light, spilling out of the lines in his hands.

He closed his eyes, eager to finish the job, and opened them again. Before him stood a young man with dark hair and the bluest of eyes.

"And what do you want?" asked Mistacles and the man said nothing.

He was slow to his feet; his legs numb from the icy exposure and a hand warm from the ball. At last standing, a giant crow with horns twisted downwards flew past and into the dark clouds looming overhead, signaling the Dark Gods farewell to which Mistacles could care less.

He wiped his head and staggered to a small hole near

the center of the mountain with the ball of light still in his hand.

"Oh, great Yexour—hear my words! Let me heal thy wounds and thy light, so you may protect those innocent of the First Crime from evil…uh…tonight!"

He shoved the light into the hole and held it there, damning himself for his poor wording.

In a flash, he became witness of the very battle that took the titans life. He saw the sword forced through the monsters back who pled with the gods. It fell to the earth and curled around the forest Garaton demanded to take as his own.

Mistacles cried at the mountains grief and stopped when it let him go. A rumble—a groan moved the ground as the Ultiquan awakened. Agonizing screams covered the sky as many dark lights, of false Magi and witches untamed, left the aura of the lovely creature in a dash.

Mistacles fell forward.

"Not again!" He screamed as he rolled to his side and allowed his body to settle there. He heard the small foot falls and subtle words of his Imagis and Magi before passing out. He was okay with it this time. Maybe he would finally get a good night's rest.

CHAPTER 20

A brutal, harsh storm hit Venlet early that morning and Agatha, who awoke as many others had at the sound, anxiously waited for her daughter who left home without saying a word of return. She stood in the freshly painted kitchen which was bigger than it appeared from outside with two children loudly eating oatmeal behind her.

She gave up staring through the window and walked to the little girl whose hair was cut shorter than a boys and set her jeweled hand on the table next to her.

"Jela, do you really have to eat like that, dear?"

The little girl looked up and laughed before slurping on her oatmeal even louder. Agatha turned her attention to the little boy who was examining his spoon.

"And?" asked Agatha.

"... I don't think I've ever seen a spoon so nice before. Maybe silver?"

She took a chair near him and joined him.

"Amazing, I never noticed, Don. You've seen spoons before, haven't you?"

"Well yeah, but back in the room we used whatever they gave us, or nothing at all."

After he spoke, the room went silent.

"Can you believe it? We live with rich people!" said Jela finally to the still confused Don who smiled at her in solidarity.

"Oh no, precious—we are not rich. The people who lived here before us had a fortune well hidden in books but most of it was taken after... you know. There are tons there for you to read when you like. Whenever Parity gets home, she'll tell you guys all about it."

"She didn't abandon us, did she?" asked the little girl, pouting.

"Not at all. She's probably busy with something. But you have me too! Grandma Agatha is here for you too!"

"Grandma Eggie!" said Don to Jela who laughed, and they repeated it till Agatha left the room.

She enjoyed spending time with the young kids but couldn't handle their edge. They weren't like other children—anyone could see that. After she cut-off most of the girl's hair, Jela spent the entire night crying in the bathroom, screaming how she wished she was never born. And Don couldn't look anyone in the face. He had said if he had done that while working, he'd get a punch to the head.

"Poor kids," she said to herself as she took to folding a basket full of laundry her daughter left unattended. After, she'd have to straighten the dishes, and sort out the children's clothes—*matters Parity also forgot to do before she left*—she thought.

She was beginning to feel apprehensive for her daughter. If she were to take these children and keep them, and raise them as her own, she'd have to do better for they'd be harder to handle than the timid and independent child she neglected.

As her mind wandered on such things, thinking again on the grandchild she hadn't seen in years, she heard the door in the kitchen open and a blur shoot through the room like a flame.

"I thought I told you not to open the door for anyone!" She turned around and saw Unta, as tired and miserable as always with the infamous spoon in his hand.

"Hmm, I think this might be real silver," he said as he gave it back to Don.

The two kids left the kitchen and ran to the sitting room where a box of toys from the previous owners stayed untouched for many years.

"Where is she?" asked Agatha with her hands on her hips.

"How did you know I had news about her?"

"Because you're crazy about her. You're an idiot, you know? So, what is it now? Did she meet some stranger and run off, or did she get kidnapped? Anything is possible with that girl!"

Unta cleared his throat and smiled in a friendly way.

"Uh, she's in the mountains with your granddaughter. She'll be coming home soon, maybe this afternoon. They were able to patch things up, but the Order is still attacking inside, so..."

He looked away, taken aback by what she said.

"Thanks, Unta. Would you like to—"

"No, I'm fine. I have my rounds to make. I'll see you later."

And he left in a flash.

The older woman leaned on the doorframe as the man walked staggered through the village streets, half-heartedly waving at the friendly faces who cared for him. She wasn't upset by what she had said, but rather the harsh truth they both knew and the inevitable he had been trying to avoid all this time.

"LILITH?!" asked Tane making a yucky face at the word. "Who names their kid that?"

The girls with aprons on moseyed upon the parts of their city clear of enemy attack, working much like every other healthy person among them. They had been given the job of taking rags and clean clothes to wounded armymen and were to bring whatever supplies the Magi needed to heal them when they were done. While one held the provisions, the other gave them out. And they did so complaining the whole way.

The Child, without thinking, walked through a large pile of broken wood set aside to repair the house it came from.

"Tane, please, it's not that bad."

"Not that bad? Do you remember the story behind that name? She might as well have called you a thief!"

An armyman near Tane raised their hand, a response for needing a rag. She took one from her friend's yielding arms and pulled hers back, whipping it at him as hard as she could.

"That's not true! And I'm not a thief!"

"Well, you probably will be now. And she didn't think she did anything wrong either!"

The Child stopped where she was and crossed her arms, dropping a lot of what she had been carrying.

"I'm not going anywhere until you apologize," she said.

Tane laughed.

"I won't apologize until you do it first!"

She then ran away, dropping the provisions she held, but the Child was quickly besides her.

"I sometimes forget how fast you are!"

"Why do I have to apologize first?" she said with arms empty as well.

"Because your stupid friend hurt my tooth!"

The Child gasped and went to hit her friend who dodged it before sprinting again.

"That's not my fault!"

Munta, resting on a makeshift chair saw the two girls' quarrel and stomp over wounded armymen, leaving the once clean rags and provisions on the filthy ground, and, at his wits ends, hollered for them to come over. He would have grabbed them where they stood but his knees were in such a state to do so would send him reeling. And his hands ached, chaffed at the palm where his axe, somewhere in the deep caves of the mountain, moved many men to death.

He had been in a small party who took a large chunk of the hidden Order by surprise. They were nestled in those cave systems to reveal themselves when the army had turned their back to them. Their plan was thwarted by the party, in part, but that wasn't what stopped the parade. As Munta gutted man after man, the mountain growled and the rock-face surrounding them turned into a blur from the loudness of its song. Many went deaf or their heads burst from their necks just being too close to it. Munta was lucky and was dead center. His ears bled, and he spent few hours upon release with herbs up them until he could bear it no more.

He sat up and, in a much stronger position, glowered at the girls skipping towards him.

"What do you think you're doing?" he asked.

"We're doing our job, Munta."

Tane's voice made the skin on Munta's back feel like it was covered with bugs.

He held back his tongue.

"Is it your job to hurt the already injured?"

"Sorry Munta, we won't do it again," said the Child as she reached for Tane's hand.

"Hey, big red—do you know the story of Lilith the White?" asked Tane, forcing the Child's wrist up in pain with the twisting of her very own. Munta pulled them apart as lightly as he could.

"Yeah, it's an old Holfenian tale. Why?"

"What happened to her in the end?"

Munta noticed the Child's face turn in distress.

"Are you okay, little one?"

"Not really, her mom gave her a name. And guess what it is?"

The Child pulled her hand free and sprung out of sight.

Before Tane could run as well, Munta caught her by her apron straps and brought her close. He wanted to squeeze her arms as hard as he could but killed the thought before it came true. Her look of shock which quickly turned to humor showed him, in fact he hadn't harmed her, and she had no idea the danger she had just been in.

"Tane, why are so mean to her?" he asked softly, regaining his humanity with every word.

"I am not! She acts all innocent and perfect, but she isn't!"

"You know, I felt the same way about my brother. He did everything right and I was the dumb one who was stronger than a horse. It wasn't until I was older when I realized he looked up to me, and everything I said to him, good or bad, he took to heart. Like I did with him. We were like twins after that, his discomfort mine and vice versa. You know, he was the first person I contacted when the first wave was over? I imagine you and her will be like that someday."

Tane stared at the smiling giant with eyes lacking any semblance of feeling.

"I don't think so," she said before walking away, without life or purpose in her steps. Munta tried to understand but knew he wouldn't.

He forced himself on his feet and wandered to where the rags and provisions were dropped. He whistled for a red-faced Pul to come over, using a fellow survivor standing up to keep him upright.

As the boy approached, he shook his head.

"No freaking way, I'm not doing that! Do you see how much crap I've had to do already?"

Munta laughed and threw the supplies at him anyways, and he caught it gracefully. He tried to walk away but stumbled, and as he felt himself losing his balance, the arms of the boy helped him up. He patted him on the back as they slowly walked, arm over shoulder and arm around waste, back to the chair he claimed as his.

"You know Pul—I am so proud of you!" Munta said as he sat down, rumbling like an old bear.

Hisousen stood over the hole Mistacles was found in when he saved the mountain. He had been in a sea of men when he felt the change take place. He searched the battle and saw the many faces of his men, of his second in commands and the ones he trusted most to bare arms with him. All but one.

He spent the afternoon after the battle wandering the

tundra surface so many Order soldiers had braved for weeks it seemed. Footprints and weapon markings took residence in the snow like the ancient etchings of the first of Man on the mountains skin. What was once an impossible endeavor, to scale the Mountain of the Predicated was now an easy task and could be done by masses of men in armor without anyone knowing.

He looked over the giant holes they made into the mountain's surface and made mental notes to have them refilled. As he stomped through snow, he tripped over an abandoned sword and landed on his hands. As he looked up, he noticed something troubling he knew had to be addressed right away.

Everything made sense then. It all started when the Order began attacking local villages near the many secret entrances the army had planned with Mistacles. There were so few who knew about it who weren't apart of the army stationed in the mountain itself.

He took the extravagant emblem in his hand and weighed it thoughtfully. From behind he heard the crunching of snow.

"I don't understand why you've done this," he said as his other hand rested on the hilt of his sword.

"What's there to understand, you've been in the Army long enough to know how much we're paid. I needed more and they offered it to me. That's all it was."

"The Order or the twins?"

"What difference does it make?"

"Marcello!" Hisousen screamed as he swung to face his old friend, his sword ringing in anticipation as he held it unsheathed. "Thousands of people have died! Their lives are worth more than your dubels!"

Hisousen moved to charge Marcello, to kill him where

he stood, weaponless, honor-less, but couldn't. He looked down as he felt the force of a blade rip through his armor and enter out his chest. Shocked, he spat warm blood onto the snow as his body was readying for death. Eyes wide, he turned to face the man who killed him and saw the null face of Ganguen, Son of Gilton.

He fell onto the snow and said nothing as he died. His blood ran wet on the orb unseen that grew bright at the touch.

Ganguen kept his eyes on Marcello who had been slowly stepping back, his blonde hair slashing against his face, untamed. He wiped clean his blade with his tunic—unaffected by the stain it left. As he peered back at his prey, he felt the stingy cool of a rock thrown at the center of his face. After shaking off the pain in his nose, he flicked his head up like a viper to find the great warrior gone and the already freezing remains of Hisousen slowly be covered in a sheet of snow.

Agatha hesitantly took the stairs of this great house, legs creaking in alignment with the creaking steps. As she reached the landing, she walked to the bedroom she had prepared for the kids earlier for Parity had not thought of it yet. When she opened the door, a little boy with bouncy blonde hair played with half burnt toys and was having a blast all by himself.

She tried to recall if her daughter had been given three instead of two children. Mind weary and her body on empty, she struggled but got down on the floor next to him and started to play.

"What your name?" she asked.

It was an innocent question, but his response would

have suggested otherwise. He gasped at her being there and screamed like a scared cloncluck for her to leave his house. At first, she was too stunned to do anything. But his face in absolute disarray made her stomach turn—something felt wrong here.

She stood up and ran out of the room as he called for someone named Cara. As the constant and unnerving screaming escalated, repeating again the name in a way that could fray the voice permanently, she took Don and Jela and ran to Unta's house without looking back.

CHAPTER 21

The Child laid across Mistacles' legs like a poor, wounded animal. She had come into his study like a bull, busting through everyone and everything to reach him and threw her arms around him as she blubbered what had happened. She collapsed to the ground after she didn't get the response she wanted but was picked up by the great Imagi who patted her head as she started to calm.

"She didn't mean to hurt your feelings, Chil."

"Yes, she did! She always does!" She sobbed some more before crawling to hug the still tired Imagi. "Why does she do it?"

"You mean, why does Tane act like Tane? Oh my, do you have all night?"

As he asked, he remembered again since waking Care was in Venlet and Parity was in the mountains. He tried to pull off the crying child, but it only made her cry harder. He asked his attendants to help remove her gracefully, but her grip was stronger than theirs.

"Sweetie, I need to go back to the village and get Care!"

"But is it true?!"

"Is what true?"

"Lilith the White was a thief?"

He closed his eyes.

"Now, I will tell you this story and I will do so quickly. Then, you will let me leave so I can bring him home?"

She nodded.

"Alright. Okay. Let's see here… Oh yes! The old Holfenian tale. A long time ago, there was a little girl named Lilith—sometimes pronounced Lilit—whose hands were little, like a baby's. She was a beautiful and kind little lady much like yourself, and everyone loved her. One day, when she was out picking dandelions, or something like that, a wolf approached her with pretty jewels around its neck. He offered her one if she let him into the chicken's pen. And she did. But she wanted another, and so he offered her another. Eventually, the wolf got his fill of chickens, cows, pigs—the lot and gave her all its jewels. But, she realized she couldn't hold them all because her hands were too small. So, she ate them, one by one.

"The following day, all the farmers went searching for the wolf who ate their animals. It returned to the girl and asked her for help. She asked for more jewels in return and it obliged. But, once the farmers came to her house, she told them where the wolf was. They dragged the creature out and it fought them with all its might. It saw little Lilith and…"

He paused.

"It's going to get gross, okay?"

She nodded.

"Okay! In its fury, it cut the girls guts wide open and out came all the jewelry it gave her which belonged to the other villagers all along. The wolf got away as they reclaimed what was theirs. And that is the end of the tale."

The Child sniffled and shook her head.

"Why would she name me after her?"

Mistacles smiled before kissing her on the forehead.

"There have been many Lilits and Liliths since her, and I'm sure there's a good reason. Why don't YOU ask her?"

The Child's eyes went wide. After their long embrace, the first they ever shared, they didn't speak a word to each other and went their separate ways. She wasn't sure what to say or if she would disappoint her by saying the wrong thing.

"I don't know how. Can you?"

He laughed.

"I must go, my precious child! And I will be taking your mother with me. I'll give you a few minutes to ask, so please use that time wisely."

She wiped her eyes and jumped out of bed. She knocked into Pul as she left, and he held her in place, worried by the state of her.

"Are you okay? Is everything alright?" he asked.

"Yeah, I got to find...uh... See ya!"

She yanked herself away and slammed through the attendant's door that led to a room where a pensive Parity sat reminiscent by a pretend fire.

"How do you get it to do that?" she asked a young Magi who couldn't hide his bedazzlement of her.

"It's magic, I guess. We imagine the flame and what it looks like. Then, we imagine its warmth and sometimes its bite!"

They laughed.

She motioned to put her hands in, and he nodded. Her

hands felt through the flame like a large wave, and it was both cold and warm.

She didn't notice the Child until she cleared her throat.

"Can I try?" she asked. Parity's ears perked at the sweet sound. She was never one to truly believe a mother's supernatural way of knowing their own, but there was no way that voice belonged to anyone else but her child.

She smiled to herself.

"Of course, come here. Let me show you."

The Child hesitantly came to, and the young Magi watched them, unaware of the distance between the two which wasn't evident. She gave her mother her hand and she took it gently.

She couldn't ever remember a time when she felt her mother's hands. They were soft, like the skin of a baby. There were no callouses or cuts on them like her Sister-maid's whose yankings and pullings felt worse with them.

She feared the flame but feared losing this moment more. Her hand went limp as Parity wished it through the fire. She giggled at how weird it felt and the two hands swam in the flame as if they were in their natural world.

Another cough from the doorway was their reminder that time was running out. Both turned to Mistacles with absolute sadness in their eyes. The Child looked up to her mother as she stood who seemed to be a tower then and wanted nothing more than to see her eyes again.

"Is it time to go already?" she asked Mistacles while holding her daughter's hand.

"Yes, and it's almost her bedtime. Did she ever ask you about her name?"

Mistacles winked at the Child who felt understood and seen in a way she couldn't describe with words. She squeezed her mother's hand and looked up at her as she finally looked in return.

"Why don't you put her to bed and then you can tell the girls all about it!"

The two didn't speak the small trip to her bedroom but their hands never left one another. As the door opened, Tane was jumping from bed to bed having grown impatient from waiting. Pul sat at the edge of Care's, watching the bright ball as she destroyed the room he wished he had.

Mistacles gave one look, and she stopped at once. The Child ran to embrace her.

"My mom's gonna tell us a story!" she whispered in her ear and they giggled as girls should.

Before the robust man could tell them to, they got into their pajamas and sat peacefully in her bed and stared down an awkward Parity to come and sit with them.

She looked to Pul whose indifference hadn't changed. She quickly went back to the girls and bounced in the center of the bed facing both of them.

"Now, have either of you heard of Lilith the White?"

"Yeah, we have! She got cut up by the big, bad wolf!" said Tane and she was the only one laughing.

"Well, I've heard what people in Venlet say about her, and it isn't entirely the truth."

Both girls moved in closer, totally fixated on the radiant woman whose voice was like a cool mist.

"Yes. Lilit helped the wolf, but she did so because she was afraid. The wolf came to her home and threatened to kill her family if she didn't. She offered to bring him jewels in exchange for their safety and he agreed. Because her hands were so small, she would eat them and then puke 'em up. She did this for three months.

"It was in the winter when the wolf decided he wanted

the Lord of the Land's ring and she had just three days to get it. She took a short path and came across a beggar whom she gave her father's white tunic she brought to keep her warm. When she reached the Lord of the Land, she was welcomed in for the beggar had been the Lord in disguise. He was testing the charity of his people. He offered her his ring for her sacrifice, and she returned home to the wolf. But, upon returning, she found he had eaten her family. Angered, she told the others where he was and what he had done—that he made her give him jewels to protect the community. That's a big deal in Holfenya.

"They found the wolf and, when cornered, he slashed the girl across the stomach and there, in her entrails, was the ring of the Lord of the Land. Upset and disgraced, believing to be tricked when in fact he broke their deal, the wolf accepted his death and no one else was killed. And in its belly were her family and the many jewels she said she gave. They brought back the ring to the Lord who was deeply saddened by this and, in honor of the little girl, planted the ring in a grove near Joneston. There, where the ring slept grew a marvelously white tree that blooms the only white apples in Zel.

"She wasn't a bad girl—she was just a little girl who didn't know better. Please, girls, if you come across a wolf like this one, don't trust 'em. Tell somebody about it."

"So," said Tane scratching her head, "the king's ring was a seed?"

"Okay, that's enough. It's time to go Parity, lovely story by the way!" Mistacles said, scratching his head at every-one's lack of get-up-and-go.

"Well, my darling Lilit—my Lilith of White—I hope to see you again real soon. You are welcome home anytime. Sweet dreams. And to you, Tane—" she said as she kissed both girls on the head, "may your dreams be as wondrous as you."

She turned to Pul and they nodded.

Mistacles took her to his study where he threw the pebble against the wall without hesitation. Parity stared at the door, wanting to run and join her daughter again, but she knew it wasn't the right time—if there ever would be. She was in good hands, and she could sleep better because of that. She walked through the portal into night in the village where a great many people stopped what they were doing as two people existed out of thin air.

"Sorry, no time. I've got to go!" he said to a woman approaching, mouth open with questions as to how they could be. Parity followed close behind.

UNTA HELD the doorknob as the young boy was having another fit of anger and was going to stop at nothing to escape his room. He had found him there after he scared the skin off Agatha and the other kids who ran away from the house. And he thought Pul was a handful.

When he tried to pick up the little boy, he was bit harder than any dog or cat ever had. His hand throbbed and bled and his anger almost got the best of him. He wanted to throw the viper boy against the wall but didn't. Instead, he locked him in where he could be away from others. Agatha helped by getting Plea Eric to send a message to Mistacles who had been incapacitated before then. He was eager to hear about all that was unfolding in that great range but could do without the scary children.

He felt the boy bash himself against the wood and he commanded him to stop multiple times. He feared he broke a bone or two by the way he thrashed in there. He heard the clatter of big things falling to the floor and many sharp things being stepped on or thrown carelessly. If he were his brother, he'd be in there and probably get himself killed by all that commotion. But he was the sensible one.

Eventually the nob stopped moving and he figured the boy had gotten tired again. It was a tug of war between calm boy and wild boy, and Unta was stuck in the middle.

"Hey buddy, can I come in now?" he asked through the wood.

"MY ROOM!" the boy sobbed, and he heard more breaking from within.

"Listen, we're not mad at 'ya. We just want to make sure you're okay. Now, I'm going to open the door…"

"NO! GET OUT OF MY HOUSE!!" he screamed, "CARA!"

He was banging on the walls now. The children who were supposed to be staying there were taken somewhere else for the night, and Agatha cowered in the kitchen near the door for a quick escape.

Unta got brave and opened the door but quickly closed it when he saw traces of blood on the walls. And it made the boy lose his mind.

He readied to overcome the boy and calm him down, but before he could open the door again, a loud sigh of relief came from the kitchen, and he heard the beautiful voice of Parity.

Still holding the door, he watched the stairs whose steps since squeaked and saw the great Imagi coming up, stopping to catch his breath at the top.

"Thank…you… for… doing this!" he said, putting a hand on Unta's shoulder. "If… I wasn't running low on pebbles, I'd… offer you to come and visit your brother and Pul!"

"Oh, they know where I am. I haven't gone anywhere!"

Without warning, Mistacles brushed Unta aside and

threw open the door. He took into his arms the very image of a broken boy much to his broken heart. His bloody frame flashed briefly across Unta and that sour image, so close to the faint one years back, resembling the bruised and bloodied babes taken from their beaten parents and thrown into a cage to suffer and drown in a sea of their friends in unending despair, was to stick with him for a while.

"Okay, Unta, I've got it from here. You can go now!" said Mistacles through gritted teeth as a mumbling, angry boy punched and kicked his way through him.

"No, I'm staying tell he's okay."

"I swear, you and your brother are twins—both thick-headed and stubborn...and kind of stupid."

"Gee thanks!"

Unta stepped aside, keeping his eyes on Mistacles who rocked the boy in his arms, humming an exotic melody as he went limp and snored.

CHAPTER 22

The remaining of the ten thousand Order soldiers were neutralized by nights end, many losing their lives in the endless dark zone of the cave they assaulted, fleeing for their lives to only have it end where no one could save them. Some of their young men who survived, inexperienced and desperate to live begged for mercy and were sent, still in chains, to Allsingdale where the Army of Miracon trained their legion. The blues lost only a tenth of their men, but it was still a bigger upset than anyone could have ever imagined from a threat that should never have been.

"We had no idea!" Jusceanous murmured repeatedly to himself as Marcello and Reine paced Hisousen's tent.

"How in the hell did we not hear them? Not a single villager, traveler, not one?"

Though Reine's question was not said to be answered, he still looked expectingly at the young captain, hoping he'd have some solution to his own internal mess.

"They were paid off or bullied. That seemed to be the case near Glenloch when we tried to infiltrate them from the sea. Oh, glory be to Miracon if she wasn't disappointed that day!" said Jusceanous.

"Was that not the time when sailors and slaves with boats buoyed them in such a way we couldn't get past? Putting themselves in harm's way? I mean, how could a man with any conscious ever allow such a place to continue to exist, anyways? Did they not know what they did to the children, to their own people?" asked Reine running a hand over his head.

"So many questions," said a voice from the tents opened flaps.

Standing in the doorway was a young armyman whose eyes were shut. His arms did not move as he walked in stiff, like one of the dead. The three men watched in horror as the moving flesh stopped short of them and, like a string on each side of his mouth, simply smiled.

"What are you?" asked Jusceanous, reaching for the long sword at his side.

"This one?" he asked, finger to his chest. "Who knows, he was coping a feel with a young maiden down one of the alleys a few moments ago. I'm only borrowing him while we talk. No harm to him, I promise."

"Dreqtaton!"

"Nope, I mean kind of, but still a nope. I am the great Ganguen, son of—"

"We know who you are, a pathetic worm whose nothing like his father!" Jusceanous screamed with a sincere rage such a calm and reserved man rarely showed.

Ganguen laughed.

"Okay, sure. Whatever you say. I'm not the one with moles on my side!"

"What are you talking about?" Jusceanous asked,

staring at the smile growing on the poor armyman's pained face.

"Don't listen to him, sir. He's a liar. And is wanted in every province in Zel. His bounty alone could build us our own city!" Marcello mused.

"I'm afraid, dufus, that won't be happening. No, I've come to discuss a few things instead. You see, my brothers want me and will do anything to get me; like, stop a war from happening, perhaps?"

"It's already here, Ganguen! Name your price or leave!" Jusceanous rose to his feet as he spat his words. His strong arms tensed as he grabbed the sides of the desk.

"Give me the girl, and I'll walk down the long road to Gilton City as your prisoner, with her and my partner by my side. This is the only way we can have peace."

Jusceanous laughed. "Leave now! You must be joking! That girl isn't going anywhere. Tell your Dark God to get his own kid!"

And with that, he jumped over the table and cold-cocked the poor armyman in the face. His body hit the ground with a thump and he awoke out of breath, wheezing and turning red as he gasped for air.

As some Magi took the boy to be examined, Jusecnuous meandered to the giant map Hisousen had hung when he first came to the mountains. He examined every city and province marked as allies and squinted.

"Sir, he's trying to rip us apart. Please, trust me when I say we have no finer a team than now!"

Reine patted him on the back, but it gave him no comfort. They were searching for their lieutenant whose wise counsel was needed more than ever now. They were waiting on Mistacles but it was taking him all night to return.

Jusceanous thought on the offer.

"Guys, let's think about this for a second. If they got what they wanted, would they finally leave us alone?"

Marcello's heavy armor made no noise when he approached for its steal was one of a kind, forged from the very hands of a godkin from iron no longer found in this world. He sat at Hisousen's desk and collapsed in the seat.

"Well," he said, feeling its exquisite details, "I think they would recount their offer and come at us full force. And we would lose. They'd turn us into slaves, forcing the women to breed and the men to die on the front line. And that poor girl—they'd kill her, no doubt about that."

"Reine?"

"It's not even up for debate. Plus, Mistacles would lose his shit if she were gone. We have to wait for Hisousen— he's bargained with them before."

"I hope he's alright," said Marcello, holding the very dead lieutenant's emblem in his hands.

Tane and the Child wouldn't leave the more disciplined and very serious Pul alone and thus neither of them got a wink of sleep. He threatened to beat them up multiple times if they didn't stop harassing him but that just made them torture him more.

Tane stood over the floor Pul insisted he sleep upon, and the Child whacked him with a pillow.

"Isn't this fun, Pul? Just like old times. We never got a chance to have a sleep over so, why not now?"

He eventually grabbed the pillow from the Child and hit her with it, and she laughed so hard she nearly peed herself.

"You had better get to sleep, Tansey-lion, or I'll give you one too!"

And both girls oohed at his empty threats.

"Come on, guys, I've got training in the morning! I need to get some rest!"

His voice sounded younger than, like when he'd bargain with his brothers for his time in the bath only to get in when it was less than warm. He smiled at the memory until the girls bounced on him, causing his back to crack in ways he wished it hadn't. Finally at the end of his rope, he took them both in his arms and slammed them against Care's bed with all his might.

"Now look what you've done!" he screamed as the bed's legs buckled under and broke. "Poor little guy! I hope he doesn't hate me more for this."

"What the hell does that mean?" asked the Child getting her unbrushed hair out of her face.

"He hates me because you, me, and Tane been friends longer."

Both girls scoffed.

"That's the most ridiculous thing I've ever heard."

Tane put her hands on her hips and the Child followed.

"It's funny, actually. I used to play with him and Cara all the time—father would allow it. I thought we were friends then. She was a nice girl, you know. I hope she's alive."

The girls looked at each other before the Child spoke up. "She isn't, Pul. She was killed in Glenloch…"

"Poor guy…"

"Well, we'll make his bed as fresh as new before he comes back. And, we'll have to get you your own bed now since you'll be with us forever!"

Tane shot up and ran to the broom cupboard and the Child followed. Pul held out his hand with his mouth open but gave up trying to stop the pair. He sat back helpless as they changed the bed spread and took books from Mistacles' study to level the wooden legs. They also took pages from some of the books he seemed to like and stuffed a sack full of them. Eventually, Pul offered to help when they needed to move the bed, and helped make cute butterflies to hang above the bed though he would deny it if Munta ever asked.

AGATHA HELD her daughters face and let out a sobering cry, both happy and angry at her for her small rendezvous.

"How dare you leave me like that? Again, my girl?" she asked.

"I had to go, I needed to see her and be around her a little longer. It was worth it, momma. You—"

Her eyes became red and full of tears, and her voice got caught in her throat.

"You should see her, she's grown up so much and her hair..."

She wiped her tears and Agatha hugged her close.

"Maybe next time, I'll go."

They both laughed and hung in the kitchen and would shoot random looks at the bedroom where shocking noises came. Mistacles had been up there for hours and the boy's fury came in waves, but not once did they hear the Imagi raise his voice.

They had prepared him coffee and then dinner and both went cold. Parity felt a need to get up and check on the two, but her mother's eyes insisted she stay where she is.

Unta, who had left sometime prior to get some rest, returned with a new set of clothes, and rushed upstairs. He had already gone and grabbed a few other sets, but they were ripped or stained by the boy's savage outburst.

She wasn't surprised when the screaming began and

seemed to be at its worst when Unta showed up. He was down the stairs faster than he went up and stopped by the women half-dazed and half-sad every time.

"You okay?" asked Parity. She held out Mistacles' cup and he accepted it.

"Ick, it's cold. Maybe I should go home."

"You can stay, that's not a problem."

Her eyes were inviting and somewhat untrustworthy to the hardened man who looked over at her mother and nodded in understanding.

"I'll be by in the morning to bring the children, unless you're going back to the mountain, or wherever. Good night!"

And he left without a response.

"What's his deal?" Parity asked, sipping her coffee as a loud thump came from above.

"I think if the boy doesn't stop soon, we'll have to give him something."

"Mother!"

As the two women bickered over the boy and how to deal with the matter, a tired and weary Mistacles, covered in blood and other excrements walked halfway down the stairs. He waved his arms as if he was signaling defeat, but his words were anything but.

"By Yexour's glory—he's almost ready to come home. Do you mind if we use your bath?"

Both women raced to meet him and offered a hundred times at least to bathe the boy but he declined.

"Then we'll clean the room and you guys can have mine," said Parity.

"It's beyond cleaning now, dear. I'll deal with it when he's in the bath. I would ask then if either of you would make us some food. Your patience will be rewarded."

And they fought, like two hungry clonclucks in heat on their way to the kitchen and each grabbed a different skillet and tool the other needed. They raced to see which would get the better burner and Agatha lost. But she took rain over the sink and was overzealous with it. And they made the best dinner either ever had.

FOR HOURS, Mistacles spoke calmly to Care and received vitriol in return. By luck or Care's own disinterest in fighting the old man any longer, Mistacles convinced the boy it would be best for him to bathe. He had been itching at his sides and legs where he allowed himself to defecate, and they were turning red. He asked the boy if he needed any help for which he refused. All bath times at home were like that as well. There were only a few instances when they had to go in and clean him when he came to bed smelling just as awful as before. And that was an ordeal in itself.

But Care washed himself without resistance, and as he did, Mistacles crept to his room and sighed. It was a small space but looked more like the destroyed den of a fox. The walls were covered in terrible smells and there were giant holes where Care tried running his head through. Fragments of his fingernails were carved into wood like a sword stuck in stone. The bookshelf at the center of the room was taken apart and all his toys were beyond repair.

Mistacles almost cried when he noticed the large pieces of glass resting on the soaked floor where he found the boy. He had tried to cut his arms and cut himself deep on his legs and on his neck. Never in his life did Mistacles think he'd ever see anything quite as horrible.

When Care felt like talking, Mistacles was able to understand how angry he was for Cara hadn't come back yet, and how mad he was people invaded his home. He couldn't see reason or the truth. And when he was told she wasn't there, he flipped into madness again.

Mistacles heard the water drain from the bathroom and knew he had little time to work. He did a quick spell that made all the damage Care had done undone, to his body and his room and the mess he left was no more. But this cost Mistacles greatly. His energy supply was already dangerously short. By the end of the spell, he felt a part of his chest harden into black obsidian and his grey, sprinkled hair acquired a white streak down the side, from his temple to the ends. He would be foolish to do magic again for a while and he was ready for the break.

He left the clothes Unta brought in the bathroom hoping Care would see them and forget about the man altogether. The boy emerged clothed, wearing the threads without issue. He stomped past Mistacles and walked through the doorway of his old room without noticing the mess being gone. He sat in the middle of the room and grabbed a perfect teddy bear waiting for him and played with its eyes.

"That's a nice bear," said Mistacles.

"It's Cara's. She'll want to see it right away when she gets back."

"My son, she's gone from this world and is in the next. She is where you cannot go. Please, we need you home with us."

"I am home!" he screamed, taking the bear and smashing it against the floor.

"Okay, that's fine. Why don't we go downstairs and have some dinner, hmm? Are you hungry?"

Care nodded and the two walked slowly downstairs.

Agatha and Parity waited like two servers and smiled at

the angry-faced boy unrecognizable moments ago. They ate and said nothing. Care then got up and went back upstairs and Mistacles followed. He watched as the boy got into his old bed opposite the empty one his sister slept in without incident.

Mistacles closed the door and rested against it. The boy then fell asleep and Mistacles could have brought him home without him knowing but he didn't want to do that to him. The mountain could be collapsing but that wouldn't change his mind on the matter.

He got comfortable and fell asleep against the door only waking when it opened in the middle of the night.

"Sorry!" whispered Parity.

She brought with her a blanket and some pillows and gave it to an appreciative Mistacles. He slept soundly and the busy world stopped for the night.

CHAPTER 23

The moon spilled through the simple home where all were asleep, except for Care. He had slept well and dreamt of his blue dressed sister when he suddenly awoke to the sound of silent singing drifting from his room to the next. At first he was frightened and moved to wake Mistacles but let go his fears when the old songs it sang—songs he sang as a little boy—opened his heart in the way his mother only could.

Like a moth to a flame, the boy crept out of the room, sneaking past an exhausted Mistacles, touching the white part of his hair affectionately. He would have stayed to wake the slumbering man, to ask and to worry for the new stain on his hair, but lost his focus once the singing whipped in his ear, like lull bells bringing cattle home.

He wandered down the stairs after dancing the halls to music only he could hear. He snuck past a sleeping woman, the same who bugged him in his room earlier. He sneered at the thought and would have screamed for her but stopped once a faint hand, unseen, lured him from the door and he followed it without question.

The moon was so bright his eyes hurt from staring—it was the brightest he had ever seen it. He could recall one other time, when the moon blinded them, and he and Cara were gazing at it from her side of the room where it was most clear. They'd stay up all night just to catch a glimpse of her before going to bed under its bright lights, soundly as if she were their far-away grandmother.

He would have remained there, like a sprout in the earth, staring up at her if it weren't for that tender hand pulling him away again, this time north, outside of the village's graces.

He walked heavy footed, slapping bare feet on the cobbled roads newly planted to replace the old ones. They weren't ever this nice before that Eleventh Day and he much preferred the way they once were. He dug his heel into a loose cobble and kicked it out of place. The singing stopped and he whispered his sorry's, praying to it to not stop. And as he walked by that cobble, he picked it up and stuff if into his pocket.

He noticed then, under the moonlight, those charred marks of that dreadful storm the day before. It had made the earth black, separating the good and evil in equal jumps as short as those in hopscotch.

"Chil…" he whispered, bending down to feel the rough grass cocooned in whatever metal enveloped it.

"Come here!" the voice, finally speaking, said in a soft, child-like voice.

Care sprung and forgot all about the world and followed it, doing summersaults and cartwheels as it led him further into the Black Valley. He stepped away only to see every place within an acre or two was covered in the black death.

He lifted his foot as it grew irritated, and he wanted to

itch it but stopped when he saw the ash and instead started to cry. He fell to his knees and tried pulling out his hair, harder than he had earlier and Mistacles wasn't there to stop him this time.

As he felt the skin under his hair start to rip, he heard another voice as clear as day above him, and he froze.

"My son—please stop that."

Her voice was like that of a mature mother, an honest friend, and of an understanding father. Her voice was what he wanted love to sound like and he let go of his hair and cried some more.

"I'm sorry!" he screamed, holding out his hands full of small lumps of fragile hair.

He closed his eyes and held himself. Time slipped by before he felt that soft touch again sweep the hair form his hands and held them in theirs.

"Open your eyes, my son. Open your eyes and you will see your heart's desire."

He was slow to open them—not a lot of good came from seeing. And he had seen plenty of things he wished he could forget for the rest of his life. But as his vision came clear, he saw before him Cara, or the very likeness of her to utmost perfection. She didn't look the way she had in Glenloch, rather, her hair was brushed down and had small butterflies fixed in it, and her dress was like that of a lady's, full of gems that sparkled against the moon's pale rays.

Care cried, in an agonizing way, squeezing his sister's hands with the intent of never letting go.

"Care, what have you done with yourself?" she asked, gleaning over his many cuts and bruises, seeing deeper than what had already been healed.

"It's nothing; I'm okay. I'm so happy your home. I knew you would come home!"

He reached to give her a hug, but she pulled away.

"Care, I'm not going to our old home. I'm with mom and dad in the Afterlife—we're all there waiting for you. Even Uncle Koja's there!"

Care shook his head.

"No, you're not dead! When you were thrown from the window, you survived and—"

"All my pain and sadness is over, Care. I am free, as is all our people who suffered."

"But you weren't given the Rite! How can that be?"

"There was a man who found my spirit and put me to rest. I wasn't anywhere bad before, but I was alone. Thank the gods he saved me."

"So, why have you come back?"

Cara, who was there as real as when she was alive, was beginning to change. Her colorful dress and pretty hair began to fade, and her skin was slowly turning into nothing. She was becoming unseen and no longer a part of this world.

She watched her brother stare at her concerned and smiled at him with tears in her eyes.

"I've been watching you. All this time. I am so proud of all you've done, you're stronger than I ever was. I love you so much, but you have to let me go. Your life was never meant to endure all this pain and suffering. They told me so."

"Who? Mom and dad?" Care asked through rivers of tears.

"No. You see, brother, your pain and suffering are so great the goddess Amacon brought me back to see you one last time, to help ease your troubles. She wishes you to be happy and live freely. I wish that, too. Live for me, for mom and dad. Live for all of us children who couldn't make it out of that horrible place. Live to see Gilton City for me, or the unending snow drifts in the north. And tell me all about it when you come home."

Care smiled.

"But I thought you're watching over me?"

"Not all the time! We are all laughing and singing up here, living each day as if it were Santif's Dream and it never ends!"

Cara looked past Care and he turned around. A wispy light showed vaguely the silhouette of a woman, shrouded —whose face was hidden by fabric not of this world. He had only heard her name but to see her was something else entirely.

He turned back to Cara and hugged her.

"Until we meet again, sissy."

"Don't forget to wash behind your ears, brat!" she said, pulling away but not before kissing him on the cheek.

He instinctually knew to close his eyes and when he opened them, they were gone. He spun around, eyes open, searching for them and fell to the ground crying, one last time, alone under the Moon.

As the Sun rose above the sleeping village, Mistacles shot up with hands ready to hold back a spastic Care. They fell when he saw the boy's bed empty. He listened closely and heard the taps of pots and pans with muffled voices and ran downstairs quickly. He stopped on the bottom step and held his obsidian spot as it throbbed like iron hitting shaking iron.

"Oh look, he's awake!" said Parity with a skip in her step.

He observed the table and saw Care sitting opposite

Agatha, smiling, looking sweeter than any kid ever should. He stomped to them with his arms crossed, glaring at each of them, skeptical.

"What's going on here?" he asked, and no one responded.

Parity fixed another plate of food so hot it steamed.

"Well, I guess it is what it is!"

He sat down and examined Care. The two women had no doubt covered him in nicer clothes than what was laid out.

Mistacles pointed at the boy's new wardrobe and Agatha sighed.

"We went to the merchant right before he set up. Got a great discount for being his first customer!"

"Wh—! It's barely morning, woman. We can't accept this!" said Mistacles slightly mad he had to wait for his food to cool down.

"Yes, you will. It's our gift to him for letting us live in his house!" said Parity, dumping a few more pieces of bacon on Care's empty plate.

The smiling boy swallowed them faster than he breathed and continued to watch Mistacles' frown at him.

"You okay son?" asked Mistacles.

Care nodded.

"I thought long and hard about it," Mistacles said as he touched the flaming eggs. "If you want to stay here, you can. I would never make you do anything you didn't want to. Well, I do but this is a different thing. It won't hurt my feelings at all if you stay."

The room grew quiet. The first sound heard was laughter, and it came from Care.

"You're such a funny man, Mister Mistacles!" he laughed, hitting the table.

Agatha's eyes shot up and she grew tense. Care stopped when he noticed their change in demeanor and Mistacles grew all the more suspicious.

"Alright, let's go. Into the main room, just you and me, boy!"

Mistacles got up and Care followed. They sat on the large couch and Care spoke first.

"I saw Cara last night."

Mistacles moved in his seat.

"She came to me as a spirit. Her and Amacon, I think. She said she was in our Afterlife, and she would be waiting for me. Isn't that great?"

Mistacles rubbed his chin and smiled before speaking. "What a beautiful prayer to be answered! I mean, you really saw Amacon—thee Amacon!"

"Yeah, she watched us as we said our goodbyes. She was like, a light but also a woman, I think. It was so hard to tell!"

Care sat back and put his hands on his belly.

"Thank you, Mistacles. I know it was you."

Mistacles didn't turn to face him.

"When did you go?" Care asked.

"Oh," Mistacles said choked up, "shortly after you guys arrived. I sent a few Imagi but they didn't come back. That was when Miracon's legion tried to take the city by sea. It was when you guys were shown the whole place, I was only gone a few days. I found most of the children—their spirits and snuck them back here. Siracon does not like me very well!"

"Why?"

Care sat forward and watched intently the big man wipe his eyes dry.

"Because she's—I don't know, it's hard to explain, son.

She's a greedy god, that's all I'm gonna say. She'd take every soul if they weren't already claimed!"

"Is Amacon greedy?" Care asked timidly but he relaxed a bit when Mistacles let out a relieved laugh.

"No, heavens no. Quite the opposite, actually. Those in her domain must really go out of their way to find her. Millions have tried but few have made it all the way. She's probably the nicer of the Seven but I still wouldn't trust her. You hear me? They've all got tricks up their sleeves. So—," he patted his legs and finally looked at him, "where 'ya going to live?"

"With you and the rest of my family."

He reached over and gave Mistacles a big hug and the great Imagi thought he was going to faint.

JUSCEANOUS WAS a statue as he stood, exposed among the mass of army men waiting to hear his words. They had been through hell and lived. Too many were boys who had never seen death firsthand until this fight. They had yet to know the real world outside of their quick training from boys just as young as them. He thought heavily on this as he stepped forward, and the crowd quieted at his approach.

"My friends and family. We have done this together. We have conquered the calamitous hand of the Order of Garatos, and we have saved this sacred mountain and the people therein from certain death. You have guarded your brothers and they you. They are now the closest people in the world to you. No one else will know what really happened today but you all, and no one can diminish that bond, not even you yourself.

"My first war was much like this, outside of Allsingdale in an island city crawling with Umeki. There was help coming, and no way of escape besides...death. My brothers in arms, the ones who saved me and allowed me to save them have remained my family since. Lieutenant Hisousen, Chief Officer Reine, Chief Officer Marcello—and there were other's we've lost along the way. But that is the life we've chosen for ourselves. It is a life in constant remembrance of death, but that is what makes it worthwhile.

"The world will never be the same after today. Some of you who have fought to live here, in this very mountain can stay here until you die, rotting of old age. But consider a life full of adventure, where you live like a lord and die when you want, on the field in battle or old and grey and full of stories to tell your grandchildren!

"We are leaving soon for our capital where you can receive the best training in all of Zel. Come with us, live your life the way you want to, and save those who can't. Sleep by your sword, and may a thousand Blessing of Miracon find you, my friends!"

Jusceanous waved at the crowd of armymen, innocents, and boys in bandages clapping for him. Another man in charge went to speak next but he had no interest in hearing it.

"You okay, friend?" asked Marcello from beside him.

"Are you late again? Where do you go all the time, it's crazy!"

"Jusceanous, I'm taking Hisousen's disappearance very serious—"

"Yes, I know, and don't you worry. Miracon will help us once we return home to Allsingdale."

Marcello cringed at his words. The goddess' Whirl of Truth showed her the entire life, from birth until death of the person standing before it. No magic could hide memories from her glowering gaze.

She would ask him to step forth just as she would Jusceanous or Reine, thinking him to be an ally among allies when he was only an ally to himself. And his truth could not be revealed, not for a long while. He needed to do something and fast.

SARTY STOOD BY A TIRED PUL, listening to the speakers speak their peace.

"This is absolutely insane," said Sarty. "We've just fought a war and they're already recruiting for those lost? Disgusting, man."

"Well, how else do they grow their armies to be so big? They speak at every town, village, to every person they meet—everyone is welcome to join and for good reason. Their fights are usually in the right," said Pul with his arms crossed.

"Usually?" Sarty scoffed. "How can they afford all of this?"

"They don't," said Pul, stepping off the wall. "They pay their men practically nothing, and they borrow a lot of their money from different places."

"Places? Oh, did you mean from gods?"

"Sarty, it is what it is. Regardless, we'll probably have to go and serve, at least for a few years."

"Excuse me?" Sarty put a hand to Pul's chest. "Last time I checked, the Prophezier didn't have to join any army to get the job down."

"Prophezier? Are you serious?" Pul looked Sarty up and down. "Who says you're the one, anyways?"

"Everyone. And the last time I checked, I was the bigger of us two."

"Barely, but I can grow."

"So can I!"

"Boys!"

The thunderous voice of Munta took them by surprise. "These long speeches are killing me! What are you two bickering about now?"

"Pul thinks he can beat me at the training center, and we all know that won't happen," said Sarty and Munta stared him down, more confused than he had ever been in his life.

"We don't know that. Does that mean you will come with us?"

Pul held a smile waiting for a response from Sarty who rolled his eyes and stormed off.

"Figures."

"So, is that where you're headed next, hm? Back to that stinking, fish town?" asked Munta, robbing his nose.

"It's not stinky! That's not fair! They train all over the peninsula," said Pul defensively.

"Wow, peninsula—that's a big word! When was the last time you read a book, hm?" Munta asked, slapping him on the back. The sound it made had everyone looking.

"I read all the time. Now quit that! I'm thinking of leaving after Malkeevs is over. What do you think?"

Pul expected an answer but didn't get one. Instead, the big man raised his shoulders and walked away.

Pul watched him drag his feet all the way to his chambers where he wallowed until dinner since the battle officially ended. He would have ran to cheer him up, but knew it was no use. There were some things only time could heal.

CHAPTER 24

Mistacles watched as Care followed a mangy dog running along a newer made stone fence just outside the village. He smiled faintly, returning to the task at hand. He stood by Plea Eric's door and, after a pensive moment, knocked.

A clatter of what sounded like books falling and a swearing man forced the Imagi to step back. And he stepped further back as the door finally opened with an intensity unbecoming of a holy man.

"Uh—hello?"

Plea Eric was tired and seemingly hungover. As his eyes finally fixed on Mistacles, he shot back and closed the door.

"Just a moment!"

It wasn't long before the door opened again, and a fresh-faced Plea Eric appeared before him.

"You know, you're the first Grand Eunich I've ever seen with hair," said Mistacles, rubbing his beard.

"Well, the goddess can be lenient when the time calls for it! What can I help you with today?"

Plea Eric hid the inside of his home from Mistacles'

investigating eyes. The slightest of movements made by something bigger than a pet gave away a dishonorable pastime for such a high official.

"I am under the impression Siracon attacked us—myself and some small children—two days ago. And I would like to know why."

Mistacle squinted, turning his judging eyes to Plea Erics whose own moved over everything but the ones opposite his.

"I have no idea what you are talking about," he replied tight lipped and fidgety.

"Excuse me, Eric, but can't you see the scorch marks leading from near here to the center of the village?"

"Oh! Those!"

Plea Eric raised his arms.

"But that was from a storm! Siracon would never attack anyone, especially children whom she loves—"

"Yeah, yeah. No matter how many times you Pleas say it, it doesn't sound any more believable. Listen—if you won't tell me, at least tell that monster this—she would be wise to never try to hurt the girl again."

"Is that a threat, Mistacles?"

Plea Eric for the first time flashed a small but frightening smile and the air got thicker. He blinked a few times before returning to indifference as Care approached.

"Can we keep him?" asked the bouncy boy with the dog smelling of garbage at his feet.

"Sure."

Mistacles' eyes didn't leave Plea Erics and as Care scurried off, he whispered, "Remind your goddess who will always be above her, and how he would feel if his child were to be harmed. Does she not remember how he reacted with Gilton? I'm sorry, Eric, but your goddess is a dim-bat!"

Mistacles stomped towards a playing Care before Plea Eric could respond. He turned back once and screamed into the sky, "And she is LUCKY I wasn't here when she smote Marcus Daniels!"

Plea Eric closed his door shaking and kicked a shelf into a pile of dusty wood. The young woman, barely old enough sat on his bed, terrified. The bruises on her arms and legs were evidence of a long night not worth what she had been paid.

He smiled at her before nodding for her to leave.

He sat at a small table and lit a candle.

He closed his eyes.

The sound of his door closing sent him closer into his deepened mental state. He fell into his mind where he could beckon the goddess to speak. He had given his soul many years before, but not for being a Plea. He, like most of his family for generations were true followers of Siracon, who received her secret messages, her oracle callings to correct those who have harmed her, and they never failed. He may have been the weakest in his family, but he certainly held the most power as Grand Eunich.

He sat cold and hungry in a wagon outside of Gilton City when he was first called to act. By her will, he went from human to Grand Eunich in waiting overnight. He would be her shining star sans the treacherous Plea Marcus Daniels who couldn't get the job done. But there was one person standing in his way.

A wispy voice shimmered from one of his ears to the other.

"Yes, my hethathy?"

He breathed in.

"My lady, Mistacles has spoken poorly of you. What would you have me do?"

"And what did he say, hmm?" the voice purred into his mind. *"I will be sorry for what I've done? Pathetic—"*

"He said Garaton would be upset if his—"

"It's not his! This is ridiculous—the LIES you humans spread! And he took to form to see her and won't see me?"

The voice tingled down his spine, and he felt his nerve endings pinch in a terrible but pleasurable way.

"Please, my lady, I am not the one to be punished."

"No, my hethathy. You are doing your job and well. Soon, you will act. And I will have an Imagi's skin hung on my wall!"

CARE's journey back to the mountains was uneventful. The armymen who knew him and were awake picked him up and shook him, saying with great joy how much bigger he hadn't gotten much to his chagrin. He ran home where the attendants who had survived, including Maggie nearly cried at his cuts and marks, begging him to never leave again. By the time he reached his room half the mountain showed him their love left idle all this time.

As he entered his room, he was taken aback at the state of his bed. At first irritated, he stopped when noticing the books and pages crafted in his honor. He closed his eyes and caught a glimpse of his dear sister winking at him, and he knew she would be with him forever.

He cheesed over the bed and went to jump on it but froze before he could step over his still sleeping friends. They all laid on the floor—Chil, Tane, Pul, and a lumbering Sarty sat sleeping up with the girls crawled up by his long legs.

Finally feeling at home, he squeezed in the middle of the girls and took a peek at Pul whose one eye had opened.

He winked at Care, and Care winked back. They both fell back to sleep, and they all slept together, for the first time.

Mistacles entered the room shortly after and called for another Imagi to come over as soon as possible. The still tired Imagi, young but talented, followed Mistacles' command and put a spell over all the sleeping children.

"Be sure to bind them together, no matter what happens. And bring peace, love, and luck to them wherever they go. And let me be with them forever as well."

As Mistacles spoke his spell, he reached for his obsidian chest and ripped out a big piece. Breathing heavily, he broke it into five pieces. The frighten Imagi begged to end the spell, but the greater Imagi insisted.

"I will live through this, son—don't you worry!"

Mistacles took the Imagi's hand and sent the power into the pieces. He held them close to him, to syphon as much of him into the pieces as was possible. When the spell was over, the Imagi fell back panting and Mistacles stood tall, feeling better than he ever had in his entire life.

Ganguen paced in circles at the top of the mountain, anxiously waiting for the meditating Dreqtaton in the form of a young serviceman to wake up.

"How long will it be this time, hmm? How is this supposed to work when you're out to pasture days at a time?!"

"That's enough!"

The god opened his bright eyes and stared tyrannically at Ganguen.

"Do not forget your place!"

"Or what, are you going to send me back to my brothers? Ha! No, that wouldn't please your lovely lady too much would it?"

Ganguen's words shot like a javelin he wished he could recede, and the Dark God rose into the sky like a flaming bird, his form obliterated in a black fire and emerged gigantic, his black armor and helm shiny from the flame.

"What did you say?!"

Dreqtaton leered towards the cowering godkin whose defensive hands, moving as if weakened by the raging winds, signaled defeat.

"At least... I'm not afraid to tell the truth."

"The truth?!"

A black smoke whirled around the god and his voice returned back to that of a young man.

"The truth is—my time to rise is close at hand! And your grandfather will not stop me this time—this I swear!"

"Okay... So, what's next?"

Ganguen had learned quickly to never irritate the Dark God for his fate rested in his hands. He had promised him freedom, for which he was given, and further promised him dominion of Zel as new High Guardian if the plan was realized in full. And so far, by at least his account, things were progressing well.

"We are to leave the mountains and head east," Dreqtaton said as casual as any human would.

"East? But we just came from there! What the hell are we?.."

"Listen. East it is. We are to raise a legion of our own... They will never see us coming!" Dreqtaton laughed and Ganguen followed him down the mountain side, damning the day he took the deal.

. . .

Sᴀʀᴛʏ sᴀᴛ ʟᴀᴢɪʟʏ in the wooden chair in Hisousen's tent. Next to him were the other kids he didn't know too well. They had grown up in the village him and his family traveled to twice a year, to sell their produce and livestock and buy the luxurious his new friends no doubt dismissed daily.

He stared at the glowing Tane who bounced in her chair as they all waited for further instruction. She snarled like a dog when she noticed him watching, and he laughed in return.

"Is she feral?" he asked, and the Child spoke up before her friend made it worse.

"She's hungry. You had better watch out."

"You know, you and I with our dark hair are outnumbered with those three and their light," he whispered to her and she giggled.

"That's not true. The dog's got darker hair too!" she said and the others turned to her.

"What'd you say about Riki?" said Care with his arm rested on the dog's neck.

"Maybe you should let the poor guy breath," said Pul sat back with his arms perpetually crossed.

"Maybe you should stop trying to tell us what to do! You're not much older, Pulseph," said Tane, petting Riki sweetly.

"You know, you are nicer to that dog than you are to me, your oldest friend!" Pul said with big eyes. "And, what the heck is a Pulseph?"

"Tane, you and your names are just too much for me," said Sarty taking his attention away from the feuding kids beside him and staring at the giant map at the back of the tent. He could see from where he sat many red markers in the south and west of their part of Zel. Further west past the sea and further east past Allsingdale was not in view.

There were fewer blue markers than red, and he noticed with every one blue there were at least four red.

He squinted.

"Hey, Pulseph, which do think is the red on the map?"

Sarty's question stopped the arguing and Pul sat forward to squint at the board himself.

"Shit—" Pul said out loud, "that's got to be the Order. Shit!"

The Child reached around Tane and hit Pul in the arm as hard as she could, but as she hit his arm, he flexed and she retreated back before he could reach over to her. But unfortunately for Tane, she sat back as he went to retaliate and got a big punch in the back.

And this sent her over the edge.

Sarty laughed as a giant pile of fighting kids made the adult meeting not far off break them apart.

"That's enough!" said Jusceanous as he held a biting Tane from a pummeled Pul.

She mouthed—*I'll get you later*—before sitting on the other side of the Child next to Sarty where she showed her teeth again.

"Okay, really, that is enough. Okay," Jusceanous caught his breath, "as you all know, the mountain is again safe for you all to stay. And it would appear the mountain spirit accepts you all and wants you to remain if you so please. The Army of Miracon will be leaving, most of us anyways, in a week's time. Mistacles has given us permission to take you with, any of you if you so shall please. But, it will be under strict rules. We will be heading to Allsingdale where you'll meet the great Miracon who is eager to shake your hands."

"I don't want to go!" said Tane to Mistacles surprised. "You can't make me!"

"Well, sweetie, I've realized keeping you all here hasn't been very fair to any of you. I've spoken with the goddess who is our ally, I promise you. You don't have to stay there —you can come and go whenever you want."

"But what about you?" asked the Child whose eyes were turning a lavender that broke his heart.

"Well, you guys don't have to go anywhere, of course. But, if you do, I will always be with you. And with that, a gift!" he screamed as he reached into one of his satchels and revealed the five obsidian necklaces. "I had Munta forge them. These will never break, and the chain will never rust. Wear it and I will be with you always."

"A necklace? Why couldn't it be a belt or something," said Sarty, reluctantly putting it on.

The Child hit him in the side and gave him a quick look and he fell back.

"I know Pul and Sarty are planning to go with the rest of the party. I would like to personally welcome both of you back anytime you like, and I hope it will be fewer than once a year."

"But Mistacles, getting here is impossible!" said Pul whose eyes showed a weariness only men knew.

"We'll work it out, son. But it's still Malkeevs—the celebration of peace in the land! We will wine and dine and have fun while we're still alive. Come on guys!"

And Mistacles left the tent with the children and dog soon after, except for Sarty. He slowly stood up and walked to a pensive Jusceanous.

"Are you in charge here?" he asked.

"For now, yeah. Why, what's up friend?"

"Well, I'm not sure I want to join the army. I feel like it might be a waste of time."

The tall teenager hovered over the experienced armyman, looking down upon him. But the captain turned away and paid him no mind.

Sarty pointed to the wall in the back, desperate for the attention. "It seems you're fighting a losing battle."

"Young man, you think you know everything, don't you?"

Jusceanous laughed.

"Those don't mean what I think you think it means."

"Oh yeah? The red ones are of the Order and the blue ones are the Army of Miracon, am I right?"

"Sort of. It's more complicated than that." Jusceanous ran to the map and laid his hands over a cluster of markers. "You see, the smaller markers signify a smaller force, maybe ten to twenty thousand men, we anticipate."

"Ten to twenty thousand?" Sarty stomped to be by the board and marveled at it's design.

"Yeah, and as you know from experience the Order doesn't train theirs like we do so they have the numbers but...wait—" Jusceanous stepped back, "you like this kind of stuff, don't you?"

"Hell yeah I do!"

"Language son. I can teach you more...in Allsingdale. Come on, what have you got to lose?" Jusceanous smiled at the young man who smiled back.

CHAPTER 25

The Child laid in bed, shivering to some unnameable cold that crawled into her chambers and attacked only her. She held the top of her blanket up to her chin, teeth chittering, wishing for the intolerable night to end and a new day to begin. She could sense sleep was soon to come and was regretting the inevitable.

She whimpered.

While her world fell apart yet again; while her friends were in danger and the Order of Garatos pointed their swords in their faces, again, her night terrors returned. She suffered this truth alone. She should have told Mistacles but chose not to, honoring his time while he was at rest or off taking care of matters only he could. And she didn't want to bother him anyways—there was little he could do to stop it. Everyone seemed so happy, for the first time in a long time. She didn't want to ruin that, like she had everything else.

She wagged her head until it hurt, and she could feel it while she dreamt. The master of sleep had gotten her, and his grip was the strongest. She would beg to be freed, to wake up and it be morning which hardly ever worked.

Resigned to allow what she avoided to unfold, she descended into her mind and fell through the clusters of her thoughts like a jagged rock thrown too fast—faster than any dragon could fly. No image or memory came to her mind and she could care less if it had, preferring the black nothing her tired eyes loved as it was a silent friend who never hurt her.

As she tumbled through air, flares of hot red jumped in her line of vision which would have made her sick if she were awake. But while she dreamt, she was mostly invincible.

She finally landed in something warm, like a gooey lake of odd tastes and smell which held her under even as she squirmed to breathe again. Whatever tortured her, waiting for her day and night to endlessly lead her into torment, knew she couldn't die here and made good use of this.

She scratched through a thin layer of slim and crawled out of it, gasping for air. She would have cried and screamed for help if the sound of the all-too-familiar mean birds weren't so close, with their talons always pointed towards her face. She dipped back into the gelatinous pool after taking a big, deep breath and could see from above the cloudy ooze a cluster of black and red blood spatter from the sky and land where she had been.

She smiled as three feathery carcasses fell on the spot she had just took air and knew she was safe for a little while longer.

When she squeezed out of the pool, she crept low to the barren earth as a solitary, dusty wind slapped her incessantly. Another adversary. She allowed wind to rake her back, ripping comfort from her skin and leaving scars that would leave once she awoke. She looked everywhere for a safe place to rest but found nothing past the brown horizon, leading her in circles no matter where she turned.

She came to stop short of a familiar tree where she etched her name with her nail a few months before, when the Darkness had found her and hurt her as it did more times than she could count. She had put her name on thousands of trees, but that entity destroyed them all.

She had thought for a few years her Otherworld had been destroyed, infiltrated by a new, horrible host. But, on one such occasion when Mistacles gave her a longer session of hypnosis, an application that worked as often as it didn't, her Otherself called out to her and found her for the first time since leaving Glenloch. She took her to her Otherworld which was exactly the way the Child left it, and not a single shred of its beauty had been tainted.

"Where was I?" she asked her Otherself.

"It took you to a different place—you cannot trust it! Try to leave as soon as you can and call for me if you need my help!" she replied.

She thought on that as the also familiar rumble of the dark clouds came in. She closed her eyes to cool them from the never-ending dust. A low growl came from where it grew and she tried to think of her Otherself—she tried her best. She wished she knew what she looked like—IF she looked like anything. Her voice, her laugh—all of it! But no matter how many times she tried, she couldn't get her to come.

She held onto the tree as the Darkness picked her up and yanked her into its nimbus. She flew past innumerable clouds that burned her skin and scorched her flesh. In their round reflection she saw so much evil, and this is what she hated the most. She saw the many hands and pointed fingers of the villagers, long lost now, who beat her and scolded her for any reason they could find. And then she saw the soldiers in Glenloch, with their swords pointed, threatening to cut her flesh as they had Big Dade. And a fearful Tane reached for her, and she couldn't get to her, no matter how she tried.

The fire, the pyre part ended then, and then came the cold. She shook as she floated helplessly in a chamber of ice with her mother's angry face opposite hers no matter where she faced. The woman was drunk and angry, glaring her down worse than one would their enemy. The dark and twisted face of Parity moved to grab the Child but fell on her face and cried for her bastard to go away.

The Child cried until she couldn't anymore. She knew at any moment she would wake up or another atrocious thing would happen.

It was when all hope had been lost she saw her—a mass of black hair coming into view. She was faster than a flash of lightning and jumped through the painted cloud and into the picture of Parity on the ground.

And she kicked her.

"Get up!" she said, kicking the drunken woman rolling on her side. "Get up or i'll kick your ass!"

The Child forgot about her pain, astonished by the girl who spoke like an adult and kicked the drunken woman until she got up.

"Stop, okay. I'm done!" said Parity, falling asleep on the chair she managed to climb upon as the Otherself walked out of view, not knowing the Child could see her as plain as day.

The Child took a deep breath and screamed, "Hey, get over here and help me!"

· · ·

Munta stood lazily as battalions of men ran amuck, clearing up their stations for the long trip east. He breathed in, clenching a long chain of white gold in his tight fist. He wasn't an old man—his father, who died much older than him, was considered young on his Rite day—but Munta wasn't getting any younger. He felt it most in his knees— two balls of rigged bone, worn down from years of smithing with such a carelessness he'd do anything to go back and shack himself. How he would twist them and pop them as if they would never change—as if he would never change. But he had, more than he realized.

That damn battle got to him, more than he would ever admit. He was in the thick of it, with men and boys less experienced, with quickly made piece of metal, not ready to see another woman or child hurt if it came to that. His eyes glossed over as he killed, like some wolverine with no other option but to destroy. His axe, thought to be made of some magic steel, was lost in the bodies of dead soldiers; no better than any other piece they carried. But that didn't stop the hungry for life armymen from guessing how amazing it was. Though the younger armymen thought him some sort of iron god, the seasoned men who fought more times knew better, thinking his form too unsafe and reckless.

He had enjoyed the thrill of taking another's life at first, a wish he had asked the god's when his heart was lost at the killing of his people, but that high receded and left the same hollow feeling he had for many years before. Even before the Eleventh Day. And somehow the hollow depth grew.

But something changed.

He took to heart the very task of making special necklaces for Mistacles and enjoyed it more than he thought he would. It was the simple things most took for granted he wanted more than anything. He had always made weapons and armor and did so expertly, but never did he think forging such a small jewel could feel so...rewarding.

He released the excess of the chain he didn't need for the others and let it roll over his large fingers. He didn't notice a curious Tane approach, eyeing him like an emerald hawk.

"Whatchya doin' there, Munta?" she asked with an especially annoying voice.

He barely moved and said lowly, "Nothing."

"Did you get a necklace like us?" she asked.

"Nope."

"Do you want one?"

"Nope."

"Then why are you holding that ugly thing?" she asked with such disgust knowing it would get a reaction.

He looked up.

"It isn't ugly, my dear. It is small, yes, and maybe not all there, but that can change. Over time, I can turn it into something great. It could be the strongest band in all of Zel. What do you think of that, little one?"

His words hit hard, and she said nothing, nodding more than once in agreement.

"Good girl. You and I are a lot alike, I think."

She looked up confused and his gentle palm up stopped her from interrupting.

"Just—I'm big and old, and you're young and precious. Hope hasn't always been our ally. Do you think we have a chance?"

Tane smiled. Tears long held in her eyes ran down her face.

"I don't know if it's worth trying..."

"If I promise to try, will you, sweet Tane?"

His dark eyes lit up and if there were any power behind them, then it would have healed the girl, of all her wounds both inside and out.

She jumped into his arms and squeezed tight.

"You've got a deal!"

She was slow to let him go and slower to keep her eyes off his, alive for the first time since he arrived. He watched as she ran away, smiling like when she was little, like when her mother and father took her to the river to play.

He felt a pain in his chest and nearly fell forward. After he realized it wasn't death, he hollered with joy at every person who walked by, and they jumped at his intensity.

It was well into that same night when he finally found Pul and had gotten the words he wished to say to him together in the way he wanted. The boy stood among men with a tankard in his hand. Munta took it from him and drank it in one gulp as the rest of the men scattered at his arrival.

"Hey! That was mine!" said Pul who was still reaching up to stop him well after the cup ran dry.

"You're only twelve, get over it! Plus, I need this now!" Munta said avoiding the young man's eyes.

"What's your deal?"

Munta with no grace led him to an alleyway where no one else could listen.

"Alright, here it goes—you are going to Gilton City!"

Pul's face turned dead white.

"What?!" was all he could say.

"Shit! No, that's not what I—ugh! Okay, let me try again. Uh..."

"Are you crazy? I'm never going there! That's where our people were slaves!"

"Yeah, like a long time ago. It's not so bad, you know..."

Pul's shock turned into sadness.

"Wait, you want to...?"

Munta nodded and both stood silent until a passing cat spooked them out of their pants, breaking the ice.

"Listen Pul, I want to go there, I always have. I promise once I get myself situated, I'll come and see you in Allsingdale!"

"But... you've always been with me!"

"Son, you are far more independent than you know. I haven't even seen you all day! You've been, uh. Wait a second, what on Reicher's Realm have you been up to?"

He put his hand on his hip and the young armyman smiled a little.

"When do you leave?" Pul's voice had fallen to a whisper.

"When you do. And I plan to spend as much time with you as I can until then. Unless you find a cute girl."

Munta walked after Pul who had put his hands over his ears at the mention of girls, and he was nowhere near stopping. They walked the streets all night like brothers and drank until they could no longer stand.

Tane woke up early that following morning. She shot back to her pillow and would have kicked out if the Child wasn't sleeping next to her. She had tried to wake her when she was shaking in her sleep and was surprised it stopped as quickly as it started. She wanted to rest but couldn't and she didn't know what to do with herself.

She sat up and looked for Care who was sleeping legs out of his bed, like normal.

She groaned.

She skipped her warm feet over the cold ground until she found her shoes. She left the room expecting a few attendants to be awake. But there was nobody. She began to panic and ran to Mistacles room but stopped shy of the knob. She breathed in deeply and stepped away, sure nothing was wrong.

She went into the kitchen and ate some bread, but her stomach continued to growl. She thought then how Munta and Pul had food in their tent and decided to sneak off. She wouldn't be long, and they'd still be asleep while she was gone.

She walked along the empty streets and enjoyed every step—she picked the most perfect time to be alone, right before everything opened and was awake for the day. She made every intention to follow the path she marked for herself but stopped at the spot where Care and her used to hide. It was a cozy place to run away to when the mountain got too busy.

She walked closer to it, compelled by some reason she couldn't explain. She furrowed her brows and opened her nostrils. She took in the fresh fragrance of eggs and sausage unlike anything she had ever smelt. She glided her way towards it as if she were floating on air. She didn't realize how far into the mountains lengthy caves she had gone until the light she used to find her way back was but a dot. She turned to walk back, before it was too late, but stopped at a new sound, heightened by her eyes resting.

A new voice sang to her.

"Come, my child, come and see us"

And then there were two. She froze and felt the need to

run. She reached to her side and found the cold rock surface and used it to move forward. The voice called to her and didn't stop.

"Come, my sweet. Let us show you the way!"

She knew better than to run and was thankful she hadn't when she tripped over a large mass she couldn't see. Arms out, hands reaching, she felt flesh and stiffened backwards. She felt her way along and as the small light grew bigger, it than disappeared.

She screamed.

"Don't be afraid, little one. Let us help you!"

From besides her, she felt the mountain rumble like it had before. There, an opening emerged with a light so bright it hurt her eyes. She covered them with her arms and was too afraid to bring them down.

"I said don't be afraid. We won't hurt you."

The voice seemed human then. She peered through her folded elbow and saw a smiling older woman with long, bushy gray hair and more winkles than she could count. She motioned for Tane to follow, and she did.

They walked through a rock hole that led down a narrow path. The woman's constant reassurances kept the lost girl moving. And when they did leave the path, they stood upon a ledge, overlooking a hamlet and its small rolling hills and small buildings—of cottages and barns. Over a small bridge made of wooden planks of blonde ash they went before entering an opening full of rainbow-colored trees and animals, as wild and monstrous as one could imagine, roaming freely—as peaceful as the prey grazing besides them. Tane screamed again, but this time with delight.

At the woman's subtle jab, Tane looked up and saw the opening—a small oculus above them that let in the outside world, where snowflakes fell like they had many Malkeevs before, back home.

Her eyes followed the flakes as they fell upon a lonely stone tower, magnified by the light from above, humble with flowers and ivy-like veins on its skin.

She took in the sweet cold air from outside and wanted more but shivered at its embrace.

"Oh, my dear, come this way. Let us get you warm!"

She followed the woman to the tower as curious bunnies and bears watched her and she was none the wiser. They entered the tower, and Tane felt it's wonderful warmth, and thought back on a memory once thought to be a dream. How her mothers' workers would enrage the flames of their home's hearth to grow it into an inferno, even while the cold outside turned skin black and cursed it otherwise was her favorite part of the holiday.

How could she forget?

The woman led her to the kitchen, not far from where they entered, where another woman sat vigorously pummeling spices in a mortar, her black dress moving as she did.

"Sister, look—a little girl has come to visit!" the sweet-voiced woman said as she set the lantern on the table.

"You idiot!" the other woman, just as old and grey said reaching for the lantern. "Don't leave that there. What, do you have—worms for brains?"

Tane laughed, and her two hosts stared at her inquisitively.

"I'm sorry my dear, we have been so rude. My name is Minerva, and this 'bright' woman who brought you is Duot, my sister. Pleasure to meet you."

Tane bowed before them and spoke quietly. "Pleasure to

make your acquaintance. My name is Shane, and I live in the mountains."

"Well of course you do!" said Duot, laughing until she looked at her mean-mugging sister.

"We are happy to see a new, shiny face in our home. Come, sit. We won't keep you long. Tell us all about the going-ons of the thermopolia! We heard all the commotion —was a war afoot?"

"Uh, well, I don't know—"

The two women laughed which made Tane feel uneasy.

"I would think you were a smart girl if you hadn't gotten stuck in the cave," said Duot.

"Stuck in the cave?" Tane asked.

"Well, yes! You are very lucky I was looting the dead soldiers when you—"

"That's enough, Duot—don't scare the girl! Now, tell us everything and don't leave a single thing out," said Minerva with her big eyes stuck on the ever-clever Tane.

CHAPTER 26

Jusceanous the Bold was again a vision—a figure resolute as he stood before a crowd of hungry, young faces near the great thermopolia known to those outside the mountains only in songs and books.

"As we celebrate Malkeevs in this most holy place, let us remember again all those who gave up their lives for the cause and those who were taken too soon. It shouldn't have been this way."

He held back his words as a lump formed in his throat.

"Just this morning, my dearest friend was found. He was left, cold and lifeless, like he was nothing. But he was something—our hero...my hero. Not a day will I rest while the Order of Garatos continues to exist without proper punishment. We will see a time when all their debts will be paid, and those who come with us to Allsingdale will help us see it through!"

His words, like fire, caused all those watching to whistle and clap in triumphant agreement. They cried for revenge and scrambled to reach the grieving man whose words captivated them so.

Mistacles looked on with a heavy heart, amazed by his friend's strong declaration no one else could have said better.

"So, Reine—what do you make of all this?" he asked.

Reine had been in a state of distress—holding his hands on his face, worried and frustrated, having bitten off most of his nails by the time the speech had ended.

"Eh... Don't know," he said as he gnawed on his fingers.

"Would you stop that?!" Mistacles said, slapping him on the back of the head. "There's something amiss—I can feel it."

"Yeah, it's all very peculiar." Reine got closer to Mistacles, whispering in his ear. "I fear even speaking up around my very own friends. What's a man to do?"

"Investigate," mouthed Mistacles, vigilant with his stares. "Find out whatever you can and report back to me—only me."

The two looked back to Jusceanous who was hugging and shaking hands with adoring patrons as he appeared to be crying. They turned at one another once more before parting ways—Mistacles went back to his chambers, and Reine nosedived into the crowd.

Behind the many young and older who wanted more than ever now to be a armymen was the hardened army. They stood tall, stone faced and forward as their new lieutenant spoke. They were to wait, unmoving, until further command.

Reine came upon the line and snuck to the side of a clumsy armyman, one who was known to break rank and not know it.

"Psh!" he screamed into the confused man's ear who turned to face him upon approach. His fellow armymen snickered but didn't break rank.

"What you want?" the armyman asked, lifting his eyebrows in surprise.

"Do you happen to know who—"

Reine stopped when a small chorus of shushes came at him, he lowered his voice and started again.

"Do you know who found him?"

"Found who?"

The man was unspeakably confused and his comrade nearest him laughed without moving a muscle.

"Hisousen!" Reine whispered loudly with large veins popping out of his neck..

"Oh, yeah. Um—Macy in armory, I think. Is that right, Joshua?"

The armyman leaned into another just as their sergeant arrived. Reine noticed the approach and slithered away, behind the long row of armymen until the harsh yelling's of the sergeant could barely be heard. He eventually found a corner, dark and empty enough to settle in and took that moment to breathe.

He watched as wandering souls walked by unassuming and without a care in the world. They had just been through a siege and survived. And yet, they were laughing and carrying on. But he couldn't for his heart was broken.

When he caught his breath, he ran for the armory, but they told him to see the infirmary, and the caregivers there told him to go to the barracks. By days end, he had been all over the army's camp and not a single person he spoke to knew who found the body.

Discouraged, he took a stroll to Hisousen's tent. He hadn't fought a single battle without him since he joined the army. Even as a small, whiney errand boy—Hisousen looked after him. He couldn't fathom life after this—after he finds his murderer. But he knew this day would come, but it felt too soon.

As he reached the tent he froze, thinking ghosts were calling for him from within the abandoned sheets. He traveled to the side and could hear the voices louder, only one sounding as demonic as the imagination could allow. He tried looking under but stopped when, upon his touch the entire side of the tent waved. He squirmed to find a place to hide but stopped when he found a small hole torn into the fabric, revealing enough of the inside so little of the outside could be seen. He swallowed his fear and took a peek.

The space was dark with not a candle in sight. The voices once ghosts were human—two men standing near Hisosuen's desk in wild conversation. He recognized the ever-shiny armor of Marcello, but the other man was unfamiliar, his gloves a daring ebony with a stature well above the aged officer, hovering like a father his son. Though they stood in the shade, flashes from the cave light squeezed from above showed Reine who the other could be. And his eyes went wet at the realization.

He composed himself the best he could, breathing low though a roar was wishing to be freed. He listened closely, picking up only a few words he could discern like feud and earth. Whether the words made sense made no difference as their conversation appeared to be a cordial one when it should have been hostile.

They eventually shook hands and the man with the black gauntlets disappeared in a plume of black smoke, further plunging the sword of Marcello's deceit into Reine's heart.

He watched with unending rage as a nonchalant Marcello sat at Hisousen's desk with a stack of papers in his hands.

"Papers?" he asked out loud.

He covered his mouth but the sound already alarmed Marcello who turned to face his direction. He fell back and scurried to a small corner hidden by wooden beams, concealed in total darkness among the spiders and their webs.

Marcello approached the hole from outside with his sword drawn, gripping it tightly. He pivoted with a menacing stare, searching for anything that breathes in all directions. When he stopped on the dark corner, staring at what could have been a man's foot, stepping to attack whatever was on the other end of it, another voice, like some saving grace, came from somewhere unseen and Marcello quickly sheathed his weapon and left.

Reine, pulling his boot in closer and smacking his head with the palm of his hand, realized his moment to run had come. He snuck out of his corner and sprinted passed the tent, eventually entering the safety of the city streets. He stopped only to catch his breath, sweating like a warlong who survived the hunt and booked it to Mistacle's office.

"I saw him and another. They were exchanging papers!" Reine shot through Mistacles office, breathing heavy, shutting the door quickly behind him.

"What do you mean exchanging papers? What are you—"

"Ma-Marcello!" He bent over, gasping for air. "He was in Hisousen's tent and made some sort of deal."

"With who?"

"I mustn't say! But he had black gloves; like a monster's if you ask me. If I say his name, I'll be damned!"

"Shut up, you idiot! This is concerning!" Mistacles lowered his voice and scratched the top of his head vigorously. "Our own chief officer, making deals with the Dark God himself!"

"Whoa, whoa! I didn't say that! Maybe I'm wrong. The room was dark; it was hard to tell!"

"Well, I said it! Did he disappear in a cloud of smoke? Of course he did! I must go and see Yexour at once—this is not happening!"

Mistacles threw his bear robe over his shoulders and went towards the door before it swung open. Before him stood Marcello, smiling and as ordinarily plain as usual.

"What's happening guys?" he asked.

"Nothing, we were just about to go have some ale at the bar. You want to join?" Reine gritted his teeth.

"Reine, my good friend—you know I don't drink! I did want to speak with Mistacles alone, if you don't mind."

Marcello smiled even wider.

"Can this wait till morning? I'd rather relax for the rest of the day."

Mistacles reached into his pocket where a small dagger rested, waiting for these very moments.

"Okay, it can wait. I will see you two tomorrow then."

Marcello smiled at Mistacles before leaving, closing the office door delicately.

Both men had held their breaths and gasped when the menace left.

"He did it, he definitely did it!" said Reine in almost tears.

"You don't know that! We need more evidence. We'll sneak out of the bar and head to the burial pit—can you handle that?"

Reine shook his head and the two walked through crowds of welcoming people, softly hitting their shoulders as they passed as a way to show a pray meant for them for good health and happiness. They smiled in turn and gave up returning the gesture when it slowed their pace.

When they finally made it to the bar, two piercing eyes surveyed their every move, and Mistacles had to act as if he were unawares—laughing and hitting tankards with Reine, who looked as pale as a fish. Though they drank round after round, it was never of ale but of water much to the sadness of Reine who foot the bill, very much charged as real ale. It was hours later when their pursuer gave up his pursuit and left the shadows, both men tired of the act and nearly at their wits end.

But though they knew he was gone, the pair left through the back, careful not to raise alarm to anyone but perhaps the alley cat eating scraps to their surprise. And they jumped and held their chests at the sight of it.

Most folks had gone to dinner or home by the time they made their made-dash to the barracks where they found Marcello, speaking with a fellow armyman. They wordlessly nodded as it was their time to investigate.

Though Mistacles was slow to jog, they found their way to the burial pit Hisousen's remains, wrapped in linen were displayed alongside his army brothers of lower rank. This was his will in death, executed by Jusceanous himself.

With little effort, Mistacles waved his hands and raised the body to a lonely slab and allowed Reine to beat him there, still tired from all the running.

"We're not gonna unwrap him, are we?" Reine asked, with his Adams' apple high in his throat.

"Don't be stupid!"

Mistacles lowered his voice as Reine looked away embarrassed. "I'm sorry, friend. This whole situation has me rattled. Now, let's see..."

He waved his hands briefly over his body, stopping over his chest. He closed his fists and shook his head.

"This doesn't make sense!" Mistacles exclaimed.

"Why? What happened?"

His eyes went black. And very slowly, a red plume came from the bottom of his vision. He waited patiently, hearing the distorted sound of crying, not knowing if it be from demons or innocents. And as the cloud came to form, he saw the very image of two young girls, not much older than his own.

They became clearer the longer he stared, and he noticed their distress was least he had witness. He was seeing through Hisousen's eyes. His very daughters were begging him to stay, to forget the army and pick them instead. But he turned away and the scene turned black once more.

And quickly after came the moment of Hisousen's death. Mistacles saw through the lieutenant's eye as he looked down upon the blade. As he lifted his head, perhaps showing the murderer, Mistacles vision went black.

He cursed until Reine put a hand on his shoulder.

Mistacles spoke through gritted teeth, "A long dagger, made not of this mountain killed him. It's wielder has not been shown to me. It could be Marcello, though he wields a saber, I believe. Or it could be another… Yexour will not tell me."

As he braced to leave his spell, he heard laughter from a malignant voice and strengthened the connection.

"Dreqtaton! Is it you who's done this?!" Mistacles screamed.

The Dark God humored himself in quiet laughter before answering the frenzied Imagi, "I'll tell you if you give me the child."

Mistacles opened his eyes and shut down the spell with the twist of his hands. Reine stared, astonished by the revelation.

"Dreqtaton...did this?" he asked as meek as a mouse.

"He will not tell us until we forfeit my child. The only way to know now is to ask Marcello outright, or take him to Miracon to stare into her Whirl of Truth. Either unlikely to happen."

"Damn it all!" Reine yelled as Mistacles placed the stiff corpse of their friend back in his grave, neither any closer to finding the truth. They left the pit and went their separate ways, both pledging to the other not to speak of this to anyone—not until the time was right.

THE KIDS WERE ALLOWED to stay up until the end of Malkeevs celebrations a few days away. Afterwards, everything would go back to normal, if they decided to stay.

Tane had been especially quiet whilst the Child could not shut up.

"Did you guys see that one guy with the weird, teeth thing on his back? How do they do it? And what about the girl with the legs and the arms and—"

"Please, Chil, for the love of the gods, we were there!"

"So?" she asked arms crossed and defiant.

"Shut up!" The three boys barked at the same time which made them laugh.

With her arms crossed, she nudged her pensive friend who was continuously braiding the hair on a doll she had recently found.

"Where'd you find that thing again?" she asked.

"Oh, just around. It's cute, isn't it?"

Tane looked up briefly and her eyes were glazed over. She hadn't been that way since their time in Glenloch.

"Are you… okay?"

"Yeah, why do you ask?"

"You seem, troubled. Did something happen to you again?"

The Child's words sparked a familiar rage in the once subdued eyes of Tane.

"Why did you have to bring that up? Is it not enough the very sight of you reminds me of it? What—you want me to be hurt again, so you can be better, and better, and better than me?!"

The room had gone quiet as the mad, golden girl with crimson cheeks loomed over the retreating child who sank where she sat and stared at her feet.

"What's going on?" asked Pul with a soft voice.

"Nothing. You don't know, you weren't there!" Tane's words were poison but Pul was having none of it.

"We've all had a bad time, you little brat. What makes you think you can talk to her like that?"

He sat at the edge of his chair and stared swords into her eyes, but she did not retreat.

"Again, she is in the right and I'M in the wrong! How fair is that? Oh, wait, before I say anything else that might make YOU feel sad Pul Venam—the least of my friends whose seen me a handful of times since then!"

Her face had distorted into that of anguish and so did Pul's. The Child took to pinching her leg to help stop the pain she was feeling within.

"Ouch! Stop that!" her Otherself said as tears ran down her face. "Don't be sad, Lilit—we'll get through this together."

The Child nodded and sat up, wiping her eyes as Sarty

held back a blazing Pul from a screaming Tane. She looked to Care who was as carefree as ever, smiling at no one in the room.

"Enough!" screamed Mistacles who had entered the hall with a sweaty Reine at his side. "What's going on here?"

The Child shrunk as Tane took the doll into her chest and held it close. She looked at her, searching her eyes for any comfort, and she glared in return, much to the deepening of the sadness in her heart.

Her Otherself growled at the look, beckoning her to come to the Otherworld, but she refused. She watched as did everyone else as Mistacles picked up a crying Tane who spat and scratched at anyone in her path. And she screamed in a way so troubling even Care looked when they tried to take the doll away.

Pul escaped the long arms of Sarty and followed Mistacles out of the hall where he, no doubt, was taking her back to their chambers. For the first time ever, the Child didn't follow. Tired, she turned to Sarty who took a seat beside her, refusing to blink even at her alarming stare.

"Are you okay there, missy? You're acting weird—just like the other one," asked Sarty bewildered by the whole ordeal. "Does this happen often?"

"All the time," said Care.

He whistled for his dog who came galloping to sit where Pul once had.

"That's rough. I, uh, may have been a slave for longer but I would never say I had it harder than any of you."

Sarty played with his hands, rubbings his fingers so hard they turned white.

"That's big of you, man. I really appreciate it. Say, why

don't we sneak into the bar and catch us a few bottles of ale?"

Care was as light as air. The Child eyed him suspicious as the three went to the bar where they, no doubt, would fail on their quest.

PUL, Mistacles, and Reine held down the wild girl who wouldn't stop thrashing.

"Just let me go!" she screamed as she wiggled in a most uncomfortable way.

"Calm down first, sweetie. We're not gonna hurt you!"

Mistacles held down one arm and waved a free hand over her mind to calm her, but she kept moving and his spirit was still weakened.

"Let me go or else!"

Her voice changed and the Imagi stopped.

"Or else what?" asked Pul.

"I swear I'll kill each and every one of you!" she screamed, growling like a wolf.

They stared at one another in shock before Mistacles spoke. "Sweetie, please don't talk like that! Why would you say that?"

She struggled until she broke down once more, this time giving up the fight and collapsing into the bed finally.

"Please... I beg you... Please stop!"

Her cries broke their hearts, and they left the bed immediately. Mistacles stared down at the beautiful girl whose scars would never go away. He picked up the doll and gave it back to her. She cradled it as she curled up in a small, green and gold ball. She didn't open her eyes and instead counted quietly.

"1...2...3..."

They took their time to leave, making not a sound. Outside the room, Mistacles grabbed Pul by the shoulder and squeezed.

"You better not do that again, young man."

"Do what? I didn't do anything!"

"You upset her, that's what you did!" Mistacles blinked at his own words and wished he had not said them.

"Listen, I don't know what you've had to go through with my sister here, but please stop egging her on."

"Excuse me, young man?" Mistacles asked but Pul walked away. "Do you have any idea what happened to her at that place, hmm? You'd never sleep again if you knew!"

"Mistacles!" Reine screamed, stepping in between the two.

"No, it's okay Reine. Tell me, tell me!" screamed Pul shaking. "Was she raped? Was she tortured? Was she cut up into pieces while she was still alive?! Our mothers were! My baby sister was! She's been abused, yes! Miracon help me— I will destroy the men who did it! But not a single person in our lives HASN'T been defiled by those WRETCHED MEN, so don't you DARE put this on me! Don't you DARE!"

He breathed deep before speaking softly, "She's stronger than she looks. Please help her before it's too late. Please, I beg you!"

He stormed out before another word was spoken.

TANE HAD STOPPED CRYING by the time she heard what Pul said. She hadn't known all that had happened to her village until they had gotten acclimated in the mountains and were making enough progress to be told. She had thought all that time it was just a nightmare. She thought the screams and agonizing moans, and the begging's to die were just a figment of her imagination. But indeed, they were real. She got worse than, worse than she had started to become.

Not a single aspect of her life before survived besides her and her friends. What had been left was unrecognizable. And when she was in Venlet, a few days before, she felt out of place. Glat the Bakers had moved and half of the homes she used to scamper by were gone. She would have gone to her home if there were more time.

If only I had never been taken.

She clenched her doll tighter at the thought. She would rather think of anything else than of her time at Glenloch. Anything else.

Her mind became clear over time and the face of the Child ran across. She snarled almost by instinct at the sad, little girl. She turned in her bed hoping to see something else. She was everywhere in her life and was with her no matter where she went. She wanted to be free of her—of the memory and of the pain. Care understood but not that...thing.

She pressed her face against the doll and began to hear the voice of Minerva singing a distant song she made for her that would help ease her troubles:

> "My sweet, my lark,
> Don't cry when it's dark,
> I'm not very far—
> I'll protect you.
>
> My sweet, my heart,
> Don't hate who you are,
> No matter where you are—
> I will find you."

CHAPTER 27

The open corridor was bustling with every person with thread and sheets pulled wide, preparing for the biggest night of Malkeevs. During festivities, a large banquet was displayed for all to take from and everyone who attended had to bring a contribution. The children had all brought a roll to contribute so they could have their pick of the delicious foods. And there were endless entries for them to try! Care had taken a particular fondness to Huburthian cuisine, always lathered in the hottest of sauces, and Sarty couldn't keep his hands off the Four-Fined Salmon fresh from a river near Fairful. The Child ate scraps and preferred the treats while Pul ate everything in sight, like a wayfaring horse. But Tane was the only one who didn't eat. Instead, she kept her doll close, and her eyes were ever distant.

The Child reached for her a few times to get her to eat but her friend pulled away instead and looked the else-where. In the past, she would have informed Mistacles but she didn't feel like it, not right then. She was enjoying her time with those who didn't bring her down. And she was getting tired of always being Tane's punching bag.

Munta sat closest to the children, next to Pul who didn't protest. The longest table in history that waned from the darkened caved north to the ones south gave space for anyone to sit and chat awhile, no matter who they were.

Mistacles sat across from Reine, Marcello, and Jusceanous. His constant stares at each of them caught the attention of Jusceanous who was just as weary of the company he kept.

"What seems to be the matter, Mistacles?" he asked, mouth full of food.

"Nothing. Nothing at all. I guess I'm just a little curious as to what you all have planned for your last day in the mountains."

"Who said anything about leaving?" asked Marcello with a cheesy grin. His eyes were sharp on Mistacles who own hardly left his plate.

"Marcello, you silly fool! Anyways, Mistacles—the plan is to gather as many armymen as we can and send them out during the day to get a head start. There's a small chance a small charge may be met where we wish to travel. They'll send word when it's clear and we'll proceed. Otherwise, we'll take an alternative route."

"So, food for the slaughter?" Mistacles question made the army men look up in confusion. "What if they die, Jusceanous?"

He laughed.

"They won't, Imagi. The size will be too great. And if there are any causalities, it'll be because of their own misstep, I'm sure of it."

"Is this because of the Prophezier?" asked Marcello.

Reine met the eyes of Mistacles filled with worry.

"Of course. We have them both and the Order would do amazingly well if they had them at their disposal. It's all tactics, I'm afraid. But, we'll probably spend the day resting and gathering supplies for the long journey home."

Jusceanous smiled and continued eating as the three other men grimaced.

TANE AWOKE on the day of Malkeevs to the sound of hammers and quickly left her room. It still echoed in the house but wasn't in it. Outside men in uniform were preparing to leave. Tents were taken down and boxes were put together to carry the many essentials needed for the long hike.

The Imagi's spent the night guarding the mountain side from anymore unforeseeable attacks. To their east, where a secret passage led to Beningdul was a small upstart of Order soldiers but not enough to stop the thousand and some odd men from carrying on. They were to leave very soon, haggard and hungover, but not all would go. Half the men plus those young men who wished to stay and train remained, to protect it from future attacks if possible.

Jusceanous stood resolute as his men prepared to leave without him. He was to take Hisousens place but was commanded by Miracon to stay put. She also commanded to speak to Marcello whom was nowhere to be seen.

"Gone again?" asked Reine as Jusceanous moved stiffly.

"He does what he pleases. But he never loses contact with the goddess. Should I be worried?"

Reine held back his prejudice and answered, "No, he is an able man. He'll come back and get the message."

"But she has to speak with him now, before we leave."

"On all days for him to be aloof..."

Reine surveyed the crowd and noticed Mistacles standing alone near an alleyway. His slight nod gave Reine justice to leave Jusceanous and sneak to where he was. Besides a building, he heard the low murmurs of two men.

"It wasn't me, dear friend. Surely you know that."

Reine could hear Mistacles sigh before speaking.

"I know you are a wonderful man, but I don't know you well enough. But no one is blaming you."

"But what of Reine or Jusceanous? Weren't they gone when all were looking for them? Why am I suspect?"

Mistacles shushed Marcello.

"You are not. If you didn't kill Hisousen, go to Miracon and speak with her. All will be well."

"Will it?"

Reine walked away and took residence in a nearby store. He approached the shopkeep and picked out a bagel, as anxious as a possum.

"How much do I owe you?" he asked.

"Nothing. Thank you for saving us," answered the man whose worn eyes were bright.

Beaming, Reine left but not before running into Marcello.

"Friend, why do you mistrust me so?" he asked.

Gulping his food, Reine smiled and shook his head.

"I trust you Marcello—always have!"

Marcello, who held him at the arm let him go before stomping away.

Reine searched for Mistacles and found him heading to Jusceanous, surely to tell him of his suspicions of Marcello. Like a jack rabbit, Reine beat the Imagi and pulled him aside.

"Don't do it!" he whispered adamantly.

"What?! Why not!" Mistacles answered through gritted teeth.

"We need more evidence. This isn't enough."

Mistacles scratched his beard before sighing. "We need the Dark God."

THE CHILD ROLLED her eyes as Tane sang to her doll, treating her better than her. She rolled her eyes before leaving her to play with the others. She found Care in a clearing near the foundry playing with Riki. They were alone and happy, and she didn't feel like interfering. She ran to Munta and Pul's tent but upon entering was forced out.

"Why can't I come in?!" she asked the giant man.

"They're getting ready to leave. It's not time yet but soon, okay?"

"But I want to play!"

Her words hurt Munta but he still turned her away. Lost and confused, she walked through the many alleyways and streets once filled with many simple people and now filled with them among armymen, conversing and gifting as if they were sending off long-lost loved ones.

She ventured forth until she reached where her and Mistacles had gone when she wanted to see the Sun. That seemed like so long ago, but was it? She had forgotten how to go up so she stayed near the magical transportation portal, hoping someone would come looking for her.

Nearest a rock wall she felt a cool breeze hit her back. She walked slowly towards it, where light was still visible and she found a secret pathway. Smitten, she walked closest to the wall and entered into another space. The hallway was narrow and winding, but it led her outside with no doors closing behind her. She was safe and she could find her way back.

Although morning, the clouds outside made it appear darker than it was. She had wished she took her jacket and shivered as the tundra hissed at her. Undeterred, she examined the space carefully, deciding where, in the future, she would have picnics and play dolls when springen and the warmer months surely came.

As she walked onto snow, shivering and confused, a bright light caught the corner of her eye. She looked down onto a sheet of snow where light ebbed from underneath. She got down and brushed the snow away. Under was an orb surrounded by blood.

She sat back, scared and grossed out. But she felt compelled to touch it and she did. As she touched it, her world turned white. She was somewhere else—a room in the shape of a circle with a giant orb at the center—much like the crystal ball in Mistacles study.

She saw no way of escape and began to panic.

"Do not fear me, Go-ges-ta! I will not harm you!"

Its voice was like rock and rumbles in low pitches she couldn't not understand.

She thought on the name. "Gogesta?"

"Yes, you are a go-ges-ta! Half-born! Half-light!"

She was without words.

"I am healed, they say, but blood was spilt where my spirit lays. What is the cause of this?"

She stammered, "Th-th-the Order of G-g-garatos broke into the m-m-mountains, and k-k-killed and..."

"Yes, but whose blood was spilt here?"

Confused she shook her head, "I don't know. I'm sorry."

"Yes, but you can know."

"I don't understand."

"Yes, think of the blood. This, of the blade. This, of the death. It will come to you, go-ge-sta!"

The Child reluctantly closed her eyes and recalled the blood and the snow. How cold they must have felt as they died. How they would have known the one who took their life. She could feel the long dagger in her hand and it was heavy. Shocked, she wanted to open her eyes.

"Yes, don't open them yet. Can you hear their voices, little one?"

She turned her head instinctually as a man spoke, heartbroken but angry at another. And another one hid, not far away.

"Yes, now open your eyes and tell me what you see!"

She flicked her eyes open and saw Chief Officer Marcello and Lieutenant Hisousen speaking, both with their hands ready to take arms. She felt herself move and looked down at her hand—it was a man's that held a dagger familiar to her, somehow. She leapt and dug the dagger into Hisousen's back and she shuddered.

It was then she pulled away and fell back into the circle room, crying on the ground as a blue orb danced above her.

"Yes, thank you for your help. Go now and rest within my home, go-ges-ta, until you are no longer welcome!"

She found herself back on her bottom but in the snow, cold as ever before. She got to her feet and headed for the passage but stopped when a chorus of angry grunts came from it. She hid behind a rock and waited for the incoming force. Marcello, with his gallant, bright boots, came through, a dust of snow strewn on his path as he stopped shy of the orb. He looked down upon it, its crimson a burning glow, and his face changed into something distorted and ugly. Without warning he stomped on the orb but fell onto his backside. Undeterred, he got back to his feet and kicked snow upon it, again and again, until snot fell from his nose and a loud sob came from his throat. The blood remained and the orb shined an even brighter crimson.

He had lost.

Seemingly alone and without spectators, he stumbled back, collapsing on the hard rock wall. He held his head up, clearing his sinuses as tears fell.

"Why, brother? Why did you interfere?!"

He kicked the snow again before forcing himself to calm at last. As plain as ever, a pale and stoic Marcello walked through the passage, into the secret tunnel with the Child staring from behind, unblinking and cold.

CHAPTER 28

Munta fashioned himself a nice harness to take to a horse waiting for him at the bottom of the mountains. He only planned to go himself with a few dubels to his new life, but felt the boy missing would never make him feel complete again. But no measure of reason could explain why he must go but not going would be his biggest regret. This task was what he was meant to do, whether he understood it or not.

Their day together was spent telling one another stories they lived through together: of Pul's healing from the Seeress; of their first time on a mission; and the last time they fought in battle. Pul was only thirteen but was more a man than even he could ever realize.

Munta's job was done.

Pul was well on his way of being an armyman, and had no one in his way to get there. He kept in his hands the necklace Mistacles gave him. He had only known him through visits but respected what he did. Regardless of how he treated them, he was happy he kept his friends—his sisters safe. But to wear his necklace felt... strange.

He shoved it in his pocket as he examined his bag for the hundredth time. Sarty watched him, dismayed by his efforts to stall for time.

"I'm pretty sure we're all waiting on you to leave, princess."

But Pul didn't stir at his words.

Irritated, Sarty left the tent, bag already packed and ready to go, and went looking for the Child. The name Lilith he practiced saying a hundred times though it felt weird leaving his lips. By the time he reached her, still sulking in her room, he had already grown tired of it.

"So, uh, what's going on now?" he asked, rubbing his head.

"I'm sad to see you guys go," she spoke honestly, and he sat next to her.

"But why? Aren't you going to Allsingdale as well?"

"Yeah, but not with you guys. They say it's not safe," she pulled her knees to her face and was going to bury it but Sarty stopped her.

"Don't."

"Don't what?"

"Don't give up."

"I'm not giving up, I'm just sad."

"There's no time to be sad. We've got the rest of our lives, as adults, to be sad. Let's be happy and have fun. Enjoy ourselves and learn everything we can. Aren't you to learn magic with the goddess herself?"

The Child nodded.

"Well, what a dream come true! See, no reason to be sad."

"But I'm going to miss you guys."

"Nah!" he said while he whipped his long legs up and

down. "You'll be too busy. I know I will. But you can write me if you want."

"Really! But..." she fell back again, "I don't know how to write."

"Then, learn."

He jumped and landed loudly which shocked the girl. He had been like a breath of fresh air since he came, even during the mountain's upheaval. His energy, gravitas, and his strength were unlike anything she had ever seen before. Hardly had she seen him sad.

So, she thought, *why should I be?*

As he left the room, she sprung from her bed, smirking like some awful pirate ready to break sea. She ignored her friend who spent hours talking to her doll, whispering short stories and giggling though only her voice could be heard.

The men rallied their things unto horses and donkeys brought with them and prepared to leave. Malkeevs was over, the celebration was at its end. Banners of holly and red berries were to be taken down, but not until the party left. Thankful mountain-dwellers gave their praise and love to the passing armymen, shedding tears as they left until no longer seen. Everyone participated, except for Tane.

She watched as Pul hugged the Child, and then her though she did not hug back. He begged for her attention with sad eyes, but her heart had little room to care. Her doll told her to say her goodbyes but she didn't want to. Sarty gave Riki a good pat as Care sat in a horse, ready to see the rest of the world at Reine's side. Such a big task for such a hardy man, but he could be trusted, even Tane could agree. But Care would return once he arrived in Allsingdale.

The only of the five to stay in the mountains was Tane. Mistacles had implored her to take the trip and offered to send her with the Child, but she refused. Instead, she wished to stay with her dolls. Finally, it had been settled she would go with Mistacles wherever he went, a far better deal than what the others got, at least that's how she saw it. She couldn't leave, she had to see her friends deep within the mountain.

The Child held back weeps as her friends grew smaller the further they ventured from the dining halls of the thermopolia and into the great abyss leading to their escape. She held onto Munta who grabbed tight the shoulder of Jusceanous who kept telling him to be brave.

When they had finally gone, the Child ran to her room where the present Pul left stayed untouched, even by the falling mountain and rough hands of the Order soldiers. She was to open it in her bed but feared Tane would come in and take it from her. Paranoid, she took the small box and left the house without being noticed.

In a small patch of green, right below the grand opening above, she opened her box. Inside was a small, gold bracelet with a small heart etched into it.

Her heart sank.

She wished her best friend could stay with her, like when they were little.

She put it on and ran to show it to Mistacles who would smell right away the enchantment it possessed.

"Who gave this to you?"

"Pul!" she answered, jumping up and down.

"He gave you that? Well...that's a pretty big deal."

"Why?" she asked, red in the face and neck.

Mistacles chuckled.

"That's a magical bracelet. It can do many things and is very valuable. Maybe the goddess can show you."

"But, why can't you?"

Her eyes looked for his but he couldn't keep her glance. Had she known it would be sometime before they were again together, she would have searched harder.

"Well, Tane, Maggie and I are going on a vacation. Probably to Salmer's Thame!" he laughed but the Child didn't. "We will come see you in a fortnight."

"Wait, when am I leaving?!"

"Uh, in a few moments!"

She ran from the Imagi as he yelled for her to get back. She ran past the armymen, now residents of the mountains, asking for a high five and ran past the everyday people going about their life in the alleyways nearest her escape. As she left through the passage on the side, she could hear the murmurs of armymen soon approaching, ready to bring her back if she wanted to escape.

"I thought I was finally free, but I'm not!" she said out loud as she got close to Yexour's Orb and touched it.

She waited to be taken from there, but nothing happened. Defeated, she turned to face the armymen soon to arrive, no doubt sent by Mistacles when a feather fell from the sky above her. It fell down so gracefully, it took her breath away. It landed in her hands she held out as if on instinct.

She grinned for it was a white-gold feather as silky as milk and as pure as snow. Above her came the rolling growls of giant beasts she recalled once gave her peace.

She hid the feather in her dress as armymen approached, sighing in relief as they gently pulled her back to safety within the mountain.

．　．　．

She looked indifferently in her sacred hole, full of warm, bubbly ocean as the events of all that happened passed through, like a flashing of fire in a lightless room. Not a single tear she shed for the men in the army who fell to protect the mountains. Had she known how badly they would fail at losing, she would never have agreed to the attack with her sister. And she wouldn't have involved that pest, Marcello, whose own motivation eluded her, who couldn't uphold his end of the bargain.

She, whom they—her brothers—hadn't desired was desperate to keep the peace with her sister, Siracon, though, she despised her just as much as everyone else. Her own Army, in their name is her namesake, were supposed to give the monster up. But they couldn't get the job down. But she couldn't tear down Yexour with her own hands; Garaton would rip her apart. His own wife he disowned for their botched attack on the mountains already deteriorating, among other reasons.

The Order left, well before signs of their losing was evident. The fire breathing Golden God forced their hand, ensuring their deaths if they persisted further. His High Guardian grandsons, who promised to helm the battle, were no where to be seen. Though it is believed they went back to Osir once the mighty dragon's roar obliterated the sky.

And Siracon was silent then. Not a storm or a cloud riddled the sky for she knew better than to test his will. And into Malkeevs, not a scream left Osir.

Miracon, a fissure of blue light scoffed.

What had seemed impossible had been made so. Though her efforts to take the girl were futile, the Great Imagi Mistacles was sending her to be her charge—to learn from the oldest goddess. She had been in competition with

Dreqtaton, the Dark Pest for dominion over the monster, and soon she'd be the one laughing at her kin.

She chuckled but stopped when the door to her chamber opened.

"Madame—your highness?"

"What?!"

"The girl has arrived, and she is accompanied by Jusceanous who will be returning to the mountains at your command."

The priest bowed and closed the chamber door, knowing well than to expect an answer.

"Hmmm..."

Her light dimmed and in the shadows came lurking a grotesque figure, of clawed hands and wet, scaly skin. Its hunchback uncovered as the rest of the deformed body was in netting and wire. Twisted and disturbing, it breathed heavy, smacking its lips as wet as a fish tail out of water.

It dragged its feet to the throne where a chalice of purple and pink bubbly liquid waited for its master. It took it into its maimed, webbed hands and chugged it in one gulp.

It opened its eyes, a fierce silver in a blackened room and breathed in. It clapped its hands together and the magical flames of the room went off.

Where the creature sat now lived a beautiful woman— the Miracon known to her flock. She flicked her fingers and the door opened again, this time—the girl was on the other end.

"Come in, my beautiful niece. Don't be afraid—"

I will hurt you.

EPILOGUE

The grey sky had gotten darker as the days after Malkeevs got colder. The harbor was in rough shape. Ambec had taken out her anger on the capital city as the Order went in for their assault on Yexour —her once lover. No ship dare come from Glenloch for they were smashed to smithereens. Gilton City was without it's sea trade and were fairing worse on land, where eastern cities like Hulbrind refused to send their wares out of fear of looting and Eleventh Day festivities, not practiced on the sea.

Too many already starving laborers were forced to move out of their homes and into the streets, where they were kicked like rats for existing there. And many went to the High Guardians, hoping to speak with them personally, but were shooed away.

Children died. The elderly died. Little hope remained in the city of endless possibilities.

Yet, the puppeteer continued his show, forgetting to leave hit hat on the ground for dubels, or so he told the poor folk and their kids on Malkeevs who couldn't afford presents. How he made the grim laugh was a hallmark on the south-side of the city, where the poor were the poorest.

It was an odd day after Malkeevs when the puppeteer found his lively street empty. They first he had seen it since he was a boy. Even as the great god Gilton and his son cleared the world of the Darkness, there were still people out of their minds, too terrified to do anything but wait to die.

He shrugged off the feeling something was amiss and continued to undo his box, making his miniature theatre as spectacular as ever.

But as he went to fashion the curtain onto his box, he heard a horn—a warlongs vocal cords spraying through the streets. Frightened, he threw all his things into his box, clumsily dropping fabric and puppets and picking them up as clatter of armor was soon approaching.

He finally got hold of all his possessions and held them close, running to a dark alley, behind a trash bin only a fool would look around.

He poked his ahead out and noticed the soldiers—all in new, gold armor, with helmets of warlong tuft at the top.

His eyes rolled up as he counted out loud.

"The twenty-seventh, the twenty-eighth...There's still three days until the Eleventh Day!"

He held his most and shivered, sweating like a roasted pig.

He heard the armor of a single soldier walk slowly in his direction. He breathed heavy, hoping for once in his life to be invisible.

He heard the hammering of iron against brick and waited for what seemed like the end of times for the amor to clatter away, with a chorus of more armor singing their menacing song down other streets in the distance.

He searched the area to be sure the coast was clear before he jumped to his feet and prepared to run. He stopped once he saw the poster.

"All manner of men, young and old, must surrender to the Order to be drafted into their legion... What in the blazes—"

He felt a rough pull at the back of his tunic and was turned around, dropping his life's work to be destroyed upon impact. It was a soldier whose weathered eyes said it all.

"It's time to gear up, old man!" he said as the puppeteer reached for anything to hold him back. He screamed for help and none of the onlookers, hiding in their homes above moved—scared themselves of the newly sprung draft. He gave up fighting once he was forced in a caravan, with the young man—the fisherman's boy—beside him.

He regained his composure.

"You're Sephen, correct? Son of Uba? What a fine young man to have in such unpleasant company."

"I'd rather die than work for them!" screamed the boy.

The puppeteer held his hand over the boy's mouth.

"Shhh...Don't give them what they want. Do as they say, and you might live. By the way, my name is Paul— pleased to meet you, at last."

The pair shook as the rickety caravan moved along the empty streets, heading to their new home in the barracks.

GLOSSARY

Afterlife - A paradise made for the people of Oxem after their death; can only be reached by the Rite of Oxem.

Agatha Hollon - Grandmother to the Child; a Creature-whisperer and breeder of clonclucks in Holfenya.

Bart - Parity's ex-fiancee; the man she wished was the Child's father.

Amacon - Goddess of Tears.

Amao - The sixth god; formless and terrifying.

Ambec - The Ultiquan name for the Red Sea.

Apontaceus Marcello - Chief officer of the Army of Miracon; the Shining Knight.

Army of Miracon - Special forces sent by Miracon to stop the Order of Garatos.

Cara Venpas - Sister to Care who was murdered in Glenloch after she was abused.

Care Venpas - Friend of the Child; survivor of Glenloch.

Cloncluck - Vicious bird-like creatures whose feathers have magical capabilities; only found in Holfenya.

Debusse of Glenloch - Currently named Mika; in charge of business in Glenloch; supported by the High Guardians and the Lords of the Land.

Don - One of the lost, Venetian children taken back to the village after years of slavery; adopted by Parity.

Dreqtaton - The Dark God; the Dark One; bringer of darkness; destroyer of all things created; and malevolent to all —including his followers.

Eternie - The goddess Siracon's unsightly afterlife.

Ganguen - Son of Gilton; grandson of Garaton and Siracon; Lord of the Land in Bruselet.

Garaton - The Greatest of the Golden Ones; Leader of Man; God of Strength and Steadfast in War

Gargo - Son of Gilton; grandson of Garaton and Siracon; high Guardian of Zel alongside brother Girgo.

Gilton - Child of Garaton and Siracon; favorite High Guardian of Zel; Only Born God; sacrificed himself to stop the Darkness.

Gilton City - Once called the Golden City, the capital city of Zel where the High Guardians reside.

Girgo - Son of Gilton; grandson of Garaton and Siracon; high Guardian of Zel alongside brother Gargo.

Glenloch - Port City to Central Zel with a road made of white gold.

Glinton - Son of Gilton; grandson of Garaton and Siracon; sacrificed his life to the Darkness along with his father in The Great Sacrifice.

Gogesta - Name given to Lilith by Yexour; meaning half-born and half-light.

Hestha - Once an Ultiquan; a lush island, since destroyed.

Hethathy - Secret avengers of Siracon.

High Guardians - The leaders of Zel; in charge when Garaton is away.

Holfenya - City north of Venlet, hidden by the Mountains of the Predicated.

Imagi - Nomadic magic wielders who could manipulate anything in Zel without the aid of Dreqtaton.

Jela - One of the lost, Venetian children taken back to the village after years of slavery; adopted by Parity.

Jusceanous - Captain of the Army of Miracon; member of Mal Three.

Lord of the Land - The authority of a region and/or city appointed by the High Guardian.

Man - The men and women of Zel.

Malkeevs - Festival of Stars; the cold holiday celebrated in Zel; where family and friends gather and exchange gifts and be merry.

Margaret - An attendant to the Child, Tane, and Care in the Mountains of the Predicated.

Munta - blacksmith turned member of Mal Three; is Pul's companion and protector of the Blood of Oxem; brother to Unta.

Order of Garatos - The military force of the High Guardians, sent to protect the people of Zel; practitioners of the Eleventh Day.

Otherself - The only person other than the Child in her Otherworld; only exists there.

Ozerith - Tower in the Realm of Light.

Osir - Tower in Gilton City; the Eye of Zel; sister to Ozerith.

Paul - The puppeteer; taken in by the Order to serve.

Plea Eric - The Plea to take Plea Marcus Daniels' place.

Plea Marcus Daniels - The once Grand Eunich; long-lost friend of Mistacles.

Pleas - Extreme followers of Siracon.

Prophezier - Destroyer of the Darkness; born to die, to save all for another generation.

Pul Venam - Potential Prophezier; member of Mal Three; protector of his friends.

Red Sea - Also known as Amber; the sea between Central Zel and the wild lands west where sea monsters dwell.

Reicher's Realm - Also known as the Sixth World. The worst world in creation.

Sarty - Survivor of the arm of Garatos; one of two potential Prophezier.

Sephen - Son of Uba; young sailor taken in by the Order to serve.

Siracon - Goddess of Love and Fertility; Goddess of Marvels; sister-wife to Garaton.

Tane Venal - Friend to the Child; survivor of abuse with a heart of a wolf.

Tel-nequri - the harsh, tundra land north of the Mountains of the Predicated; home of the Umeki people.

Tentactacon - A treacherous sea monster that deceives its victims by appearing as a beautiful women; child of Miarcon.

The Child - creator of the Otherworld; daughter of Garaton and Parity.

The Darkness - An abysmal black cloud that consumes all life.

The Eleventh Day - The ancient practice of the Order of Garatos and extreme followers of Garaton that allows them to commit any crimes they wish without punishment.

The First One - The Creator; Our First Father.

The Moon - Created by the First One; the companion to the Sun.

The Mountains of the Predicated - The mountain range that circles the Valley of Venoxem; a sacred place where many people live safely.

The Nine Planes - The nine worlds (realms) made by the First One.

The Seven Golden Ones - The seven gods: Garaton, Siracon, Dreqtaton, Miracon, Amacon, Amao, and Yecon.

The Sun - Created by the First One; the light source of Zel.

Tom - The human form of Dreqtaton.

Ultiquans - The spirits of Zel slain by the gods.

Umeki - People north of the mountains.

Unta - Councilmen of Venlet restored; brother to Munta.

Valley of Venoxem - The area within the Mountains of the Predicated first found by the ex-slaves of Gilton City.

Venlet - A small village at the entrance of the Valley of Venoxem.

Warlong - A giant boar-like creature with massive tusks; sacrificial animal of Garaton.

Zavai - A volcano at the edge of the world.

Zel - The world.

ABOUT THE AUTHOR

K.C. Nuzum is a storyteller who uses literature, music, and sketches to bring her stories to life. Born and raised in beautiful Minnesota, she spent most of her childhood outside in nature where her imagination bloomed. She started writing when she was little, with her first book being a handwritten one at the age of nine. She went to school to be a singer, but her heart wasn't in it. Rather, it was in the telling of tales. She currently spends her free time outside in the Pacific Northwest, listening to the birds and looking for feathers. If you'd like to hear more about K.C. Nuzum, her music, and read some of her other writings, visit kcnuzum.com.